TALES *from*
GRANDPA GREG'S
FIRESIDE

BOOKS 1-3

ADVENTURES IN OTHERWORLDS

*Leandra
Massengill*

KING'S COMPASS
PRESS

Edited by Misti Moyer, Sunshine Pencraft, LLC, MistiMoyer.com

Cover & interior design by TLCBookDesign.com

ISBN: 979-8-9989226-0-2 (paperback)
ISBN: 979-8-9989226-1-9 (ebook)

SOLI DEO GLORIA

To my mom, for fighting dyslexia with me,
though it wasn't her fight,
and for working to make this book a reality,
though it wasn't her dream.

CONTENTS

BOOK 1
Behind the Forbidden Waterfall

BOOK 2
The Island of Thanatos

BOOK 3
The Griffin Key

1

BEHIND *the* FORBIDDEN WATERFALL

1

THE GREENWOODS

"Are we there yet?" asked six-year-old Natasha Greenwood as she and her family drove to her grandfather's house for Christmas vacation. Natasha was the youngest in her family. She had green eyes and rosy cheeks; her red hair was always tied in braided pigtails.

Jonny, her brother, rolled his bright green eyes. "That's the tenth time you've asked that! So stop it!" He, unlike his sister, had dark brown hair and pale skin.

"You can't tell me what to do," Natasha snapped.

"Oh yes, I can," Jonny said in a know-it-all sort of tone. "I'm oldest."

"By—by two years!" Natasha said, irritated.

"Now, now, children," their mother, Amy Greenwood, said soothingly, "there'll be none of that."

Rae, a seven-year-old girl with dark brown hair and blue eyes, listened quietly to her brother and sister quarrel. She never desired to pitch in when Natasha and Jonny argued, which they often did. Instead, she stayed silent and minded her own business.

She gazed out the car window, watching the snowflakes fall lazily to the ground as the car zipped along.

At long last, they reached their grandfather's house. The children scrambled out of the car and hastened to the door. Bouncing on the balls of his feet, Jonny eagerly rang the doorbell. An old man with grey hair and gentle blue eyes answered the door, leaning on a walking stick.

"Grandpa Greg!" the children cried in unison.

"Children! Welcome! Come inside and get warm," said Grandpa Greg with a big smile. "Welcome, Amy."

"Thank you, Greg. How have you been?"

"Good, good," he answered, still smiling. "Well, I see Mrs. Greenwood, but where is Mr. Greenwood?"

"He couldn't make it, I'm afraid. He got held up at work. His boss dumped a bucketload of assignments on him at the last second. Sorry to say he won't be joining us till Christmas Day."

"What a shame, what a shame. Well, I'll be looking forward to seeing him on Christmas then. But now for dinner!"

After they ate, Rae and the rest of the family went to the sitting room. It was quite a cozy room; there were two battered armchairs with a small coffee table between them, a sofa with pillows, a large dusty bookshelf, the tallest and most beautiful Christmas tree Rae had ever seen, and an enormous fireplace. This was Rae's favorite room and her favorite part of the night. It was story time, but this was not just any old story. This was one of Grandpa Greg's stories. Every evening for the five evenings leading up to Christmas, Grandpa Greg would tell the children a story. In Rae's opinion, they were the best stories ever told.

All three children plopped down on the floor in front of the fireplace and crossed their legs, waiting excitedly for him to begin. Grandpa Greg settled down in his favorite armchair and scanned the children's faces.

"I guess you want me to tell a story," he teased.

"Yes!" the children burst out in anticipation, Rae being the loudest.

"Ok, let's see then," he mused. "What to tell? Where to start?" There was a moment's silence.

"Oh, the first story of Christmas vacation," Rae whispered to herself. "I can't wait!"

A wide grin spread across Grandpa Greg's face, and then he sprang into a story: "Once upon a time," he began in a mysterious tone, "there was a fairy—"

"Aw, man," Jonny groaned. "A fairy? That's so *girly!*"

"Shh! Shut up!" Natasha snapped, hitting Jonny on the back of the head. "Let him tell the story."

"But this wasn't just any old fairy. Oh no," Grandpa Greg went on as though there wasn't an interruption, "she was the size of an average fifteen-year-old girl. She had magically bright blue eyes, light blonde hair tied in a braid that fell to her knees, and fair skin. She wore a simple dark blue knee-length dress and no shoes. Her blue wings were as outstanding as an eagle's. They looked like water flowing gently from above her shoulders and down her back until they collided with the ground in misty clouds.

"She was the very last fairy, it was said (though no one told her how that came to be), but she wasn't lonesome. She had all sorts of friends: bunnies, deer, birds, foxes, unicorns, and all the animals and magical creatures you can think of.

She lived in magical garden-like woods. These woods were glorious, but there was one place in particular that entranced the fairy so. In a clearing with dainty flowers and luscious grass, a large and magnificent Waterfall poured into a sparkling pond. Unfortunately, the fairy only had one single rule given to her by her friends: never go behind the Forbidden Waterfall.

"The fairy's name was Sky, and her life was good. But still, one question had nagged her all her life: What's behind the Forbidden Waterfall? Little did she know, her life was about to change forever..."

2

ANOTHER WORLD

"Wonderful day, isn't it, Ms. Hops?" Sky cheerfully asked her best friend, a rabbit whose first name no one knew.

"Yes, it is," replied Ms. Hops. "It is indeed."

The friends sat on a rock next to a pond, Sky's feet dangling in the water. The Forbidden Waterfall rushed into the pond, sending tiny waves skipping over to tickle Sky's toes. Like thousands of jewels falling off a cliff, the curtain of water glistened. What wonders did it veil? Curiosity was like an excited little girl within her that wouldn't stop chattering about all the possibilities.

Sky started flicking the water with her toes. Should she ask again? She was desperate for an answer, but all her inquires in the past had been unsuccessful. Would this time be any different?

She cleared her throat. "Ms. Hops?"

"Yes, my dear?"

"Could you *please* tell me why the Forbidden Waterfall is—well—forbidden? What's behind it?"

Ms. Hops sighed. "Fairies, always so curious."

"Come on," Sky said. "Don't I have the right to know?"

Ms. Hops wiggled her nose as she always did when she thought matters over. But she was thinking too long. Was it possible to just skip over the waiting and get right to the interesting part?

At last, the rabbit replied, "Well, I guess you do. I think you're old enough—and ready—for me to tell you."

Sky's heart leapt and never came down. It just flew up and up and up. This was it. Finally, she would know the mystery of the Waterfall.

"A long time ago," Ms. Hops began in a hushed voice, "there were hundreds of fairies—a whole kingdom. But one day, a fairy named Vivian stumbled into the Waterfall and found a new world. Instead of trying to befriend its people, she wished to rule over them. Vivian came back through the Waterfall and asked the fairies to join her, thus the fairy kingdom was divided. Vivian and her followers went through the Waterfall and ruled over the humans. However, the fairies on this side felt they couldn't stand by as the human's suffered under Vivian's harsh rule. And so, there was a war. Many fairies went into the Waterfall to face Vivian. None came back. So, that's why you're not allowed to go through the Waterfall. That's why you are the last fairy."

Sky stared wide-eyed at Ms. Hops. A war of fairy against fairy? An entirely different world behind the Forbidden Waterfall? A billion questions zoomed around in her head like pixies. She didn't know what to ask.

She finally broke the silence. "Wh-what happened to Vivian's followers? Are they still with her?"

"No, Vivian was the only one left when the last of the fairies went through the Waterfall."

"How come I'm the only fairy left? Surely there were other children at the time."

The rabbit's eyes dropped. "The war took them, my dear. Vivian raided this world after the first group of fairies tried to take her off the throne. When that happened, all the children were killed."

"But *I* survived."

"Your parents hid you well. It probably never crossed Vivian's mind that fairies would trust a 'lowly' rabbit to protect their child."

Sky's heart dropped like a stone in water. Slowly it sank to the bottom—alone, cold, and empty. She couldn't think about her parents. She couldn't. It hurt too much. But she'd always wondered how they died. Did Vivian kill them? She wiped a tear away before it had the chance to slide down her cheek. She needed to know.

"What happened to them?"

"They died fending off a second raid on this world, fearful Vivian might find you. They asked me to take care of you if anything should happen. And so I have."

Sky turned toward the Waterfall. Did Vivian still have the throne? An angry spark ignited in her chest, but it was just a spark. The really important question was: What was this other world like? What untold beauties, stories, and adventures lay just behind that Waterfall?

The rest of the day passed by uneventfully, but her people's history never left Sky's mind. Question after question floated in and out of her brain. But there was one in particular that really bothered her. How could Vivian do such a thing—to their people and to hers?

At twilight, Sky lay in the leafy tree, her curious mind still yapping at her. What was behind the Forbidden Waterfall? Surely a little peak wouldn't hurt. She peered over the tree branch to check if the animals were asleep before flying over them and landing noiselessly in the pond.

Sky glanced over her shoulder, ensuring no one had awoken. "Ok, how do I get through? Maybe...could I freeze it? Part the water?"

Making an arrow shape with her hands, palms facing up, she put them into the Waterfall. FLASH! The water stopped in its tracks. Sky peered through the split she had made. She couldn't see a thing.

"Don't get scared now, Sky," she whispered to herself, then took a deep breath. "Ms. Hops is going to kill me." And she stepped into the Waterfall.

There was a blinding flash of light. She blinked and squinted to see what was in front of her. It was—

Her jaw dropped.

"I'm going on an adventure!"

It was morning, and she was standing on a hill. Square structures with pointed gnome-like hats were clustered below. Horrifying peaks made of many smooth stones stacked one atop another towered over the structures. Stretching out from every side of this place was a clearing full of withered grass, a river winding through it. After a while, thick woods began growing in every direction, stretching on forever.

The sun reached around the haunted-looking peaks and hit Sky's eyes. It cast spooky shadows over the pointed squares below. The place didn't look very lively: the people were gloomy, going about their business with their heads hanging low. Everyone was dirty and wore ragged clothes. Everyone, that is, except these men in hard, shiny clothing on horseback. They seemed to be making everyone's life miserable, like nasty little goblins. Nevertheless, the place was incredible.

Sky could hardly hold still. She had to go explore. Just a few minutes wouldn't hurt. She bit her lip and glanced over her shoulder at the frozen Waterfall—which apparently existed in this world also—with a split that led back to her world. She had come for a peek. Well, this was a peek. She should really go back, but look at the place. How could she not explore it?

"Hmm." Sky studied the people below. "No one has wings or colorful clothes. I'm really going to stand out. I need a disguise."

She clapped her hands twice. Immediately, her wings and clothes vanished and were replaced with a ragged dress. (She still had no shoes.) Her hair flipped up into an untidy bun, and dirt covered her body. However, her radiant fairy eyes could still be seen as that was something she couldn't change. Hopefully, these people had bright eyes too.

"Ah, that's better. I'll really blend in now. No one will ever know I was here."

She approached the Waterfall and touched the frozen water. The split closed and the water rushed on. She then set off down the hill.

The people didn't give Sky a second glance as she rushed past them. Traveling to and fro, they carried large baskets or stacks of wood on their shoulders. Sky marveled at each face. Everyone looked like her, with the exception of wings. The animals present were few in number and kind, and they didn't talk to anyone.

I wonder why they're so quiet...maybe they're just tired.

Sky bounced over to the center of the place. A lady there sold carrots and radishes and all kinds of food. The cluster of veggies was a burst of life amidst the gnome-like structures. A little girl scampered to the lady and, holding a snail, said, "Mama, look what I found!"

Ignoring the tightness in her throat, Sky moved on. There was a lot of racket coming from a structure on her right. She stood on tip-toe to look through a square opening in the structure. Inside, men beat on glowing metal then plunged it into water.

Sky cocked her head. *That's a strange thing to do.*

Suddenly, a shriek cut through the clang of metal.

Sky gasped and whipped around. "Horses!"

She scurried over to the animals, one welcoming her with a nicker. Beaming, she patted the beast on the neck.

"Hello there. What's your name? I've been exploring your home. Do you like it here?" She noticed some hay at her feet. "Oh, are you hungry?" Sky tried to feed her new friend. Oddly, though, a local shooed her away. It didn't matter, however, for she was certain she had caught the scent of flowers.

She wandered over to the structure full of plants and was gazing at the blossoming roses when someone yelled, "Hey you!"

Jumping halfway out of her skin, Sky dropped the flower she had been admiring. One of the silver goblins was coming up to her, nostrils flaring like a dragon disrupted from sleep.

"Who are you?" he shouted. "I have not seen you here before."

Sky took a step backward and stumbled over a pot of daisies. Everyone stopped in their tracks, gasping and gaping. The fairy's brow furrowed. What were they all staring at? She looked down, and her heart skipped a beat. She had turned back into her normal self. She clapped her hands as quickly as possible and changed back, but it was too late. They had already seen her.

The silver goblin started inching towards her, and Ms. Hops's words came flashing back into her mind, "*None came back.*" Panic-stricken, she got up and ran for it. Her heart beating so hard her ribcage could barely hold it in, she hid in a narrow gap between two of the square structures.

A small opening appeared in one of the structures, and a girl's voice came from the darkness, "Psst! Hey! In here."

Sky hesitated, unsure if the voice could be trusted. But going through the opening was more appealing than being captured by the annoyed, silver goblin, so she darted inside. The opening closed with a soft thud.

3

TWO NEW FRIENDS

"It's ok. You're safe now," said the voice. "My name's Harper, by the way. So, you're a fairy?"

Sky, standing with her back against the wall on the opposite side of the wood structure, heaved and said nothing. Her eyes strained against the darkness, but all she could see was a vague outline of the girl in front of her.

"No one's seen a fairy for *years*," the girl continued. "That's why they were so afraid of you. See, the queen gave the order to kill any fairy that enters the kingdom. She thought all of them were dead, but...I guess not."

An uncomfortable silence followed that was only interrupted by Sky's quick breaths.

"So, what's your name, newbie?" the girl asked.

"S-S-Sky."

A little flame suddenly popped into existence, revealing Sky's surroundings. The girl, who had lit a white stick on fire, had a freckle-covered face and long brown hair that was pulled back with a much-worn cloth. Though scrawny, there was a weary but determined look to her face. The fire, somehow contained in a tiny, dancing ball atop the stick, pointed out the calluses on the girl's hands and the scars marking her arms.

Many strange objects surrounded her. There was a flat, fluffy-looking thing low to the ground, a thin piece of wood balancing on four sticks, wooden boards sticking out from the side of the structure that held up other odd things, and a stone arch with piles of wood under it. Sky forced herself to look away. She didn't have time to wonder at these things. She needed to find out more about this queen and this world.

"So," Sky said, tucking a wayward strand of hair behind her ear. "What's the rest of the story of this place?"

"Well"—Harper sighed—"Queen Vivian came to our village and *dazzled* the king (I think Vivian just wanted the throne), so he married her. Shortly after, they had a son, Prince Anthony. The king died a few days after the prince was born. Rumor has it that the queen killed the king to get the throne *all* to herself and that she married the king only to have a son of royal blood, so she and her little *prince* could rule together.

"Many fairies, over the years, came out of *nowhere* to try to overthrow her, but they were all captured and put to death or killed in battle. Or like I said—I guess not." Harper stared at Sky for a moment, as though trying to read her thoughts, then added, "I just hope one day someone will come and save us from her evil rule. She'll *kill* us all; I just know it! Maybe even the prince, so she'll still have the throne to herself. Yeah, her *own* son! That's what *I* think her plan is. A rumor's been going around, and I can *definitely* see her doing that."

There was a moment of silence before Sky slowly said, "Not from nowhere."

"I'm sorry?"

"The fairies. They didn't come from nowhere. They came from behind that Waterfall on the hill. Behind it is a whole other world. That's where I came from. I'm the last fairy—ever."

Harper blinked several times before whispering, "So, you've come to help us?"

Sky opened her mouth, but no words came out. Help them? How? She had only come to explore, but all those people were suffering under Vivian's rule. Her parents had tried to help. They had stood up against the evil queen, refusing to accept the injustice. How could she stand by and do nothing?

Sky swallowed. *Help them by confronting the woman who wiped out my entire race.*

Her lungs stopped working for a second. Anxiety pushed against her ribcage, demanding for more room to spread. She closed her eyes. Inhale. Exhale. In. Out. Courage played hide and seek with her heart, but she was determined to help these people. If she didn't, who would?

"I didn't come here to dethrone Vivian, but I will help you. No people deserve to suffer like this. However, I'm not familiar with this place. It is all very new to me. I'll need some help." Sky looked pointedly at Harper.

"Me?"

"Yes. Will you help me?"

Harper stared at her. Sky braced herself for a very harsh "*No!*" but at last, Harper replied, "Ok, I'll help you. It'll be kinda cool to have a fairy as a—as a *friend*, perhaps?"

Sky's heart calmed at those words. She smiled. "A friend."

"One question, though. How are two girls going to wipe out a horribly powerful queen?"

"We need a plan. And some more help would be nice."

"Well, we can't make up a plan here. The knights might overhear us. Let's go into the woods where no uninvited guests will pop in." As Harper walked to the opening, a long, shiny object on the four-legged piece of wood caught Sky's eye. She picked it up and ran her finger across its glittering edge.

As soon as Harper called, "Careful with that!" a sharp, stinging sensation zapped Sky's finger and blood began to ooze out. Sky dropped the shiny stick, and it clattered on the ground.

Wincing, she studied her finger. "It bit me!"

Harper giggled and picked it up. "It didn't *bite* you. It's not *alive*. It's a knife. It's for cutting things and defending yourself." She began stabbing the knife at some invisible attacker. "You know?"

Sky's eyes narrowed as she glared at the knife.

Harper looked around her. "I guess a lot of these things must look pretty weird to you, huh?"

"Could you tell me what they are?"

"Sure. That there's called a bed. This is a table, and that's a fireplace. What we're standing in is a house, and inside it is called a room. The horrid looking 'house' outside is called a castle. The man that shouted at you is a knight, and he's dressed in armor. That's a door. Coat. Plate...." Harper went on and explained several of the unfamiliar things Sky had encountered on her journey.

"That's some of the basics for now," Harper said, then frowned when she noticed Sky gazing out the window. "What's wrong?"

"It's just"—Sky took a deep breath—"your world seems so dark. Don't get me wrong, I think it's spectacular. I've never seen anything quite like it. But when I look at the people.... How can anyone live under such oppression? How could anyone have a happy day or a joyful spirit with such difficulties?"

"It's not easy," Harper admitted. "But you know, joy isn't the absence of pain and difficulty. If it just disappears at the sight of a small cloud, then it's pretty weak. I've had a difficult life under Vivian, but I've learned to find joy in spite of it. We all have. That's what you have to do in times like this: find joy in the pain."

"Aren't those things contradictory, though?"

Harper stared at some unseen thing, the corners of her mouth curving upward. "No. Not when you really think about it."

Joy with pain—it didn't sound right. But the words whispered in the back of her mind like someone was whispering a secret to her, but it was too soft for her to hear.

After sliding some shoes onto her feet, Harper piped up, "We'd better get going." So the two friends crept their way through the village, dodging the knights' watchful eyes every so often. From one of their hiding spots, Sky watched a father and son play together. Harper must have caught sight of Sky's watery eyes, for she asked, "Hey, you ok?" Sky dismissed it and arose from their hiding place. Slowly but surely, they made their way into the woods.

When they could no longer see the castle through the trees, they settled down onto the grass.

Sky breathed in the familiar smell of grass and bark. The birds played hide and seek with each other in the leaves. A group of squirrels argued over who got the last nut as the tiny flowers tittered at them. It was as if Sky's world had been blended into the human world.

What if we could live in the same world?

Harper rubbed her hands together. "So, what's the plan?"

Sky pulled her wandering mind back into focus. "Do you think we could *reason* with her? I mean, I still struggle to believe that anyone could be that evil."

Suddenly, someone in the woods burst into laughter.

"Oh, as if!" said a male voice. "My mom's a psychopath! She'll kill you on the spot with you being a *fairy* and all."

Both girls sprang up and whirled around. The owner of the voice was leaning against a tree. He was a handsome blond boy about Sky's age. With his hair combed back and his clothes clean and colorful, he appeared very different from the villagers. His eyes especially set him apart due to their brightness.

"My prince!" Harper gasped, whiter than lilies, and she dropped to her knees. He stared at her for a second with an ashamed countenance.

"Oh, please," the prince said, blushing. "None of that. I don't really get into all that formal, royalty '*you must kneel before me*' foolishness. Just...stand up. Please?"

Harper stood up slowly as though she did not want to.

So, this is the prince. He doesn't seem too bad.

Sky asked him, "How'd you know I was a fairy?"

"I saw the whole incident in the village from my bedroom window and thought I'd come down to see why in the world a *fairy* is in our kingdom," the prince replied. "I didn't know there were any left."

"I'm the last one," mumbled Sky, and the prince's gaze dropped. "How did you find us?"

"I saw you leaving the village," he explained. "So, you want to overthrow my mother? Talking to her won't work. She doesn't listen to anyone—not even me. The only way is to attack."

Sky and Harper glanced at one another. Even the arguing squirrels dropped their last nut and stared.

Harper blinked multiple times before saying, "You're *helping* us?"

The prince nodded grimly.

"She's your mother," said Sky. "Why would you help us?"

He sucked in a shaky breath. "My mother has been ruling these people, *my* people, cruelly, murdering *anyone* who stands up to her. She needs to be stopped. I've also been getting this eerie feeling lately. I don't feel safe around her. But, as you said, she is my mother. I will help you *only* if you promise not to kill her. Deal?"

Of course, I won't kill the queen!

A zap of anger struck her heart. Through her mind's eye, she saw her parents standing before her, smiling at their daughter as they should have been. The weight of their absence flooded her. Vivian had taken them away from her.

The small sparks of anger burst into a raging fire. Like a furious, wounded dragon, her soul roared at the idea of not taking revenge.

"Sky?" said a muffled voice.

Sky gasped and unclenched her fists. What had just happened? What was she thinking? The dragon's roars hushed. The fire extinguished. Her heart plummeted and smashed into the ground. Her spirit, like a scared little girl, wept bitterly within her.

"Sky?" Harper repeated.

The fairy blinked a few times. She refocused on the question at hand. Could she trust this prince?

"Ok," Sky agreed. "I need all the help I can get."

It's a deal. Of course, I don't want to kill the queen. Right?

Sky said, "You're Anthony, correct?"

"Yes." He looked in Harper's direction. "And your name is Harper, right?"

Harper nodded. "I am confused about one thing though. Why would the queen do this to her own people?"

BAM! It hit Sky like a lightning bolt, like a smack in the face. She stumbled backward a few steps. Could it be true? She wasn't the last one.

"Unicorns and pixies! It makes perfect sense," the fairy blurted. "They're not her people. She's not from here."

Anthony's brow furrowed. "Excuse me?"

"Your mother isn't from here," repeated Sky. "She came from behind the Waterfall—from my world."

"Ok," Anthony bit his lip. "Wh-what are you saying?"

"There's no humans in my world."

Now the prince was whiter than lilies.

"Wait a minute!" Harper exclaimed. "That means—the prince is—he's a—"

"You're half-fairy, Anthony," Sky whispered.

He leaned against a tree for support, looking at her with an expression that said, "You're crazy."

"Think Anthony. Did your mom ever ask you weird questions or keep a way-too-close eye on you?"

"Always." He grunted. "She would stare me down like a hawk when I was playing, and she'd ask the doctor to check my back a lot. It was for my spine, she said. But that's nothing too—oh. Oh, my gosh...oh, no."

Staring at some unknown thing in terror, Harper said, "She was checking to see if you were growing wings! But watching him play?"

"Magical abilities," Sky explained then asked, "What's a doctor?"

"Oh, right, I didn't go over that one. It's someone who looks after your health."

Anthony sunk to his knees, still holding onto the tree. "I never...I never..."

A wave of pity washed over Sky. She knew what it felt like to discover some ground-shaking truth that completely changed one's outlook on life. It must feel the same for him to learn that he was not completely human as when Sky learned the fate of her people. She almost wished she hadn't said anything.

"Are you still going to help us?" Harper asked gingerly.

The prince took a deep breath. "Yeah. Being half-fairy isn't the worst thing. I'm just taken aback, that's all." He smiled at Sky. Why did she get the feeling that his smile had another meaning beyond "Don't worry, I'm not against fairies"?

Her cheeks started burning. "It's hot out here, isn't it?"

Harper's gaze darted between Sky and the prince. She cocked her brow. "Sure, Sky. It's a little warm."

"So"—Anthony cleared his throat—"do you have an—um—army or something? How are we going to attack?"

"I don't have an army," Sky admitted. "But I do have some friends that can help us."

4

A CALL FOR AID

They walked along the woods' edge, heading for the Waterfall. Sky told her new friends about her world, her people and their history, and her journey to the human world through the Forbidden Waterfall. After her story, they traveled in silence, except for the prince's grunts and winces. What was wrong with him?

The lack of conversation left room for Sky's busy mind to talk.

You are horrible, a furious voice declared inside her head. *Why would you even have an impulse to take revenge? Why would you let yourself get that angry?*

But then another voice retorted, *Do you forget? Murder. Suffering. My parents.*

At the words "my parents," her temper rose rapidly, fingernails digging into her palms.

See, I told you. You're no better than her.

Her heart dropped like a bird with a broken wing. She felt uneasy, almost sick.

This internal argument was still raging when they reached the Waterfall.

Anthony asked, "So, how do we get into your world?"

"Huh?" Sky struggled to emerge from her thoughts.

"Um—your world? Are you ok?"

"Yeah, I'm fine."

Sky lifted her hands, but the prince interrupted her. "Before we go, I've been wondering, why do you want to help my people?"

With the internal argument lingering in the back of her mind, she replied, "No one should live like this. When I saw the people, I knew I had to help them."

"I agree. But still, they never fail to amaze me. I sometimes catch a glimpse of a smile or a gleam of joy in their eyes. I have learned from them that pain enriches joy. For how can you know what true joy is if you've never suffered? Even so, a relief from this oppression is long past due."

Pain enriches joy? His words filled Sky's mind as she clapped her hands twice. Her wings and blue dress reappeared, and her hair fell out of her bun. The prince's jaw dropped.

"Woah," he murmured, then, recovering himself, added, "Um—so this is what you—er—normally look like?"

Sky nodded and stepped through the Waterfall.

Cheerful sunlight and the sweet smell of flowers greeted her. Harper and Anthony stood by her side, looking around in amazement.

"It's so *beautiful*," Harper breathed.

"Yes, it is," whispered the prince.

"It's day already," Sky said. "Time must travel faster here."

Suddenly, a voice boomed, "Where *have* you been?" It was Ms. Hops, madder than a werewolf at full moon. A large group of animals and magical creatures accompanied her.

Sky held her breath and waited for the lecture to come.

The rabbit took several angry hops toward her. "You did the one thing—the *one* thing—I told you *not* to do!"

"I know, I know."

"*What* in the *world* provoked you to—" Ms. Hops stopped short, staring wide-eyed at Harper and Anthony. She and all those with her began to back away.

"It's ok," Sky assured them. "They're my friends, and they need our help. Yes, I went through the Forbidden Waterfall, and I found the evil fairy you told me about. She is ruling their world *harshly*, without mercy. She thinks she's won, but I cannot let that be the end of the story. I cannot stand by while these people suffer. We need to free them from the fear and misery Queen Vivian has brought into their lives.

"She doesn't know of this plan. Hopefully, that will give us an advantage. I know this seems rash, but we need to do this so the people can have their lives back. This terror came from our world. Though not our fault, we need to fix it. And then, maybe, we can be friends with the humans."

Instantly, there was a great uproar, all the animals screaming reasons why this war shouldn't happen.

"Listen to me," Sky bellowed. Anthony and Harper cast startled looks at her, apparently taken aback by her sternness. "I'm not doing this out of hate for Vivian. I just want to end the suffering."

Or, at least, I think I do.

She continued, "Look, I don't know what made you so afraid of the humans, but this is what my people, your friends, fought for—to protect them from Vivian's rule. Just because the fairies are—are *gone*, doesn't mean we should abandon what they fought to save. We have a chance to make it all mean something. So, will you help me?"

No one moved or said anything for what felt like a millennium, but eventually, one by one, they all agreed. They were going to free the human world from its slavery.

Ms. Hops said, "That's my girl. Isn't she so brave?"

Sky grimaced. Was it bravery? Was it noble? She had almost gone crazy with rage after merely promising not to harm the queen. She glanced at Anthony. What would he say if he knew what was brewing inside of her? All the hate, all the fury. How could she desire such a wicked thing?

She inwardly ordered her queasy stomach to pull itself together. *Everything's fine. I'm doing this to save the humans.*

Anthony's voice startled her. "What now?"

"Oh, um...they'll spread the news and get more help. It won't take them too long. We will all go back to your world soon."

Too soon for me to figure all of this out.

Ms. Hops sat ten feet away, giving the little critters instructions on how they would assist in the upcoming battle. She then turned to Ember the phoenix and ordered him to spread the news to all flying creatures. Ms. Hops always knew what to do in every situation. In *every* situation. Of course! She was a wise rabbit. Surely she could help Sky with her predicament.

26

"I have to talk to Ms. Hops for a minute," Sky told her new friends and walked over to the rabbit, who had just finished her conversation with Ember. "Um, Ms. Hops?"

"Yes?"

"I couldn't help thinking that—well, I may be doing this for the wrong reason. I have so much hate for Vivian—pure *fury*. It's almost torture to think of not—of not...she's hurt so many people: the humans, the animals, the fairies, my...*my family*. And I just...I just...I want to—"

I want revenge. I can't let Vivian get away with this murder.

There was no more denying the malice living in her soul. She could already see herself with blood-stained hands, the keening of a Banshee saturating the air. It would summon a death but not Vivian's. It was the death of Sky's own heart. Vivian had not only taken her family, but her soul as well.

That vengeful poison spilled out of Sky's eyes in tears, burning their way down her cheeks like acid. Despite years of trying to keep heartache at bay, it filled her to the brim and her joy dissipated. Was this who she was? She was no better than Vivian.

Furry cheeks damp with tears, Ms. Hops said softly, "Don't cry, my dear. Being angry is natural. Anyone would be. But having the impulse to seek revenge is not equal to the action itself. Just because you have the thought doesn't mean you are guilty of the crime. Our impulses and emotions—whether good or evil—are always going to be a part of us. Whether we choose to act on them or not, however, is another matter entirely. We must not let such emotions control us. We must not let them eat away at us. Don't dwell on them, my dear. There are times to listen to the heart, and there are times to listen to the mind.

"But I will say this, hate and revenge only hurts the person who seeks revenge. It will fix nothing. You must *let go*. Though it seems impossible right now, you have to learn to forgive—yes, even Vivian. It won't make the pain go away, and it certainly doesn't make what Vivian did right, but it frees you and often those around you.

"But Sky, do not worry. Our impulses don't make us who we are. I know you wish to help others. You're a good person, but you had a bad impulse. You're imperfect, like the rest of us. What else did you expect, my dear? This is a matter of choice, not feelings. You must *choose* to forgive and *choose* to do this for the humans."

Sky sniffled. "Choose?"

"Of course. Our emotions don't control us, not unless we allow them to."

An invisible load that had been pressing down on her shoulders suddenly lifted. Joy zoomed into her chest like little pixies and ripped despair to shreds. Yes, she would fight for humanity, and she would keep her promise to the prince. But could she forgive Vivian after all that had happened?

That was a question for another time. She sighed, relishing in the lightness of her heart. "Thank you, Ms. Hops. I don't know if I would've actually done anything, but the fact that it was in my mind...it scared me."

"It's ok, my dear." The rabbit smiled. "We all face these difficulties in life. It's a good thing too, for if one is wise enough to allow it, there are valuable lessons to be learned from these things. Very valuable, indeed."

Meanwhile, the prince was enduring a splitting headache and an aching back. Harper was talking to him, but he was in too much pain to listen.

He interrupted her, "I don't feel so good."

"What do you mean?" she asked as he sat down on a rock. "What's wrong?"

"I feel nauseous. My head is throbbing. And my back is *killing* m—"

"Still?"

"How did you—"

"You keep rubbing your shoulders, and you were moaning all through Sky's speech."

"Sorry."

"I didn't say it was *your* fault."

"Shh! Here comes Sky. Don't tell her I'm not feeling well."

"Everything alright?" Sky asked as she approached.

"Yep," Harper lied.

"Ok, good. I'm going to go see if the others need any help."

Once Sky was out of earshot, Harper turned back to Anthony. "I really think you should tell somebody. Maybe they can help."

"No, I'm fine. Just give me a minute to catch my breath. You can go see if Sky needs any assistance."

Harper seemed hesitant to keep Anthony's condition quiet, but she respected his wishes and went to join Sky. He took several deep breaths, willing himself to recover, but the clamor of the bustling creatures was making his headache worse. He needed to get away from all the noise, so he staggered into the woods.

5

MORE THAN MEETS THE EYE

Anthony heaved, leaning against a small tree. *I just need to catch my breath. Oh goodness. What's wrong with me?*

He dug his nails into the mossy bark as though the prick of discomfort would distract from the searing pain in his body.

Make it stop. Somebody, anybody. Make it stop!

If relief did not come soon, he was going to die from the agony.

Something rough began slithering upward from beneath his palm.

He looked up. *Oh my word.*

The tree was growing, *fast*. Larger and taller it became until it was the biggest tree in the forest.

He jerked his hand away, and the tree stopped growing. "What—what on earth? Oh!" If someone had driven a thousand needles into his skull and scraped a hundred knives across his back, it would have been more endurable. Was this punishment for betraying his mother? Had she found out? Had she cursed him?

"I can't," he wheezed. "Make it stop." He staggered on... and on...and on until he could no longer stand. He fell on his knees and didn't move. He *couldn't* move.

A pain so excruciating it made him long for his previous misery suddenly ripped through his back. How could any hurt or ache ever reach this torturous level? There must've been a beast trapped within him, trying to claw its way out. His bones were at their breaking point. His skin felt stretched beyond its limits.

"AHHHH!" Something burst out of him. Blood poured down his back. He groaned as the darkness closed in. He toppled over. Everything went black.

A scream echoed through the land. Sky's wings stiffened. Everyone stopped what they were doing, each face wearing a troubled expression.

"What...was *that?*" Harper said.

Sky scanned her surroundings. *Where's Anthony?* Horror punched her in the gut, knocking the wind out of her. Her dizziness made it hard to see straight.

Where's Anthony? Where is Anthony? Did Vivian—

Fear, like a nasty little goblin, danced around in her mind. It taunted her with terrible images of all the gruesome things that might have happened to the prince. She clutched her stomach, willing herself not to vomit.

"W-wait." Harper's breath quickened as she wrung her hands. "Where's Anthony?" The girls exchanged panic-stricken looks, then darted into the woods. Ms. Hops followed the best she could.

Oh, no. What's happened to him? What if he's—Chimera's heads!

They came to a halt. A gigantic tree stood before them.

"Good gracious! That tree is *huge*!" Harper said.

"It was hardly nine feet tall before I left," Sky panted. "Now it's larger than any tree I've ever seen! I don't like this. This is too strange...it doesn't matter. We have to find Anthony."

They didn't have to run much further before they found another unusual sight.

"Look!" Harper pointed. There, lying motionless on the grass, were two great eagle wings—far bigger than any bird that Sky knew of.

Sky inched forward. "I don't recognize that—" She clapped a hand over her mouth. A human hand reached out from underneath the wings.

No, it can't be.

The girls rushed over to the figure, and there lay Anthony—with wings.

By the mermaid's tail, it is Anthony! And he has wings. Unicorns and pixies! He has full-blown, fairy wings.

Harper's jaw dropped. "Oh—my—gosh. What? How?"

Sky pulled Anthony's limp body into her arms. Blood trickled through her fingers and onto her lap.

Ms. Hops entered the scene and said, "Sky, you have to wash off the blood."

Sky nodded. Taking a deep breath, she placed her hand on the ground. Dew drops rose into the air and joined together overhead. She reached up and touched the ball of water. A seal broke; the water flowed onto Anthony's back.

"Woah," Harper breathed.

"Anthony?" Sky whispered, brushing strands of hair out of his face. "Anthony?"

He groaned and his eyes fluttered open. "Hey," he mumbled. "What's going on?"

Sky's voice quivered, "Um, Anthony, you have—"

"Wings?" He chuckled weakly. "I can feel two limbs attached to my shoulder blades. And with what we discussed back home, I was able to figure it out." Wincing, he raised himself up. He didn't look worried or scared, just exhausted.

"What happened?"

"After we arrived here, I began feeling ill. I felt discomfort in my back before we arrived, but it got much worse once we were through the Waterfall. My back was throbbing, and so was my head. I had to get away from all the noise, so I went into the woods, where I made a tree grow forty feet, and wings popped out of my back."

"How is this even possible?"

Ms. Hops's left ear twitched (as it always did when she hesitated) before she said, "It's because he hasn't been exposed to magic before." Everyone stared at the rabbit.

"I don't understand," Sky said.

"He grew up away from magic and thus didn't have any magic himself until he was exposed to it. Here, the very *air* is magic. When Anthony came through the Waterfall, the magic in him came to life. Like a flower needing sun and water, his magic could not grow before. Here, it can."

"But I began to feel changes back home," said Anthony.

"You were near Sky. She is full of magic. She grew up in it. But her magic alone wasn't enough to cause yours to grow."

"What about my mother? Doesn't she have magic? And, come to think of it, why doesn't she have wings?"

"When she began living behind the Waterfall, her magic began to die. She didn't know this would happen, of course. But after losing her wings, she seized the opportunity of being mistaken for a human and married the king. Her magic didn't affect you because she no longer has magic."

"So, when I go home, my magic will disappear?"

"Not right away, but yes, it will."

Sky's eyebrows knit together. "Wait, so why didn't my magic disappear?"

"You were in their world a matter of hours. Vivian was there for weeks before her magic died."

Sky shook her head. "I can't believe it." She gazed at Anthony in awe: another fairy, one of her own kind. Or, at least, he was sort of her own kind. He was different. His magic was different; his wings were different. And his eyes, his eyes were magnificent—brown now, not blue.

They were like many tree branches intertwined together, constantly growing, constantly moving. Streaks of light combed through each branch, like some magical water rushing through their veins, glowing through the bark. She had always dreamed of meeting another fairy, but this was beyond anything she had imagined.

Her excitement took a stumble, plummeting off its high cliff, abruptly ending in sorrow as reality sunk in. He hated this, no doubt. He probably thought it was the worst thing that could have happened to him.

As Harper continued gaping at him, Anthony tried to stretch out his wings. He inhaled sharply, gritting his teeth, before they had lifted an inch.

Sky grimaced for him. "They might be a little difficult to use at first."

"Did you have to learn how to use yours?" he asked.

"Yes. As you learned to walk, I learned to fly. But you don't...you don't hate being this way, do you?"

He smiled tenderly. "I could only image what this is like for you. I can't say all this is exactly comforting, but it's not like I'm going to despise my life from here on out. And magic and wings—it's cool, isn't it?"

Sky giggled. "Yeah."

"Well," Harper chimed in, "you're taking it a lot better than I would. If wings popped out of my back, I'd have a heart attack!"

"What, you wouldn't want wings?" Sky teased.

"Don't get me wrong. That'd be awesome, but I would be more shaken than Anthony here."

The prince shrugged. "Somehow, I feel I've always known. I just didn't know what I knew. Does that make sense?"

Holding in a laugh, Harper replied, "Um, no."

Sky tittered.

"I do have a question, though," said Anthony. "Why are my magic and my wings different from Sky's?"

"There were four types of fairies," the rabbit explained, "each with unique looks and magically abilities."

Sky nearly fell over. "Wait, what?"

"Yes," said Ms. Hops. "You, Sky, are a water fairy. Anthony appears to be a plant fairy. In times past, there were also sun fairies—having powers of fire and light—and weather fairies—having powers to control the weather."

"What—when—how—how could you not tell me this?" Sky sputtered.

"It wasn't relevant until now."

Sky let out a frustrated sigh, and the rabbit chuckled.

"Personally, I think this makes us a perfect little trio," declared Harper, "one fairy, one human, and one half-fairy."

"*Half*-fairy?" Ms. Hops repeated. "There's no such thing as a half-fairy. Yes, his father was human, but it only takes one fairy parent to make the child a full-blooded fairy. Even if, by your reckoning, Anthony was a third of a third fairy, he would still be one hundred percent fairy."

Harper's jaw dropped. "That's *awesome!*"

Silence settled over the group. A hawk flew by, screeching news of the war. The prince cleared his throat. "I guess we'd better get going. There's a war to be fought, and a people to be saved."

"He's right," said Ms. Hops. "We must go back to the Waterfall." The rabbit and Harper began walking in that direction as Anthony struggled to stand.

"Need some help?" Sky asked.

"Um...yeah. These things are so heavy. How in the world are you even able to walk?"

"You get used to them." Zap!—an idea came to her. It was wonderful; it was brilliant. And perhaps, it was dumb, but it would help him. And, she had to admit, she really wanted to do it.

"Hey, I have an idea." His hands tight on her shoulders, Sky gripped his upper arms and hoisted him to his feet. He wobbled a bit, but using her for support, he was able to find his balance. "I could teach you how to fly."

He laughed as though she was joking but, after studying her for a minute, asked, "Are you serious?"

"Of course, I am! Don't you want to learn?"

"Sky, I can barely walk."

"But learning to fly will help you control your wings. It should be easy to walk then."

Anthony hesitated. "I don't know. By the sound of things, I won't have these wings very long."

Sky's head dropped. The prince was right. He wouldn't have his wings much longer, and she would go back to being the last fairy.

She could feel his gaze on her.

"You really want to teach me, don't you?"

She met his eyes bashfully. "Yes, I do. It's just—I've never been able to fly with another fairy before." Ok, that wasn't the reason. Well, that wasn't the *only* reason. She just liked being around him.

"Ok, I'll try. So how are we going to do this?"

With a wide grin on her face, she clapped her hands as she gave a little jump. She took Anthony's hand and pulled him along as she skipped towards a small cliff. "We'll climb up there for starters." She halted when she heard Anthony wince. "Oh, sorry! Um—do you think you can climb, or are your wings too heavy?"

"My magic is plants and stuff, right?"

"Yeah."

"How do I—er...." He gazed at his hand then up at a tall tree nearby, biting his lip.

Sky placed her hand on his shoulder. "You can do it. Just focus on the tree. Pretend it's a part of you. Tell it to move like you would tell your arm to move."

Closing his eyes, he took a deep breath and placed his left hand on the trunk. The tree's branches groaned, and at last, one reached down and carried them to the top of the cliff.

"You did it, Anthony!"

"Yeah, I did. That felt strange." He seemed proud of himself, but his smile faded when he peered over the edge. He gulped. "I'm not sure about this, Sky."

"You'll be fine." With a flap of her wings, she rose. "Trust me." She picked him up by the arms and took off. The spectacular forest of her world stretched out before them as they glided through the air.

"Your world is beautiful," Anthony breathed, and a smile gradually spread across her face.

So is yours.

"Stretch out your wings for me." Taking him by the hand, she pulled him up so they soared side by side, hand in hand.

His eagle-like wings were slack at first, timid and frightened. They didn't trust the current to carry him. But after a few moments, they became rigid, confidently catching the wind as it pushed him a couple inches above her level. He wobbled, eyes wide, but her hand coaxed him back down. His fingers remained tight around hers as his chest rose and fell rapidly. Soon, she felt his grip relax and noted his breathing had calmed. He beamed down at the blurry landscape below.

"I'm going to let you go now," she said over the howling wind in her ears.

"Wait, what?"

"You're going to be ok. I'll catch you if you fall."

"Sky, I don't think that's a good idea."

"It's just like the tree: as you tell your arms to move, tell your wings." She let go of his hand and—he flew. He thrust his wings downward, regaining the altitude he had momentarily lost when she released his hand. Level with her, he stretched out his arms parallel to his wings, which moved gracefully up and down in time with hers.

"Oh, my goodness!" the prince exclaimed as she laughed. "This is amazing!"

They soared across the painted sky, flying over mountains and woods and rivers and creatures of every kind. The sun kissed the horizon, leaving behind a trail of brilliant colors, like every past day's sky blending together into one majestic veil, hiding the stars.

And the stars waited behind the veil, as they always did, for their turn to shine. But they could wait no longer, for something was happening that had not happened for many years. The stars appeared early, twinkling and giggling in the sky. They were unusually bright in their awe. For the first time in so long, they watched fairies play and fly together. It was like a dream from a past night. In this space between day and night, a gleam from the past reflected onto the present world.

Sky's tears blurred the scene in front of her. She had dreamed of this day all her life, but she never believed it would come. The wonder she had felt upon seeing the human world was nothing compared to this. She relished each detail: the feel of the wind between her fingers, the comfort of another fairy at her side, the sheer bliss in the prince's eyes, and the unique way he looked at her. However, a shadow came to life in her mind with folded arms and a scowl, proclaiming, "This cannot last forever. His wings will soon disappear." But Sky quickly dismissed the intruder and determined to enjoy every single detail of every single moment.

This is the best day of my life!

The Forbidden Waterfall loomed into view, and Anthony groaned. "I wish we didn't have to go."

"They need us."

"I know....Thank you for doing this, Sky. I haven't enjoyed myself this much in a while."

"My pleasure."

"Um—Sky?"

"Yes?"

"You are going to teach me how to land, right?"

"Of course, Anthony." She guffawed. "Of course."

6

THE STORY BEHIND
THE WATERFALL

Nearing the Waterfall, Anthony flipped upside-down, gazing at Sky from where he flew beneath her. The way he looked at her—an explanation began to take shape in her mind. Surely, that wasn't the reason. She ordered her fluttering heart to relax, but it paid her no mind. It was as unruly as a leprechaun.

Once they had landed, neither of them moved. Anthony shifted his weight, though he never took his eyes off her. There was something he was dying to say. What on earth could he have to tell her?

My heartbeat's too loud. Can he hear it?

He finally spoke. "Sky?"

"Yes?"

"When this is over, do you really think we have to part ways? I mean, isn't there a way we can live in the same—"

"Hey, everybody! Look!" a squirrel squeaked, and Sky started. "The human boy gots wings!"

We should've landed further away from the Waterfall.

The animals gathered around Anthony full of amazement and questions. Harper shook in her effort to keep from laughing at the prince's overwhelmed expression as endless inquiries surrounded him. An abrupt hush fell over the crowd when Anthony revealed who his mother was.

As he explained the sudden appearance of his wings, Sky sat separate from the group, staring at the Waterfall. That rushing wall of water concealed the world they were about to save, or try to save. Though her trip was short, she had seen many knights in the village. What were the total number of knights in Vivian's kingdom? Did she have an army of thousands or tens of thousands?

Sky hugged herself and glanced at her animal friends. They had no armor or war experience that she knew of. The Forbidden Waterfall had lost its alluring nature. It was menacing, its roar the shriek of a Banshee, bringing death to her world and all who lived there.

"You alright, my dear?" Ms. Hops jumped up onto the rock Sky was sitting on.

The fairy realized that she was trembling and held herself tighter, willing her body to still. "Yes...no. No, I'm not. I just...we're going to *war*. I'm *really* scared."

"I'd be surprised if you were anything else. In fact, I'd consider you a fool if you weren't afraid."

"It's just—it didn't really sink in until now."

"It's the right thing to do. Those people have suffered enough at Vivian's hand."

Sky took deep breaths and rocked back and forth, trying to appease her jitters. "Can you, p-please, talk ab-bout something else? *Anything* else."

"Well," the rabbit suggested, "I could tell you where the Waterfall came from."

"Wait, what!" Poof! The jitters were appeased. "I thought the Waterfall was just—*there*. You mean it came from somewhere else?"

Ms. Hops chuckled. "What I mean is there hasn't always been two worlds."

"You're kidding me!"

"No. The world of fairies and the world of man was once one world many centuries ago. Most humans think it's a myth. It was indeed a marvelous world, much like this one—but better. However, as time went on, men grew envious of the fairies' powers. Because of this tension, the fairies thought the humans planned on killing them. Now this might have or might not have been the case, but that is not the point. The fairies refused to help the humans after that, so the humans waged war on the fairies. Many people died.

"Hate grew on both sides—friendships ended, and alliances were broken. There was no end in sight, so the fairies and magical creatures cut themselves off from man. They created the Forbidden Waterfall and disappeared. Man forgot us. The fairies' memory of the war died out. Then Vivian found their world again and created this whole mess."

"Wow," Sky murmured. "Do you think that's why Vivian wanted to conquer the humans? You think she found out?"

"Maybe," the rabbit mused. "That just may be."

"Wait, how come you know about it and the other fairies did not?"

"The fairies kept history books, but there were certain parts they didn't want the next generations to learn. My family were the Keepers of the Forbidden Texts. However, it's possible Vivian found them anyway."

"Why were they forbidden?"

"Shame, I suppose. Fear that younger, more zealous fairies would do something rash, like Vivian did. You didn't ask, so, to try and follow the rules as closely as I could, I didn't tell you this part of the story before. But really, none of that matters now. You've grown up so much, so quickly. I wish your parents were here to see you now."

Sky took a shaky inhale. "Yeah, me too."

"They would've been very proud of you."

Wishful dreams of days with her parents danced before her mind's eye, making her heart heavy as a sack of stones. Her mom and dad were gone because of her, because they gave their lives for their daughter.

They loved me so much that they died for me.... They loved me.

Sorrow's flame bent to joy's wind in a bittersweet battle, and a smile flickered on her lips. A love must be quite mighty to not waver upon death's approach. Yes, they had loved her. But now they were gone, and she wished they weren't.

I want my family back.

Through her blurry vision, Sky could make out Anthony wrapping up his story. He was surrounded by all kinds of listening creatures and Harper, sitting cross-legged on the grass. And there at Sky's side was Ms. Hops, who had raised her and taught her so many things.

She blinked, stared at Anthony's group then at Ms. Hops, and blinked again. Then a voice sounded in her head as though it was her own thought, but it was so foreign that she startled. *Wake up, girl. You have a family.*

Somebody turned the lights on in her brain. All this time, she hoped for something she believed she could not have, but life had blessed her with a new family. Of course, she would always keep her parents close to her heart, but this wound didn't have to stay open. Though she missed them, she could still be encouraged by the fact that she had had parents who cared. She could smile at their memory, not treat it like doomsday. Is this what Harper and Anthony meant by finding joy in the pain?

But...I can't live in the same world as Harper and Anthony.

A hundred more stones were added to the sac in her heart. How could elation ever survive under affliction's tyranny? As soon as one hurt healed, another ripped open, like a vampire sucking out all the good in life. At the end of this, they would have to go to their own worlds: Sky to her magical forest, and Anthony and Harper to—

Click! Sky had an idea. *If the barrier was made, can it be unmade? No. No, that would never work.*

She asked anyway. "Ms. Hops, do you think there's any way that our worlds could become one again?"

"The Forbidden Waterfall is a barrier of hate," Ms. Hops answered, wiggling her nose. "And magic reinforced by hate is powerful. The only thing that could undo it, as I have read in the Forbidden Texts, would be the opposite—forgiveness and love. And you would have to use the old fairy language I taught you to undo the spell."

Sky turned back toward the Waterfall. Could she break the spell?

The rabbit went to help the others prepare to go through the Waterfall while Sky's mind chattered and buzzed like a meeting between little creatures:

Why are we still talking? We have the answer!

No, that will never do. Never do.

Of course, it will! Now, no one has to say goodbye.

What if they don't want to live in our world?

How could you say that? They love our world!

Ok, ok. But forgiveness? After everything that's happened?

It's...it's not impossible. No one really remembers the war.

True, true. Maybe we should focus on getting through this war first.

Good idea.

Why do you really want to break the barrier?

Their world would be better. And my friends—

It's the boy, isn't it?

Don't be ridiculous. There's Harper and—

But it's mostly the boy?

Alright! You win. It is mostly the boy.

I think he likes you.

Yeah, right...really?

I think you like him.

Shut up.

Is it just because he's the only boy you know?

No!

I think that—

It doesn't matter. You're right. That barrier will probably never come down.

It might, if we win this war and then you—

"Sky, you ok?" Harper broke into Sky's internal argument.

She murmured, "Yeah, I'm fine. Just...thinking."

Harper plopped down next to her with a strange grin on her face. "You and Anthony took your sweet time rejoining the group."

Sky squirmed in her seat. "I was teaching him how to use his wings."

"Uh-huh. Right."

"I was!"

"You have a thing for him, don't you?"

"What do you mean?"

"I mean, you *like* him?"

Sky cocked her head. *What does she mean I like him?. He's my friend, of course I–oh.* That *kind of like.*

She cleared her throat. "No. Of course not." They looked at each other for a minute with knowing smiles and giggled.

"I knew it," Harper whispered.

The girls wiped the grins off their faces when Anthony approached, announcing that everyone was ready. Sky, Harper, and the prince then went through the Waterfall, and all the critters followed them.

"Don't we need weapons?" Anthony asked.

"My friends don't," said Sky. "They have horns and claws and things."

"And what about you?"

"Don't you know by now, Anthony?" she teased. "I have *magic.*" She put her hand in a pond by the Waterfall and—FLASH!—pulled out a glittering sword made of ice. She made Harper one too.

Harper gaped at it. "Ok, you just have to admit, that's just *awesome!*"

The prince shut his open mouth. "Never mind, then."

Harper looked down at the field and her face grew dark. "Vivian's coming."

She was right. Queen Vivian was leading her army of knights toward the Waterfall. The sight was like a punch in the stomach. They were going to war.

But Sky's spirit, her resilient spirit, clung onto hope. Her confidence grew, like a flower opening up in the morning, yawning and stretching. There was still a sun behind these thunderclouds; there had to be. They were going to win, no matter what doubt's snobby voice said.

A river ran right next to the battlefield. Sky declared, "Perfect! The mermaids can help us."

Harper gasped, wide-eyed. "Wait—mermaids?"

"Yes, mermaids."

Harper shook her head in disbelief. "This is getting crazier by the second."

Before they went into battle, Anthony made a way for the mermaids. He caused the ground to sink with his magic, so the water would run down the hill and into the river below. The mermaids swam down the new river, glowing and waving.

Harper gaped at them and waved back hesitantly. "Ok, that's it! Sky, I'm moving to your world."

Sky smiled before turning to Anthony. "We need help. I've never seen war. My friends don't know how to fight an army. Is there anyone else we can call on for help? I hate to ask, but what about the villagers?"

"I don't know," the prince said. "They are terrified of Vivian. But for their freedom, it's possible. I'll go to the village and recruit some men. We can get weapons from the castle. And—um—Sky?"

"Yes?"

"I...well...um...just be careful. Ok? I'd like to be...friends for longer than a day."

The breeze did nothing to cool her burning cheeks. Sky focused hard on the ladybug crawling on her foot, but it was difficult to ignore her thundering heart. Why did the word "friend" sound so forced?

I think he likes you.

It took all the effort she could muster to keep herself from grinning.

"I'll be careful. Don't worry," she said, looking up. "You be careful too." She went off to battle as Anthony dashed toward the village.

7

BACK AT THE VILLAGE

Anthony hid in an alley. He peered around the corner. Knights paced the streets.

Oh, great. She left guards here. I need to stay hidden, or this is going to get really complicated really fast.

He glanced back at his bulky wings. It would be near impossible to hide with those things. He had to conceal them somehow.

He winced. There was an awful pressure on his back. He glanced at his wings again expecting to find something wrong with them.

Anthony flinched. Where did his wings go? Did he lose his fairy traits already? No, he had been pondering how to hide them. They simply shrunk into his back at his command, or so he hoped.

Would Sky still want to be my friend if I wasn't a fairy?

He rubbed a hand across his face. He had to stop thinking about her. He had a job to do.

Through a tavern window, he saw a group of men eating together and made a sprint for the door when the guard was looking the other way. Ignoring the men's wide eyes upon entering, Anthony shut the door and crawled to the window.

"My prince," one exclaimed. "What are you doing he—"

"Shh!" warned Anthony. "I have an eerie feeling those guards are searching for me, and it is crucial that they don't find me."

"Why, your majesty?" another asked. "What reason would the guards have for searching for you?"

"Gentlemen," Anthony said, peering out the window, I have committed treason."

They gaped at him.

Breaking the long stretch of silence, he explained, "The fairy that was spotted earlier today, I have joined with her and others to end my mother's rule. This is it, men. This is the chance for freedom. A small army of magical creatures are warring against the queen as we speak. But they will not last. Not without help. They need an army. Trained men. And I have come to find such men."

"My lord," a third gulped, "if I may be so bold to ask..."

"You may."

"Why would you wish to revolt against the queen?"

The prince didn't reply. Truth be told, there was another war raging, a war in his soul. On one side, there was a desire to free his people, and on the other, he was grieving the state of his mother's heart. Though he knew he was doing right, going through with this plan broke him. He loved her still despite all she had done to him and despite the rumors of her evil plans for him.

"I care greatly for my mother," he admitted, his voice quivering, "but I can't stand by while she rules my people in such a horrible way—not anymore. I wish it didn't have to come to this. But both you and I know, for change, for freedom, it must."

"Then, your majesty," declared the first, rising to his feet, "I will fight with you."

"I will also aid this army."

"Aye! Me too."

All the men in the tavern agreed to help Sky. The prince instructed half of them to discreetly seek out more help while he and the rest of the men retrieved weapons from the castle.

They set off, each group to their own objective. The men with Anthony appeared troubled. There were a lot of guards in the castle, even though most had been hauled off to war. But Anthony knew every nook and cranny of the castle. They would slip in easily.

Once inside, he led the way to the armory.

"It's down those stairs. Second door to the right," he whispered after they had avoided being seen by another guard. "You go on. I will meet you outside. My sword is not in the armory."

The prince strode down the corridor that led to his bedroom. Opening the chest at the foot of his bed, he retrieved his sword. He turned to leave. Two guards stood in the doorway. Their expressions were stern but disheartened.

"Good evening," Anthony finished fastening the sword to his hip. "May I help you?"

"By order of the queen," one of the guards said, "we are to arrest you for treason."

"Has this country really become that cold—that blind and black-hearted—that its men would lock up one fighting for its freedom?"

"The lives of our wives and children hang in the balance, your majesty."

"They are in danger no matter what you do."

"We cannot take that chance. We have no choice."

The other guard's eyes dropped. "I'm so sorry, my lord."

Anthony gripped his sword hilt. "So am I."

The first guard attempted to seize him by the shoulders, but Anthony spun to the side, drawing his sword. Deflecting a well-aimed punch with the flat of his sword, he ducked under the other guard's arms and hit him on the head with the hilt. That guard collapsed. The first guard lunged, but Anthony, using his attacker's momentum, slammed the guard into the wall and knocked him out.

Anthony sheathed his sword. "Sorry, guys."

I need to fly. His wings reemerged, and breaking through the glass, he flew out the window.

Thank goodness, I still have my wings.

The men were passing out weapons to a large crowd when he landed. Everyone stopped what they were doing and stared at their prince's strange appearance.

"It is a long story. Don't ask," Anthony said. "How many do we have?"

"Around seven dozen, my lord," informed one.

"It sounds like quite the battle out there," another said.

The prince listened and heard the yelling of men and the cries of animals. The horrid sound was what made it sink in: his friends were in danger. He imagined the bloodshed that must have been taking place, Sky and the animals risking their lives for his people.

Sky.

He could think of nothing else. A girl so innocent and ignorant of man's evil was fighting for her life in battle. Or had she already fallen? Had she even survived the initial impact? An image formulated in his mind: Sky on the ground, her wings streaked with blood.

He squeezed his eyelids shut, as though that would shield his eyes from it, but the image was in his mind. He could still see her.

"We must move quickly," he said, opening his eyes. He couldn't stand idle with dreadful visions of Sky's death. He must take action. "They need our help."

Anthony and his army assembled and marched into the battle.

8

THE LAST STAND OF THE FAIRIES

Sky felt as stiff as the silver goblins appeared. Her muscles were made of solid iron, her metal ribs the only reason her heart didn't shoot out of her chest.

Easy, Sky. Calm down.

She tightened her grip on her ice-sword. They were going to win. They had to win.

Like two great walls, the knights stood on one side of the valley and the animals and magical creatures on the other. The stillness was unnerving. Even the sky held its breath in apprehension.

"What happens now?" Harper whispered. "They attack first? We attack first?"

"I don't know," Sky said. "I've never been in a battle."

"I haven't either, but something about this stand still doesn't feel right."

"Let's not move until they do—show them we don't want a fight."

Harper scoffed. "I can promise you, my friend, *she* wants a fight."

The silence rang loudly in their ears. Every second lasted hours, and every minute lasted days. Then Vivian's army began marching. Their march turned into a jog then into a run.

"*Sky?*" Harper said in alarm.

"Now!" the fairy shouted to her comrades. "ATTACK!"

Her army broke into a run, barreling toward their enemy. The two sides slammed into each other. Havoc reigned on the battlefield. Unicorns charged the knights with their horns. Mermaids pulled men into the water. Pegasi, eagles, and other kinds of flying creatures attacked from the sky. Little critters—mice, rabbits, hedgehogs, and squirrels—beat on the knights' feet and scampered up to their shoulders to bang on their heads. However, the knights' swords were deadly, and they struck down many of the creatures.

It was all a blur, like flashes of a foggy memory. Chaos boxed her in. Sky deflected a strike with her sword and rammed the hilt into the knight's face. Whimpering, she backed away from where he lay limp. She bumped into something and shrieked. There was another enemy behind her. He pushed her to the ground. Her sword flew out of her hand. He raised his weapon but was snatched up by a pegasus. She scrambled over to her sword but didn't pick it up. She hunched over it, clutching her head. She squeezed her eyes shut and trembled and sobbed. It was too much. Her eyes flew open as swords collided overhead. She screamed as a spray of blood hit her.

Make it stop. Someone make it stop.

"Sky!" someone yelled. "Sky, get up! Snap out of it. You're going to get yourself killed!"

Harper.

"Don't panic. You can do this. Just focus on the fight directly in front of you." She tugged on Sky's arms, but the fairy didn't budge.

Harper paused her efforts to fight another enemy. A heap of metal clanged to the ground in front of Sky, then Harper was back on her knees next to her friend. She said calmly, "Sky, just breathe. Freaking out is not going to help anyone. Just focus on one knight at a—" A sword slashed the space between them. "Woah!"

Harper began dueling the new attacker.

Sensible thoughts returned to Sky's head. She forced herself to stop hyperventilating and breathe steadily. Harper was right: she must regain control of herself.

One at a time. Don't worry about the whole battle. Just one knight at a time.

She grabbed her sword and rose. A knight charged at her. She gave all her attention to fending him off, only allowing her mind to be occupied by that one person.

Don't think. Just fight. Just defend.

Harper and Sky stood back to back, fighting off as many knights as they could. They were doing well, considering they had no training with a sword. Whenever it became more than she could handle, she would rise and use a blast from her wings to push several knights back. She didn't dare take off and fight from the air. She couldn't leave Harper by herself.

Sky risked a glance and saw the mermaids peering over the riverbank. Water-bound, they couldn't fight. The men had learned to stay away from the river.

That glance cost her. Two knights caught her by the wings and dragged her away from Harper. Sky didn't know what was up and what was down. But her captors underestimated how strong her wings were. When she regained her bearings, she shook the men off and searched frantically for her friend.

Oh no. Harper!

Harper was on her hands and knees, trembling as she looked up at the man towering over her. The knight brought his sword to her throat.

Sky's heart came to a screeching halt. It was like Death himself was smirking at her, fingering the cord of Harper's life. He threatened to pull it, to break it, so that life might flow out of the cord as blood flows from a sword-wound. Death had its ugly, crooked claws around Harper's life, taunting Sky that she would never get to her in time. There were too many knights between her and her friend.

All around Sky, the magical creatures were falling. They were losing the battle. But wait—

The mermaids

With a deep breath, Sky closed her eyes, concentrating on the river, becoming aware of every drop of water.

Rise.

The water burst into multicolored light and rose into the air. The noise of the battle dwindled. The knights' faces drained of color as they stared into the sky. The river was floating in midair.

With a swift arm motion, she drew the river, arch-shaped, over the battle. Ice-swords appeared in the water, and the mermaids fought with them from above.

Knights began fleeing the scene.

"The fairy controls the earth!"

"There is no hope, men! Run!"

"We cannot fight the forces of nature!"

"The fairy commands the river!"

Sky stumbled back a step, gaping. "Chimera's heads!" She had never displayed such magical strength before.

Many of the knights, unfortunately, remained in the fight. Seeing that Sky was the source of the floating river, they targeted her, but the magical creatures were quick to form a protective circle around her.

A massive weight pushed her onto her knees, as though she was physically holding the river up. Her muscles screamed, threatening to give out any second. She gnashed her teeth against the agony.

I can't let it drop.

Tears burned their way down her face. The simple action of lifting her head was nearly too much to manage, but she had to see what was happening. She groaned in effort and locked eyes with the battlefield. The river had saved Harper but had driven the knights to fight harder than ever. The amount of blood their swords tasted doubled as they fought with renewed strength. Even the mermaids were taking casualties. There was no way the protective circle around Sky would hold. The knights would reach her in no time, and she would fall, along with the floating river. The battle was as good as over.

Then the sound of a horn and triumphant cries echoed through the valley. Another army came charging into battle. It was Anthony and the villagers.

"Anthony!" Sky let out an exhausted laugh. "Thank goodness!"

The knights forgot about Sky and her friends and assembled to attack Anthony's army. Many battle-weary knights fell to the vigorous villagers, but the queen's men were still winning the fight. Sky was losing her grip on the river. They were not going to win. Wait, the river...

Maybe I don't have to keep it up. But I'll need more water for that to work.

"Anthony!" Sky bellowed. "Push them back! Push the knights back!"

Anthony's men began pushing their opponents toward the river.

There has to be more water here. I need more water.

She had to focus. She had to focus hard.

An ear-shattering scream erupted out of her. Little streams of water drifted from various parts of the woods. Dew drops lifted off the ground. Strips of water slithered from the Waterfall. The river grew larger and larger, covering Vivian's entire army.

"Get out of there!" she ordered. Anthony's men fled and the animals scurried away, leaving the knights in a naive mindset of triumph.

Vivian didn't buy it. She glared up at the blanket of water. "Run, you fools! She has you trapped! This is no victory!"

Fall.

The enormous river plummeted toward them. The scrambling knights could not escape. It slammed into them, knocking them down and scattering their weapons.

Sky used her remaining strength to push the water back into the riverbank, so the mermaids would not be injured. Anthony's army and the magical creatures had the disoriented knights at sword point in a flash. The battle was over.

Queen Vivian and her army were defeated.

Sky toppled over. Her whole body tingled with the memory of pain. She was wet. How did she get wet? The river hadn't touch her. She raised her head as much as she could.

It's not water. It's blood.

The strain had been so severe it had opened wounds that immediately began to sting upon realization.

Harper dashed to her side and fell on her knees. "Sky! Oh, my goodness! You're bleeding. Someone help! Someone, over here! She's wounded! Sky, you ok?"

Sky groaned. "Fine, Harper. I'm ok."

"You—you saved my life with that floating river trick. Thank you."

Sky managed a soft smile. "You saved me first."

"Sky!" Anthony collapsed on her other side. "I want a doctor over here. Now!"

"I'm alright, Anthony. Just give me a minute."

"Sky," he insisted, "you're bleeding in multiple places."

She tried to raise her head again to get a better look at her wounds, but lightning zapped down her spine. Her head dropped with a wince. "Where am I cut?"

Harper looked her over. "You got a nasty one on your torso, a handful of tiny ones on your arms, and a great big long one on your left leg," she said. "None of them look real deep, though. You'll live. You got a cut on your forehead too, but I think that's from where that knight pushed you."

Anthony's brow furrowed as he leaned closer. "These don't look like sword wounds."

"No, they're from the river," Sky mumbled. "I don't feel so good."

"It's because you're losing blood," Harper said.

Anthony pursed his lips. "Where is that doctor!"

Ms. Hops scurried over. "Not to fear, young prince! We can fix that. Caeli!"

Caeli the Pegasus landed gracefully near the group. He held a leaf-pouch of water in his teeth. Ms. Hops poured some of the water into Sky's mouth, and her wounds began to close. Harper's jaw dropped.

"Water from the flowers of Medela, Garden of the Fairies," Ms. Hops explained. "It won't numb discomfort or renew energy completely, but it will minimize the cuts to mere scratches."

Harper's eyes sparkled. "That's so cool!"

"Could I have some for my men?" Anthony asked.

"Of course," Ms. Hops said. "We have plenty. Use all that you need."

Anthony took that water and gave instructions to his healthy men while the rabbit hopped away to find another leaf-pouch.

"How are you feeling?" asked Harper. "Ok?"

"A lot better," Sky said. "Just exhausted."

"Let's find a place where you can rest."

"No." Sky rose into a seated position. "We have to deal with Vivian."

After Harper helped her to her feet, the fairy trudged over to the queen and pointed her sword at her.

Vivian sneered. "So, *you're* the last fairy. Thought I got rid of all those *traitors*."

Sky tightened her grip on the hilt and remained silent. Vivian's eyes flickered to the sword's point.

"Are you going to kill me?" she asked, a hint of fear in her voice.

The anxiety slithered back in. Sky's heart had undergone so much turmoil, and it had left its mark. Was she able to keep her promise to the prince?

This is a matter of choice, not feelings, Ms. Hops had said. *You must choose to forgive and choose to do this for the humans.*

Choose?

Of course. Our emotions can't control us, not unless we allow them to.

Her angst dissolved. She was not doomed to take the wrong path. She had a choice.

"I am not going to kill you," Sky whispered, letting her sword drop.

"So, what then?" Vivian retorted.

"We put you in a dungeon!" Harper said then ordered two of the men standing nearby, "Take her away! Right, Sky?"

"I don't know what a dungeon is," admitted Sky, "but whatever you say."

Harper giggled. "Oh, my friend, you have lots to learn."

The two men lifted the cursing queen to her feet and carried her away. Anthony mournfully watched as they led his mother to the castle.

"Are you ok?" Sky asked as she approached him.

"Yeah. It's just—I wish things were different."

"Me too."

"But what can you do, you know?" Eyes welling up with tears, he sucked in a shaky breath. "I guess I've never really come to terms with this cruel truth."

"What truth?"

"That my mother's heart is really as black as she lets on. I ignored it. Tried to tell myself things weren't as bad as they seemed. But that lie never stilled my uneasiness. I was a fool. She never cared about...about...." He sniffled, his knuckles turning white as he gripped his elbows.

An unrelenting urge to comfort him, to tell him that it would be ok, to make everything better consumed Sky. What in the world could she say or do that would help at all? She could never numb such an agony. She wrung her hands against the tormenting itch to do something, but she couldn't just stand there.

She laid her hand on his forearm. Immediately, his head dropped onto her shoulder. He wept as she wrapped her arms around him. In the light of their victory, here stood a boy defeated. It was victory for his people and defeat for his family. It was not Sky's arms that grew weary under the prince's weight but her heart. It was her soul holding up his soul, not her keeping him on his feet.

Which is worse? Me never knowing my mother, or him knowing his mother does not love him? I don't know.

"I'm being selfish," he mumbled.

"No," Sky said. "This is perfectly natural. I would do the same. Don't feel guilty over it. Not for one second. You're not being selfish—not at all."

"Thank you, Sky." He pulled away from her, his face as wet as hers. "I'll be ok."

She added cheerily, "On a different note, though, how did the villagers respond to those new wings of yours?"

Anthony laughed a little. "They were quite surprised. You're a ray of sunshine, Sky, you know that? Never lose it."

9

A NEW WORLD

Sky and Anthony headed toward the village, and Harper joined them.

"I can't believe it," Harper breathed. "We're free!"

"It *is* hard to believe," said the prince. "I just hope the people can heal from this long oppression."

"Oh, they will. They definitely will."

"The villagers are talking about a celebration tonight," Sky chimed in.

"Yes, a long-awaited and well-earned one," Anthony said.

"But first," Sky said, "there are some questions I want answered."

They journeyed to the dungeon. Anthony and Harper followed Sky as she descended the stone steps.

The place was simply awful. It was dreary, the candles barely providing light in their somber dance. Several rooms lined the wide hallway, each guarded by long metal bars. In a room at the end of the hall sat Vivian on the floor, staring maliciously at some unseen person.

The former queen glided up to the bars as the trio approached. With a bone-chilling glare, she hissed, "Come to finish me off?" Her gaze rested on Anthony.

Sky was surprised to see her expression soften. Had his mother noticed his wings? Sky glanced over her shoulder at Anthony to find he had retracted his wings. Vivian did not yet know of her son's "fairy-ness."

"No," Sky replied. "I came to ask why."

"Why what?"

"Why you did what you did. Why murder all those innocent people—"

"Innocent? Ha!" Vivian retorted. "I'll tell you why, girl. Because humans are mindless, evil animals. But we fairies are *gods*. We should be ruling the world, not cowering behind a wall of water."

"Oh, you think you're better?" Harper blurted. "Because you can do magic and we can't?"

Sky placed her hand on Harper's shoulder and mouthed, "Deep breath," then addressed Vivian again, "How could you kill the fairies, your *own* people?"

"I didn't want to." The remorse in Vivian's expression vanished as quickly as it came, giving way to a deadly smirk as she whispered, "I slaughtered them. I slaughtered them *all*. They betrayed me. They were too weak to see what we could accomplish together."

All the hate flooded back like an invading army. Sky's nails dug so deep into her palms she surely gave herself another cut. How could Vivian be this savage and callous? What hurtful speech, what evil concoction, had blacked her heart so much?

Sky's wrath dissipated. What vile thing had turned Vivian? True the fairies had been far from perfect, but to take a path so wicked, there must be some force behind it. Who or what had caused such an ugly change of heart? Was it possible that Vivian wasn't so very different from Sky before this hideous thing had corrupted her?

Tears escaped Sky's eyes. "What happened to you?"

The former queen stared at her and said nothing. Her face was stone, but whether she truly felt nothing or was hiding some long-forgotten affliction, Sky could not say.

"You're wrong," Sky murmured. "*You* abandoned the fairies, not the other way around."

Harper said, "There's something I've got to know. Did you really plan on killing Anthony?"

Vivian's gaze again drifted over to her son, and again Sky was taken aback to see the slightest humanity in them. Remorse—and shame, Sky dared to think—returned to her face, as though she despised herself for what she was about to say.

"I wish it didn't have to be so, but he is weak from growing up with the humans. He's too attached to them and doesn't share my views. And as if that wasn't enough, he is not magical. The human blood corrupted his purity."

Sky looked back at Anthony. Jaw clenched and nostrils flaring, he glared at his mother with misty eyes, then transformed and displayed his eagle wings.

"*Anthony*," Vivian breathed, shock and admiration written on her face. The prince turned and marched out of the room. Tears dared to approach the brink of Vivian's eyes as she sank to the ground.

As Sky and Harper turned to follow him, Sky added, "If you ever need to talk about something, I'm here. Maybe one day you'll have a change of heart."

Vivian scoffed. "Right. You'll talk to *me*."

Sky stopped in her tracks. Bitterness would not bring her parents back. It would not fix the hurt or undo the cruelty. She turned to face the former queen. There it was, written in her eyes, clear as day—bitterness. It *must* have been bitterness that drove Vivian to such evil. What else could rot the heart like this? These metal bars were not her real confinement. Her soul had been trapped in a cage of hatred all her life, and resentment had slowly consumed her. If she had only forgiven whoever it was that wounded her, maybe she would be a completely different person, maybe this would be a completely different world. Sky pitied her dead soul.

"Yes, I will, because *I* forgive you. Even if no one else does, I do. I *choose* too." She left Vivian there. And as Sky ascended the stairs—whether by a freak of imagination or by a whispered truth—she heard sobbing behind her.

The girls found Anthony at the top of the stairs with his head bowed, wings drooping in a pitiful bundle behind him. His breath came out slow and controlled, but he had not mastered himself.

Helplessness captured Sky again. What could she do? What could she say? Images of the remorse in Vivian's expression, of her reaction to Anthony's wings arose in Sky's mind.

There is something I can say.

She knelt down in front of him and took his hand in hers. "Anthony, I don't think it's hopeless. I saw it in her eyes. Something's still there. She may change one day. Don't give up on her yet."

The prince squeezed her hand. "Thank you."

There was a grand celebration that night. People were dancing and singing. Children giggled and chased each other around. The air was soaked in merry laugher and friendly chatter. There wasn't a man, woman, or child who failed to praise Sky for what she had done for them. They adored her and her friends.

The children taught her a poem they grew up reciting:

> *In times of peace,*
> *Hope roars.*
> *In times of prosperity,*
> *We have the more.*
> *But in times of suffering,*
> *Joy is born.*

Harper and Anthony sat with Sky at a table. Her heart had never been so full, yet she had struggled a lot lately.

Joy in the pain.

"I love that poem the children recited," Sky said.

"Yes, but do you understand it?" asked Harper.

The fairy sighed. "I'm getting there."

Harper watched the children playing and said, "Without times of hardship, we wouldn't know what peace was, what joy was. *Because* there is a night, the day is so much sweeter."

"What about during the night?"

"Stars and fireflies, my friend." Harper laughed. "If you'll just look, you'll find marvelous things in the hard times. A day of playing in the sun. A butterfly on your windowsill. A smile from your neighbor. Feeling the increased strength of our togetherness. These things mean so much more when all is *not* well. I think they remind us to not give in to hopelessness, to remember we have a firm and secure hope—there is a sun behind those clouds. Where there's hope, there can be joy. And remember, my friend, there is always hope."

Anthony chimed in, "Wow, Harper. How long have you been hiding that wise mind of yours from the kingdom?"

"Why? You offering me a job?" Harper teased.

"Maybe."

Harper's eyes lit up. "Really?"

The prince (though Sky supposed he was now the king) grinned. "I said maybe."

"Anyway," she turned back to Sky, "you understand now?"

"I believe I do." The fairy smiled. The loss of her parents had caused her to treasure friendship. The war for freedom had made her treasure peace. The difficulties had taught her vital lessons, and there were so many beautiful moments in between. Yes, joy could be found in difficulty, and difficulty could reap a purer joy—if one was willing to search and be taught.

The friends watched the dancing villagers, whose beaming faces glowed brighter than the sun. Anthony, however, appeared downcast, quite out of place in their mirthful surroundings. "I guess you will be going back home soon, right Sky?"

Harper huffed. "This stinks! But I guess losing your magic wouldn't be much fun either."

"Actually, I might have a way to fix this little problem of ours," Sky said.

Anthony's brow furrowed. "What is it?"

"I will tell you tomorrow. Let's just enjoy the celebration for now."

The next day, Sky led Harper and Anthony up the hill to the Waterfall.

The prince's shoulders slumped. "So, you are going?"

"I'm not going, Anthony." Sky turned and pointed at the Waterfall. "This isn't just a Waterfall. It's a barrier put up by fairies, dividing our two worlds. But I think together we can break it."

Harper stared at the Waterfall. "How?"

"We represent the people that need to forgive each other—humans, fairies, *Vivian*. With mine and Anthony's magic, with our love for each other, and with forgiveness for those who've wronged us, we can break this barrier of hate. Our people will live together again."

"Forgive Vivian," Harper murmured.

Anthony bit his lip. "Is it possible?"

"Just us standing here together tells me it's possible," Sky declared. "The grandparents of our grandparents were divided against each other, but here we stand together. Not only allies, but friends. Forgiveness is a powerful thing. If that's not strong enough to break the barrier, nothing is."

A long stretch of silence passed before Harper said, "Well, what are we waiting for, then? Let's give it a go."

Anthony nodded.

Standing before the Waterfall, they joined hands. Energy zapped through them, linking them together, mind and soul, with such force no army could tear them apart. Love, as though it were a living thing, had been waiting patiently and quietly for this very moment. Its breath was nearly audible, its very heartbeat beckoning them to unravel the hatred that held the barrier together.

Sky closed her eyes. *I forgive Vivian.*

The water lit up and rose into the air, reaching for them. The earth quaked. Vines and branches sprung forth from everywhere, encircling them. When she opened her eyes, they were surrounded by a dome of water, greenery, and wood. Glimpses of her home peeked through the cracks in the Waterfall.

Together they let go. Together they forgave. Their burdens lifted simultaneously. Like evaporating water, some heaviness that had held both worlds captive vanished. Whatever offense, whatever ache, whatever bitterness had been there, it burst and was gone. All people shouted together as one. They would no longer cling to their resentment. They would forgive.

Then Sky whispered, "Duo mundi facti sunt unum."

FLASH! Anthony and Harper's world turned into the magical wood of Sky's world. The village, the castle, the whole place was vibrant, the Forbidden Waterfall standing proudly before them. The two worlds were one once again.

Misty-eyed, Sky gazed at the new world. "Now we can all live together...in *peace.*"

It was indeed a new world, healed from the bitterness that had held it so tightly. As she stood there with her new friends—her new family—she knew that the life she had before was over. And that was ok, for this would be ten times better.

She turned and again gazed up at the Forbidden Waterfall. She hadn't known its adventure would lead to a complete transformation of not only her life, but of two whole worlds. She hadn't known that the end of its mystery would be so breathtaking. Despite all the delights of her world, despite all the joys of her childhood, she had never felt happier than she did in that moment....

10

THE FIRST "THE END"

"And so, they did. They all lived in peace. Sky, Harper, and Anthony remained friends for the rest of their lives. Eventually, Anthony married Sky. She was a kind and noble queen. Harper lived in the castle with them as an honorary member of the royal family, and Ms. Hops was the leader of the advisement council that was put together after the war. There was peace throughout the land for many years to come, and they all lived happily ever after. The end." Grandpa Greg leaned back in his chair and set his glasses on the end table.

Rae stared dreamily at her grandfather. She was always the one who loved his stories most of all.

Even Jonny said, to everyone's great surprise since it was such a "girly" story, "Wow, that was good. My favorite part was the battle. Can we have one more story, please?" Natasha and Rae echoed his request.

"Now, now, children. You don't want me to tell all my good stories in one night, do you? Off to bed."

Reluctantly, the children said good night and went upstairs.

Jonny leapt into his bed. "I wonder what the next story will be. What do you think, Nat?" But she was already asleep.

"I think the journey with Grandpa tuckered her out," Mrs. Greenwood whispered with a smile. "Good night, children."

Rae pulled out her journal, as she always did before going to sleep, and started to write:

December 20, 1955

Today, Grandpa Greg told us a wonderful story about a fairy named Sky and how she found our world. She went through the Forbidden Waterfall, and she found a village under the rule of an evil queen. With her new friends she met in this world (and her friends from home), she defeated the evil queen and saved the village. I liked this story because it shows the importance of forgiveness and how we can find joy in hard times. I can't wait to hear the other stories Grandpa will tell us. This will be the best Christmas ever! I hope tomorrow comes fast.

Rae put up her journal and sank into her bed. As she drifted off to sleep, she thought, *I wonder what adventure Grandpa Greg will take us on tomorrow.* And with that, she went to sleep, dreaming marvelous dreams.

2

THE ISLAND *of* THANATOS

1

A YOUNG MAN'S BIRTHDAY

Mighty wings stretched out on either side and wind ripping through her hair, she soared above the majestical woods. The animals, the plants, and the bodies of water blurred together as she glided through the air. Suddenly, she altered her course, shooting upwards, straight into the sky. She broke through the clouds and locked her eyes on the sun, but it did not burn them. She gazed, unwaveringly, at that wondrous ball of fire without pain, without watery eyes, without blinking. She bore such a free, resilient spirit that joy did not dare try to escape her firm grasp. But then a faint voice came from far away, from somewhere beyond the sun....

"Rae! Rae! Wake up, Rae. Wake up!"

She didn't know where this voice was coming from, so she scanned the sky to find its source.

"Wake up, Rae! Wake up!"

The brilliant sun and endless clouds melted into a small, dusty bedroom—

Rae Greenwood jerked awake. Her brother, Jonny, was shaking her violently by the shoulders.

"Wake up, Rae!" Jonny shouted. "Wake UP!"

"I'm awake. I'm awake," Rae grumbled, irritated that Jonny had disturbed her wonderful dream.

But Jonny continued to shake her. "Wake up, Rae!"

"I said, I—am—awake!" Rae screamed over her brother's racket.

"Oh—well, good," he said, looking startled. "Mom almost has breakfast ready—a good, big one too. Come *on*, Rae. We all got up an hour ago, and you're still up here sleeping."

Rubbing her eyes, Rae followed him down the stairs. She took a deep breath as they entered the dining room; the smell of eggs, coffee, and bacon gave her a warm hug.

"Morning, sleepyhead," Natasha teased.

Rae yawned. "Morning."

Grandpa Greg glanced up from his newspaper. "Get a good night's rest, did we?"

"Yep."

Mrs. Greenwood came through the kitchen door carrying a plate of eggs. "Who's turning nine today?"

"Me, Mom." Jonny sighed.

"Mom," said Natasha, "everyone knows that it's Jonny's birthday."

Mrs. Greenwood dismissed the comment with a wave of her hand. "I know, I know. I'm just so excited that my little boy is becoming a man."

"Mom, you said that my last birthday," Jonny groaned.

Natasha giggled. "And she'll say it on your tenth, and your eleventh, and your twelfth, and your thirteenth, and—"

"Who's hungry?" interrupted Mrs. Greenwood.

Disliking the idea of a Jonny-Natasha quarrel so early in the morning, Rae said, "I am!"

After breakfast, the children went outside to play. The weather had had a dramatic mood swing during the night. It was nearly sixty degrees, and all the snow had melted.

"So," said Rae, "what do you want to play, birthday boy?"

"I wanna act out the 'Behind the Forbidden Waterfall' story," he declared.

Natasha gasped, giving a little jump that made her pigtails bounce. "That's a great idea!"

The children had absolutely fallen in love with the story their grandfather had told them the night before. So, for the next twenty minutes, they pretended to be the characters in that adventure. Jonny was Prince Anthony, Rae was Harper, and Natasha, having pleaded with Rae, was the fairy, Sky. Darting here and there, tittering and reciting lines, they played among the trees and bushes.

They had a great time until, as Rae predicted, Jonny and Natasha began to squabble. Rae couldn't figure out why they were fighting, but good reasons rarely seemed necessary factors in their arguments.

She sighed, grabbed the book she had brought out for such an occasion, and propped herself up against an old oak tree. Grandpa Greg's yard was her favorite place to read because it stood amidst a large gathering of trees. The woods seemed to her like nature's reading nook, as though it was specifically created for that purpose.

It was lunchtime before she knew it, and they all rushed inside. But when the siblings returned to the outdoors,

Jonny and Natasha found something else to quarrel about. Rae went back to her book.

The sun began to set, casting the trees' curvy shadows here and there. The grass grew darker as the minutes passed, and the sky was arrayed in pink, blue, and purple strips of light. Darting from tree to tree, the suddenly shy birds flew back to their nests. As the blackness of night began to wash over the top of the colorful sky, the first stars blinked awake.

Mrs. Greenwood called out into the peaceful evening, "Come on, children! Time for dinner!" The famished children scampered inside.

"What's for dinner?" Jonny hungrily eyed the pot on the stove, standing on tiptoe to catch a glimpse of the deliciousness inside.

"We're having spaghetti," Mrs. Greenwood answered.

Natasha licked her lips. "Ooo, yummy."

After dinner, Mrs. Greenwood brought out the birthday cake, and they all sang "Happy Birthday" to Jonny. Then it was time for presents. He ripped open the boxes and found a model airplane, a toy car, and a plastic sword and shield. For the next thirty minutes, Jonny pretended to be a knight and chased the girls around, calling them "vicious dragons."

"You think I'm brave enough to be a knight?" Jonny asked Natasha a little too seriously.

"Oh, *of course*," she replied. But once Jonny had occupied himself with his new toy car, she rolled her eyes at Rae. Both girls burst into giggles.

"Ok, you three, toys away. It's time for a story," Grandpa Greg announced to the room. "That is, of course, if you want a story tonight."

Rae was in the sitting room before he had finished speaking. "Oh, yes, please! Yes, we do!" She would hate to miss one of Grandpa Greg's fairytales.

"Grandpa Greg?" Jonny asked tentatively once they had all settled down.

"Yes, my boy?"

"Can the story not be about a fairy or other—er—girly things?" Jonny pleaded as though he didn't enjoy the last story. "If you don't mind."

"Of course! Why, it already is. This one isn't about any fairy or princess. No, no. This one is about a very magical and very dangerous island."

"An island!" Rae gasped, hugging her knees while rocking back and forth on the floor. "How exciting!"

"Yes, *very* exciting!" Natasha said. "Oh, do please start. I really want to hear the story!"

"Settle down, settle down, children." Greg chuckled. "Give an old man some time to breathe." After a moment, he cleared his throat and began the story.

"Once upon a time," he whispered eerily, "there was an island off the coast of Mexico. You could not see this island from land. No. You had to be out at sea to spot it. Only a choice few ever escaped the island once they had set foot on it. So, the island was called *Thanatos*, which means 'death.' The goddess of the sea, Norcepta, was the ruler of this island and had imprisoned all the magical creatures living there. She had ruled over the world of men many years ago. With her cursed dagger, Norcepta slaughtered thousands, but their bodies did not die. See, the dagger's curse was this: anyone stabbed by it—an indirect blow, mind you, not through the heart—would be corrupted with an evil spirit and would serve her forever. They were doomed to be always decaying, always on their last breath, yet never fully dying. Thus, she raised her army of Water Demons. But one fateful day, a young girl determined to stop the killing. Norcepta's dagger in hand, she stabbed the goddess. But the blade missed the goddess's heart, and Norcepta was banished to live as a dying spirit, forever bound to the sea.

"Rotting in the depths of the ocean, she and her army sought revenge on every descendant of this girl. The days bled into years, and Norcepta's hatred for her grew, spreading like an unrelenting fire. Many times, she had the last few descendants within her grasp, but they somehow slipped through her fingers and multiplied again. The teasing hand of near-success only fed fury's fire, driving the goddess to insanity. But little did she know that, centuries later, the last two descendants would journey so carelessly into the deep ocean, into her territory. Revenge wouldn't be kept from Norcepta, not this time...."

2

FEARS AND NIGHTMARES

The boat glided across the perfectly still ocean, smooth as glass. The young girl and her mother stood on the deck, watching the sun drop into the sea. But then a massive wave crashed over the deck, drenching the girl and her mother. The suddenly restless ocean tossed the boat to and fro without mercy. The girl turned and saw another wave approaching. She shouted for her mother, who was gripping the rail for support, to take cover, but it was too late. The wave collided with the deck, blinding the girl. When the mist cleared, her mother was nowhere in sight. She was simply gone. The young girl screamed in agony, tears pouring down her face. Her mother was dead, lying motionless at the bottom of the sea....

Seventeen-year-old Amber Quill awoke, bolting upright. Her heart slamming into her ribcage, she gasped for air. They needed to bring the boat around to look for her mother.

The sheet was damp beneath her. She stared at her bed's footboard as it sunk in. There was no boat, no murdering wave, only blankets and pillows drenched with sweat.

She scraped her fingernails across her wet scalp. *Nightmares again.*

Swinging her legs over the side of the bed, she gripped the mattress. "Breathe, Amber. Just breathe." The all-too-familiar fight-or-flight sensation made every muscle in her body quiver.

You would think you could just tell yourself that it was simply a dream, but these nightmares were no made-up horror film. They were memories. Amber relived her mother's death every night, watching her being swept away by the sea. And that was one of the worst things about the accident: her mother's fate was dealt by the place she loved so much—the ocean. Her mother had adored the ocean, and the family had many treasured memories on the beach. Since the accident, however, Amber had not set foot on a beach or a boat. Just the thought of terrifyingly enormous waves swallowing her, pulling her under, dark water pressing in on every side—it made her skin crawl like tiny invisible crabs were hiking up her arms. It could give a perfectly healthy teenager a heart attack.

With a childish fear that someone was watching her, she looked around. Her room was in order: a bed beneath the window; a desk in the corner with a lamp shining down on it; a lofty bookshelf up against the wall; and a large rug in the middle of the room, where her orange kitten, Gigi, was sleeping soundly.

Adrenaline subsiding and heartbeat slowing, her shaking body began to still. She went downstairs for breakfast once she mastered herself and found her father reading the newspaper. A former crab boat captain, he was an editor of the *New York Times* newspaper.

"Good morning, angelfish," Mr. Quill greeted his daughter as she walked into the room. "And how are we today?"

"Fine," Amber lied.

"All packed?"

She slapped her forehead—the cruise. She had completely forgotten.

"I guess that's a no." Her dad grinned, a bit too amused for her taste.

"No, I didn't pack," she admitted and darted upstairs to do so. Once in her room, she hastily threw things into her carryon and backpack.

"What do you think, Gigi?" Amber asked her kitten once she had finished packing. "Just one more book would do, right?"

Gigi trotted up to her and rubbed herself against her ankle. Amber went over to her bookshelf and took out her new book, *The Island of Thanatos.* Lastly, she hung her mother's locket, oval-shaped and bearing a family picture, around her neck.

"I will miss you, Gigi. Believe me, you are far better company. But in order to brave the sea, I must brave something far worse—society."

Her hand hovered over the doorknob. Was it possible that she could befriend someone on the cruise? A mental image teased her: hanging out by the pool with the girls, included in the apparently always hilarious girl-talk. But no. The picture-perfect scenario dissolved. Such things were all facades. For her own sake, on this cruise, she must keep to herself.

Misty-eyed, she yanked open the door and dashed downstairs, her carryon thunking after her.

"All packed and ready to go," she hollered.

She grabbed a banana before she shot out the door, while her dad put the luggage into their blue Ford pickup. As they pulled out of the garage, she spotted Gigi in the living room window, pressing her tiny paws up against the glass and meowing a goodbye.

The handsome white and blue cruise ship came into view, and her dad parked the truck.

"Sure you don't wanna come?" Amber asked tentatively. "They might have some last-minute tickets."

He sighed. "I'm sorry, Amber. I just can't stand to be on the water after what—after what happened."

"Ok." Her shoulders slumped. "See you in a week, then."

"I love you, angelfish."

"Love you, Daddy."

She kissed him on the cheek and hopped out of the truck. She approached the dock with a strong, steady pace, but slowed the nearer she got, finally stopping at its edge. She had said that she just wanted to relax, but, if she was honest with herself, she was going on this cruise to beat her fear of the ocean.

The water was so beautiful and calm, sunlight glittering off its surface. She still loved to watch it sway. It lapped against the poles that supported the dock in gentle thuds, the seaweed that clung there swaying in time with the waves. Watching the ocean's greenery move like a flame upon a wick, she heard a seagull call overhead. The bird, happy with a fish in its beak, landed on the railing of the ship, upon whose side the waves softly knocked.

The water's humble dance almost appeased her angst, but fear stubbornly stood its ground. She took a deep breath, the ocean's briny scent filling her nostrils. No, her angst would not stop her. She was getting on a cruise ship for goodness' sake. She was going to have a great time enjoying the sea and give fear a good slap in the face.

She stepped onto the dock.

3

THE ONLY ONES LEFT

At eleven o'clock, the crowd of people waiting on the dock started to board. Amber entered the ship and stepped into the main dining room. Sparkling chandeliers hung from the ceiling, and many chairs and tables adorned in velvet cloths surrounded a center stage. A grand staircase curved up to the second floor. A section of that floor, in the shape of a crescent, was visible from the dining room. The entrances to hallways that led to the rooms, pool, and other entertainment were also visible from her position.

Wandering down one of those hallways, Amber mumbled to herself, "Room 219...room 219...room 219."

When she found her room, she opened the door and went inside. Sunlight poured into the room from a wide window that made up the entire right wall. The ocean's reflection danced on the roof like a sea of sunbeams. A spacious, cozy-looking bed, a table with two armchairs, a few tall lamps, and a couple of paintings occupied the room. The bathroom was on her left.

Amber saw her reflection out of the corner of her eye and turned to face it.

She studied the girl in the closet mirror. *Goodness, I look like Mom.*

She had her mom's taste in fashion: a T-shirt and jeans, always. Neither of them ever had a need to wear makeup. They had natural cosmetics in their long, dark eyelashes, rosy cheeks, and pink lips. She also inherited her mom's hair. Red and straight, it flowed lazily over her shoulders, stopping at her hips. But if her mother had passed on anything, it was her green eyes, which stood out like emeralds in white sand.

Her father pushed his way into her mind. Trying to get him on the water again had been a mistake. Her mother's death had nearly destroyed him, and the ocean was a loud reminder of his wife and of all the grief.

Amber's eyes stung with tears, but she refused to let them fall. Trying to forget about her dad's suffering, she said with fake enthusiasm, "This is nice!"

Early the next morning, relaxing by the pool, she read her new book, *The Island of Thanatos.*

The survivors of the plane crash wandered through the island of death, struggling to make it through another day. Whispers and screams sounded at night, driving them all mad. Terror gripped them. Would they ever see their families again? How could there be any hope of getting off this horrid island when death herself was hunting them?

As she finished the chapter, a boy and girl (each about her own age) started clamoring in a different language. Amber tried to continue her novel, but the earthquake-loud fight was too distracting. She set the book down with a sigh and strolled over to the pair.

"Excuse me," she interrupted, "you think you could turn it down a notch? Many people came here for a nice, *quiet* vacation."

The girl turned slowly with hands on her hips, hazel eyes flashing in contempt. "And *who* are *you?*" she asked, her snobby attitude evident in her voice.

"Amber Quill. And you are?"

"Katherine Kielwein, and this is my brother, Tony." She flipped her short, black hair to gesture towards the boy behind her. Her blonde highlights were definitely overkill.

Biting back the comment about Katherine's hair, Amber asked, "I'm curious: what language were you speaking?"

"German." Katherine puffed out her chest. "But we've been living in America for years. Now what did you ask me?"

"I asked if you could keep it down. There are other people here trying to relax."

Katherine scoffed. "And why would we do that? It's an argument. It's supposed to be loud!"

"Oh, shut up," Tony snapped, rolling his eyes, which were identical to his sister's. "We can keep quiet. You know I'm going to win anyway."

"Oh, fine. Whatever," his sister bellowed.

"Thank you," Amber said with a smile.

Tony grinned a bit, and Katherine cast an I'm-better-than-you glance at Amber as she went back to her seat. The Kielweins did quiet down for a while but got noisy again after about ten minutes. So, Amber went back to her room. On her way down the hall, she collided with a boy too occupied with his book to walk straight.

"Watch it!" Amber exclaimed as the boy ran into her.

"S-s-sorry," he said.

The teenage boy was a couple of inches shorter than her. His untidy, blond hair hung in front of his eyes. How could he possibly see? He had faint freckles on his cheeks and across the bridge of his nose. His black, square-shaped glasses guarded his unnaturally bright blue eyes. And he was far too anxious considering all he did was bump into her.

"Um—what are you reading?" Amber broke the uncomfortable silence.

"Book about G-G-Greek mythology." After a pause, he added, "Oh, um—my name's I-Isaac Logan."

"Amber Quill," she shook his hand. "Nice to meet you."

"You too," he stuttered with a nervous grin.

"Well, I better get back to my room. Bye." Amber rushed off, not at all enjoying the awkward conversation, and quickly slipped through her door.

Weird guy. Cute, though. At least I'm meeting people.

Was that a good thing, though? Was it safe?

Amber sighed and sat on her bed. Friends had been in short supply ever since her mother's death. Actually, as far as friends went, she was bankrupt. They had not been there for her when her mom passed. What was the point of having friends if they were just gonna leave? No, it was best to fly solo. It was better to be alone than to have someone else ripped away from you. She couldn't afford to let someone in.

Despite her resolve, loneliness overshadowed her heart. Had she made a mistake by cutting herself off from the world? She impatiently wiped the watery intruders from her eyes and went to run a hot bath.

The next day, Amber stood on the deck, gazing at the cloudless sky. The sun's orange brilliance danced with the pink light of twilight as it hid itself behind the horizon. The sea grew sleepy; tiny, soft waves rippled across the ocean. And then, in the distance, as though inches from the sun, a dolphin jumped into the air. Nothing on the earth was more breathtaking than the sea. She had forgotten this side of its split personality, and her fear cowered under its magnificence.

Why did I ever avoid this beautiful place?

Looking over the ship's rail, Amber frowned. The tiny waves were steadily growing in size. The wind suddenly developed an attitude, whipping her hair out of her face. The boat jerked as it increased its speed. The water growled, a sound she shouldn't have heard on such a peaceful evening. The sea was awake now, and it was in a sour mood. It beat against the sides of the ship. But this wasn't a natural, rough sea. She could feel it in the pit of her stomach—it was eerie, just wrong.

Amber had experienced this sort of behavior from the ocean only once before: the day her mother drowned. She spun around to see a ginormous wave, taller and wider than the ship, barreling towards them. Preceding the ship-killing wave was a number of smaller waves—smaller, that was, compared to the monster wave behind them.

Oh, my goodness! A rogue wave.

The passengers noticed the first wall of water towering over the ship. They pointed and gaped, but no one moved.

Really, people?

"Take cover!" Amber bellowed. There was a great deal of screaming and yelling as everyone hit the deck. The wave crashed over them, but it did not deter the ship. The only harm the smaller waves did was choke the drenched passengers.

Amber gasped as another wave submerged them in watery chaos, but this wave wasn't alone. An enormous spear of ice crashed through the bridge.

"What the—" She was cut off by another wave.

The ocean ceased the havoc it was mercilessly wreaking on the ship for the moment. People, ghost-white and trembling, began standing up and looking around. Amber stayed down a few extra moments before rising, muscles remaining tense as she kept her gaze fixed on the water. Relaxing now was premature. The massive rogue wave was still coming towards them. It wouldn't be long before it arrived. Surviving that one would take a miracle.

A woman in crew uniform came bursting through the door that led inside. "Does anyone, *anyone*, have *any* experience with ships?" the woman asked desperately. "Please! Anybody?"

No one came forward.

Amber's throat tightened and she wrung her hands. She had very—*very*—little experience on her father's crab boat, but that apparently was more than anyone else.

She raised a shaking hand. "I've spent a little time on a crabfishing boat."

The woman whimpered. "That will have to do." She ushered Amber inside with the rest of the passengers and then led her to a sturdy metal door.

The door opened, and Amber covered her mouth with her hand. They were all dead. The captain and co-captains all lay motionless on the floor. The large pole of ice was jammed into the room. Damaged electronics sent sparks flying every few seconds, and the broken radio sounded its never-ending screech. If the ship had been otherwise silent, it would've made the most bone-chilling scene. The cruise ship, however, was far from quiet. Even from the bridge, Amber could hear the passengers freaking out below. The whole place was in turmoil.

"You want me to steer clear of *that* wave?" she asked in disbelief.

"Yes," the woman said pleadingly. "No one else can do it. I looked. If there is someone more qualified, they are not speaking up. Good luck." With that, she left the room, closing the door behind her.

"Oh, wonderful!" Amber dashed to the wheel. "Great! Just great!" What was she supposed to do? She could call "mayday" into the radio, but it was far too damaged to do any good.

The mega wave was close—too close to get out of harm's way. She tried steering the cruise ship to safety, nonetheless. Compared to the speed of the wave, the ship was moving maddeningly slow.

Shifting her weight, the shattered glass crunched underfoot, sending an alarming reminder to her brain. Her breath caught in her throat. *The windows are broken.*

The ice spear had bust them into a million pieces. There was nothing between her and the wave. Water would rush in, and she would drown.

The realization was like taking a torpedo to the gut. There was no escaping it. That dreadful day flashed into her mind: her mother falling over the rail, sinking to the bottom, the darkness closing in on her....

Amber shook her head, trying to push those thoughts out, but they persisted. Anxiety coiled itself around her heart, and she began to hyperventilate.

"We're dead," she whispered, tightening her grip on the wheel. "We're all dead."

The wave hit, and she was underwater. She held on for dear life, fighting against the strong current trying to push her off the ship. But she did not hold her breath.

Wait, I feel like I can—

Something slammed into the back of her head. Everything went black.

"Quill? Wake up, Quill!" came a girl's voice.

Another voice sneered, "Shouting at her isn't going to do anything, stupid."

"Quill! Wake up!"

"Look, she's waking up," stammered a third.

Amber opened her eyes and moaned.

"Aha!" the second voice exclaimed. "See I *told* you she was fine."

Amber was soaked. Everything was sore. Her fingers searched the back of her throbbing head. To her relief, she wasn't bleeding.

Having confirmed she had no serious injuries, she sat up to identify the voices. Katherine Kielwein, Tony Kielwein, and Isaac Logan knelt on the floor beside her. Her tired eyes then traveled to the sturdy door behind them.

Amber groaned. "What happened?"

"After the wave passed, we pulled you out of the bridge," Katherine said, sounding way too proud of herself. "Luckily, the wave didn't knock you off the boat."

Amber became aware that her hand was touching something. A lady was lying next to her. It was the woman who had ushered her into the bridge.

Tony's gaze dropped. "Not so lucky, that one. Something hit her on the head."

Amber grabbed her churning stomach and closed her eyes in attempt to stop her head from spinning. She was able to steady herself—mostly—with a few deep breaths.

She massaged her temples. "What's the ship's condition?"

"It's a downright nasty mess. What on *earth* hit us?" Tony said.

"A rogue wave," she replied. "They're sudden, unpredictable, and very large. They'll rise up out of nowhere, *fast*. No one could've gotten out of its way."

Tony ran a hand through his black hair. "*Jeez.*"

Ignoring her lightheadedness, she gingerly got to her feet. An abnormal tug of gravity caused her to stumble backwards. "Whoa! Are—are we sinking?"

"I th-think so," Isaac looked like he was about to be sick. "S-s-something hit us after the wave. It felt like it came from beneath us."

"It must have hit us towards the front," she said. "It feels like we're sinking lopsidedly."

"What do you—?" Katherine stopped short and gaped. "Oh! We're taking a nosedive!"

"A slow one. How long has it been since we were hit?"

Tony nodded thoughtfully. "I see where you're going with this, Quill. If we hurry, we can probably escape this death trap through the back deck. The end tail of this thing should still be above water by the time we all get back there."

"There are s-s-some life rafts we can use," Isaac said.

"Enough for everyone?" asked Amber.

"Should be. It's not a very full cruise."

"Ok, good." She wrung out the bottom of her shirt. "Where are the other passengers?"

"They have all gathered in the dining room," replied Katherine.

Amber followed them to the crescent section of the second floor that overlooked the main dining room.

Oh my goodness.

Shards of tableware covered the floor. Chandeliers had fallen and busted, sending a spray of sharp crystal in every direction. The tables and chairs were anywhere but where they should be. Bloodied and bruised passengers scurried around to aid more seriously injured people.

"We need to get these people off this ship," Amber said. She descended the staircase and walked to the center of the room. "Listen up, everybody!"

The plan worked. Within twenty minutes, twelve bright orange rafts were being loaded up with passengers and lowered onto the water. Thankfully, the boat was sinking at a slower pace than Amber originally anticipated.

Once everyone was safely evacuated, she climbed into the last raft with Isaac, Tony, and Katherine. She plopped her backpack down beside her, which she had retrieved while the other passengers were loading the rafts. They were about to be stranded in the middle of the ocean. Water and a first aid kit seemed in order. A glance at her companions revealed the boys had had the same idea.

"Oh my gosh!" Katherine stared wide-eyed at the ship. "*That's* what hit us?"

Having drifted far enough to get a good look at the ship, Amber peered over her shoulder. She felt the blood leave her face. The whole company of survivors gazed horror-stricken at the ginormous spear of ice rising from the sea, which had skewed the ship's now halfway underwater front deck. The smaller but still sizable spear she had witnessed smashing into the bridge didn't look so menacing with its big brother next to it.

Tony muttered, "That's not right."

Other than this unnatural sight, everything was back to normal. The ocean was calm, as smooth as glass.

Too calm. Too still.

"Do you hear that?" a young girl asked from another raft.

Amber turned and watched another towering wave rise. It hurried towards them, joined by a violent wind in its roar. Just as the crest began its descent, she caught a glimpse of a woman's face, sinister eyes glaring, lips curved into a cruel smirk. Her ferocity made the wave look like a harmless drizzle.

"Brace yourselves!" Amber screamed, and the wave crashed into the survivors. Once they had passed through the wave, a storm like no other surrounded them. Water towering thirty feet high circled about them in a mad rush. Lightning struck within the isolated section of ocean. The wind did not relent. Rain hammered the rafts as they slowly drifted to the other side of the circle. Through the chaos, there was another unnerving sight: bodies. Every few feet in the racing circle of water floated a body. They were human yet monstrous. They were alive yet not breathing.

Amber whipped the hair out of her face and rubbed her eyes. *What the heck?*

Her raft rammed into the opposite wall of water, and it was over. The ocean was motionless: no storm, no water circle, no bodies. Her raft was the only thing afloat as far as the eye could see.

"They're—*gone*," she sputtered, hot tears falling from her eyes. "They're all gone. We're the only ones left."

No one spoke for ages as the sea gently rocked the survivors. How could this have happened? Just like that, all those people were dead. The anger of injustice simmered in her. The little girl from the other raft—she couldn't have been older than seven.

Amber glanced at Tony. His eyelids were squeezed shut, and his hands were clenched, as though trying to not remember the faces of each and every victim. Katherine was shaking, and Isaac stared blankly into nothingness. They all felt it—the weight of unfair death. It felt like more than just a freak of nature. It felt like murder.

"W-w-we're all g-going to d-d-die!" Isaac burst into tears.

"Oh, shut up!" snapped Katherine, but her voice wobbled. "We're not going to die. Someone will find us."

They floated along, the hot summer sun searing Amber's skin. She stared at the water bottle in her hand. How long would they be out at sea? Their situation would decline rapidly once the water ran out. But even if they had an endless supply of water, the sea could become restless at any moment. She looked up into the sky as these depressing observations consumed her thoughts. Had anyone received a distress signal from the ship? Was one even sent?

Isaac's right. We're going to die.

With that miserable conclusion hovering in her mind, Tony broke the silence, "What's that?"

There, on the horizon, sat a pinprick of green.

"An island," Katherine exclaimed and began to frantically paddle with her hands.

They inched towards the island. The effort they exerted didn't seem to match their painfully slow speed, but at long last, their raft scraped against the sand.

"Thank g-goodness." Isaac hugged the ground as though they had been out at sea for a millennium.

This place looks familiar. But why?

A lightbulb turned on in Amber's brain. "Wait a minute," she said over Katherine's complaint of "It's *so* hot."

"What?" Tony said.

"Oh, what now?" whimpered Isaac.

Amber fumbled in her backpack. "It can't be."

Tony let out an irritated sigh. "*What*, Quill?"

She pulled out *The Island of Thanatos* and held it up at arm's length.

"What are you doing?" Katherine asked, sounding bored.

Amber's jaw dropped. "Oh—my—word."

"Oh my word, what? Spit it out, smartypants!" Tony said.

"This island is the Island of Thanatos," Amber said. "I don't believe it."

"The island of what now?" Katherine furrowed her brow.

"The Island of Th-Th-Thanatos," Isaac said, peering over Amber's shoulder, studying the cover of the book. The others did the same.

The cover depicted an island identical to the one they were on. Every tree, vine, and flower was in the exact same spot.

"But this book is supposed to be a novel," mused Amber. "Not real."

Her mental gears kicked into overdrive. None of this made sense: the woman, the bodies, the unnatural storm, the book—everything. She glanced at the others. If she had been an alien, they would've stared at her just the same.

"So we are on an i-i-island that's legend? Not real?"

"Well, yes. I thought. But it's obviously real." Amber bit her cheek. "And we don't want it to be real, trust me. This book is horrifying."

Tony jerked the book out of her hand and started flipping through it as she gazed into the trees, dumbstruck. *Surely, I'm mistaken. Surely, it's a coincidence. But after everything I've seen today...no, no. I'm on the wrong track. Someone probably just used this island as inspiration for the cover, surely.*

Tony closed the book with a snap. "Fairy tales and ghost stories. *Great!*"

"Oh, they are not fairy tales," said a high-pitched and over-excited voice behind them. "They weren't written by fairies."

The four survivors spun around. A tiny girl about ten inches tall stood on a rock before them. She had a green dress, dainty wings, and brown hair tied into a tight bun.

"And the island it speaks of is real," she went on. "This very one we stand on."

Katherine clapped her hand over her mouth, Tony's jaw dropped, Isaac was white as a sheet, and Amber's eyes doubled in size.

The fairy furrowed her brow and cocked her head to one side. "What's with the faces?" she squeaked.

Isaac gulped. "Y-y-you're a fairy?"

"Why, of course I am!" the fairy squealed. "What do I look like? A dwarf?"

"There's dwarfs on this island?" shrieked Katherine.

"Oh, yes! There's fairies, centaurs, unicorns, pegasi, dwarfs, all kinds of magic creatures here. That's right, even," she paused, glanced to both sides, and added in a creepy whisper, "Water Demons."

"*Ok.*" Tony rolled his eyes and turned towards Katherine. "And I thought you were dramatic."

"Oh, silly me," the fairy continued in a lively manner. "I haven't said my name. I am Olive, at your service." She gave a short bow. "And what shall I call you?"

"This here is Isaac Logan," Amber said, "Katherine and Tony Kielwein, and I am Amber Quill."

Olive blinked. "A-Amber? Your name is Amber?"

"Um, yes?"

The fairy nodded and smiled absentmindedly.

"Are you here for a specific reason," Katherine quipped, "or did you just want to scare us half to death?"

"Why, of course, there's a reason! I have come to help you off the island, to tell you about the tests. *Oh,* horrid things happen to those who try and avoid the tests."

"You can help us off the island?" Amber asked.

"Yes, yes, I can!" Olive squeaked. "Come, sit down. I will tell you everything."

They all plopped down around Olive's rock, although Tony looked skeptical.

"To get off the island, each person will need to pass a test, if you will. Games, really. (Or at least that is what my mistress calls them.) They are *very* hard. If you pass the tests, there is a magical boat that can take you off the island. According to the skill set needed, you will choose who does what test. That is the only way off the island."

"Who is this mistress of yours?" asked Amber.

"Her name is Norcepta, the goddess of the sea," responded Olive. "All creatures on this island are bound to serve her until she perishes. Her Water Demons too—they are all the people she has stabbed with her magic dagger and filled with an evil spirit. The Demons will never be their true selves again until Norcepta is gone. Only then will they rest in peace.

"My mistress has caused much death and suffering. She used to, back when she controlled most of the world, put humans on this island and watch them play her games. It was her entertainment. Very few ever left the island alive. That is why the island is called Thanatos. Or in other words—death."

"Lovely," muttered Tony.

"My mistress will not rest until she has vanquished the descendant of the girl who tried to kill her so many years ago. There's only one more, you see..."

"So, you will help us?" Amber prompted.

"Oh, yes! It seems unfair to let you try to navigate these tests by yourselves."

Tony leaned toward Amber and whispered, "I don't like this, Quill. How do we know we can trust her? This goddess is her mistress, after all."

"Do we have a choice?" she whispered back. "These are tests, she says, games. And every game has its rules. We won't make it far without her."

Olive led the survivors deeper into the island. Amber glanced over her shoulder as the beach was swallowed by the darkness of the jungle. Just then a passage from *The Island of Thanatos* popped into Amber's mind:

"*But the survivors refused the help of this mysterious guide and journeyed into the daunting jungle. As they traveled, an eerie feeling hung over them—a feeling of destiny, but this destiny was not in their favor.*"

4

NORCEPTA'S STAR

While hiking through the dense jungle, Tony exploded, "Oh, this is bull—"

Katherine whipped around. "Tony!"

"What? I said this is bull."

Katherine folded her arms.

"That was the end of my sentence!"

Amber rolled her eyes. *Sure it was.*

"As I was saying, this fairy's story is downright nonsense. It's nuts!"

"Tony," said Katherine, "did you see what happened to our cruise ship? I don't believe those ice spears were a natural occurrence."

"Fair point," Tony mumbled.

"*And* there's a *fairy*—" Katherine interrupted herself. "I'm not the only one who is seeing this fairy, right?"

"No y-y-you are not," Isaac assured her, staring at the fairy warily.

"Where are you leading us?" Amber called to Olive, who could fly a lot faster than they could walk.

"To the first test! Don't worry. We are almost there!" Olive called back with a squeak. Minutes later, she announced, "We're here!"

"Yes, we can hear you. We're standing right beside you," grumbled Tony. "No need to shout at us."

"Oh, sorry," Olive said in a hushed voice. "We are at the first test."

In front of them was a clearing. At the far end, a tall stone table stood with a crystal bottle atop it. The bottle shone like a star, beams of white light reaching out into the dark jungle.

"The star of Norcepta," said Olive.

"What's that?" Katherine pointed to something on the ground. At their feet, there was a flat stone with a message carved into it:

TO SURVIVE THIS TEST,
YOU MUST DO YOUR BEST,

FOR THE LIFE OF THE NEXT
RESTS ON THE SUCCESS OF THIS TEST.

THE LIGHT OF NORCEPTA
WILL BE YOUR GUIDE.

IF YOU WISH TO GO ON,
THIS IS THE ONLY WAY YOU WILL FIND.

Isaac bent down to study the message. "It's a riddle."

"Not a very hard riddle," Tony scoffed. "All we have to do is grab that star-in-a-bottle."

"There's more to it than that, of course," Olive said. "You have to pass the test."

Katherine rolled her eyes. "What test? The light of Norcepta, or whatever it's called, is right there!"

"My annoying *little* sister is right." Tony glanced at his sister with a smirk. "It's right there. I'm going for it."

"You're five minutes older than me," Katherine huffed.

Amber said, "I really think we should listen to Olive."

But it was too late. Tony was already marching towards the star-in-a-bottle like an—well, to say it nicely—an *unintelligent* individual. Suddenly, one of the surrounding trees swooped down and gave Tony a nasty blow to the chest. Katherine let out an ear-piercing shriek as he flew through the air and crashed at Amber's feet.

"You asked for it," Amber muttered as Tony rose to his feet, cursing.

"It's the Tree Spirits," Olive said, dread evident in her voice.

The movement of the one tree set off a chain reaction; all the trees around the clearing started swaying and stooping and hitting the ground.

"This looks like an obstacle course," Isaac stuttered, looking aghast.

"Obstacle course, you say?" Tony rubbed the back of his neck. "I do those all the time for football practice—well, *soccer* for the Americans present. I guess I have the best shot at getting through there."

"And you pretty much have to do it anyway," said Olive. "You've technically already started the test by going out there. What luck you're good at obstacle courses!"

Staring at the furious trees, he gulped. "Here goes nothing."

"Come back in one piece, ok?" Katherine stammered.

He strode toward the trees. As claimed, he was very skilled with obstacle courses. He dodged vines that came from nowhere, jumped over tree limbs that tried to trip him, and ducked as branches came swooping over his head. He was going to beat the test without a problem. He was almost—

WHACK! Katherine screamed, and Isaac covered his eyes. One of the branches had hit Tony square on the back, and he faceplanted the ground. He slowly lifted himself onto his hands and knees, grimacing as his fingers investigated his split lip. A tree nailed the space next to him. He flipped over. Another branch was barreling toward him. He quickly turned onto his side, narrowly escaping the well-aimed strike. He rolled left and right, dodging the limbs as they attempted to hammer him into the ground.

"Can't we do *something?*" Amber demanded.

"No," Olive said, surprisingly serious. "There's a magical bond tying him to this test. If you try to help him...you just might as well kill him now because it wouldn't make any difference."

Amber wanted to scream. Tony's luck wouldn't last forever. The trees would soon squash him into jelly. He was about to die. Another person was about to die. Her fingernails dug into her palms. How much more death would this day bring? She was standing right there, a few feet away from him. It would be so easy to pull him to safety, but she could do nothing. Just like on the crab fishing boat, she could do nothing. She could only watch.

Tony narrowly escaped another beating, but this time he continued rolling toward the table, the trees desperately smacking the ground in his wake. Amber crossed her fingers behind her back, muttering, "Come on. Come on, Kielwein." One tree struck in front of him, blocking his path. He scrambled to his feet, ran around that tree and ducked as another branch came at him. Lunging forward, he grabbed Norcepta's star off the table. The trees immediately froze and stood upright. Tony lay in the grass beside the table, clutching the bottle to his chest as it rapidly rose and fell with his breathing.

"You did it! Thank goodness," squealed Katherine. Once he got to his feet, she threw her arms around his neck.

"Alright, alright," he grumbled but was clearly moved by her concern. "You're gonna make me drop the star."

Olive squeaked in a sing-song voice while dancing around in midair, "He did it. He did it! He got the star. He got the star!"

Amber let out a sigh of relief and leaned against a tree.

"You alright there, Quill?" Tony approached her with a grin on his face. "You seem more shaken up than I am."

"I just—" She squeezed her eyelids shut. Why were all the faces of the passengers so clear in her mind? "I can't take anymore death today."

Tony nodded grimly. "Yeah."

This is why I don't do friends.

"Ok, players," Olive dramatically whispered, "off to the next test."

And they set off through the jungle once more.

5

A DANCE-OFF WITH DEATH

"Oh, we've been walking for miles," groaned Katherine for the five-hundredth time. *Does the girl ever stop whining?*

"Would you shut up!" Amber snapped.

"You *have* been complaining nonstop," said Tony, seizing the opportunity to nag his sister. "Not to mention those unnecessary comments you make. You know, like complaining that the grass is too green or something."

"Oh, har har." Katherine sneered.

"She never said the grass was too green," stammered Isaac, puzzled.

"I was being sarcastic, genius." Tony rolled his eyes. "Who in the world would complain the grass is too green? Not even my sister is *that* weird."

"What was that?" Katherine barked while Amber struggled to restrain her laugh. "Are you saying I'm weird?"

"Uh—*yeah*. I didn't think it was that big of a secret."

His sister glared at first, then the corners of her mouth gradually lifted. Her contagious giggles spread throughout the whole group.

"Ok, granted," Katherine said, "I can be a bit of a handful."

Tony raised his eyebrows. "You think?"

Amber chuckled then added, "Sorry I snapped at you."

"It's fine." Katherine shrugged. "I'll try to complain less. *Especially* about the grass. Right, Isaac?"

Amber glanced at Isaac to see a smile crease his face. Was that his version of a laugh?

Bringing up the tail of the group, she strolled along with her hands in her pockets. A soft smile touched her lips. The brief moment of laughter had lightened her heart, and she was grateful for it. The feeling of togetherness felt—good.

Her smile faded at that word—*togetherness*. She was letting herself get close, dangerously close. This wouldn't last. The probability they would all make it off the island was—well, it wasn't high. She couldn't give in. She couldn't become attached. It would only lead to more scars.

She trudged on, the heaviness returning. She was alone and that was what she needed to be. It was the only way to survive—not the island, but life.

Eventually, Isaac fell behind and asked Amber, "So, um, where are y-y-you from?"

"I was born in Florida," she said, "but I live in New York now. Not far from the dock."

He grinned. "I live not far from th-the dock, too. Do you go to high s-s-school there or—?"

She stopped in her tracks. "Why the sudden curiosity?" The moment the words had left her mouth, she kicked herself. *Gosh, Amber. You didn't have to be so harsh.*

He stared at her. "I-I-I just thought, since we're all stuck here, we might as well get to know each other. Especially s-s-since we seem to live close by." He paused; the longer the silence lasted, the more nervous he appeared. "I'm s-sorry. It was wrong timing. Th-that was strange, anyway. I—"

"You don't have a really high self-confidence, do you?"

He fixed his eyes on the ground. "People think I'm weird. Th-they don't want to talk to me. I g-g-get bullied a lot because of my stutter and 'nerdiness,' as they call it. I-I-I don't really have any friends."

"Yeah, me neither."

"You g-g-get bullied, too?"

"No. I just don't do friends."

"Why?"

Amber didn't reply; she just stared after Olive and the Kielweins as they walked further and further away.

"Well"—Isaac smiled—"I can be your friend if y-y-you need one."

Amber flinched inside but felt her cheeks flush. That was sweet of him. She wrestled to keep the thought at bay, but she couldn't help herself. It *was* really sweet of him.

"Yo!" Tony called from ahead. "Keep up, you two!"

Amber and Isaac jogged up to the rest of the group. She was tailing the others when Katherine fell back with an annoying grin on her face.

"Feel the butterflies yet?" she whispered.

It took Amber a minute before it clicked; her cheeks grew hotter, if that was possible. "Shut up."

"I'm just saying. Your face is as red as a strawberry."

"*Shut up.*"

Though the trees hid them from the sun, the jungle was still hot. The thick, wet air weighed down on her, so damp it almost clogged her windpipe. Drenched with sweat, her clothes clung to her body.

Mosquitos buzzed in excitement over the new feast and wouldn't leave the travelers alone, no matter how much they swatted at them. Tall grass, low-hanging tree limbs, and vines clawed at the survivors, like they were trying to keep them from the horrors within the island.

Amber took a sip of water and hesitated when putting the bottle back in her backpack. She licked her lips. Couldn't she just down the whole bottle? She eyed the precious liquid hungrily but, with a groan, shoved the bottle into her backpack. Drinking it all would be a very foolish thing to do.

"Ok," Tony broke the silence so abruptly that Amber jumped a foot into the air, "I'm starting to agree with Katherine. How much farther? How big is this downright awful island?"

"Oh, it's very big." Olive nodded her head vigorously. "We are almost there!"

After a lot longer than "almost there" should have been, they reached the next test. It was foggy and dark, so dark they could hardly see one another. All the troublesome plants had just vanished from their path, so there must be a clearing in front of them. The *plop* sound made by some small animal nearby suggested water. At least, Amber hoped it was a small animal—a *normal*, small animal.

"This is the next test? How are we going to complete the test if we can't see?" Katherine complained.

"What did that riddle say?" Amber asked no one in particular. "'*The light of Norcepta will be your guide*,' right? Maybe the star will help us. Kielwein, take the star out of your back-pack and hold it up. We might find a clue."

Tony obeyed. The light pushed against the edges of the dark, but most of their surroundings remained unclear. A curtain of fog shimmered before them. Beneath it lay a bank, a gigantic lily pad floating in the water, and a riddle etched into the ground, the letters reflecting the starlight.

"Quill, you are *brilliant*," Tony said as he knelt down to read the riddle aloud:

GRACE IS WHAT YOU WILL NEED FOR THIS TEST.

HERE, YOU MUST DEFEAT DEATH.

YOUR SURVIVAL MEANS
THE LIFE OF THE REST.

POUR THE POWER FROM YOUR HANDS
INTO THE WATERS OF DEATH,

AND BE LIGHT ON YOUR FEET,
AS LIGHT AS A FEATHER,

CROSS THE LAKE AND
PULL DOWN THE LEVER.

Tony stood up and scoffed, "A five-year-old could have written these riddles."

"Yeah," said Katherine. "We have to 'defeat death' every time. Like *duh*."

"We know we have to use the star in one way or another," mused Amber, ignoring the siblings' ridicule.

"I-I have an idea," Isaac said. "The star is liquid, right? Th-the riddle said we need to '*pour the power from our hands.*'

What if we pour the s-s-star into the water? We m-m-might be able to see better if nothing else."

Amber bit her cheek. "I don't know. If it really is a star, they are *extremely* hot. We could seriously hurt ourselves—or worse."

"Makes sense to me." Katherine shrugged. "What else can it mean?"

Amber frowned. "Oh—well—alright. I guess we need to try *something*."

"Ok then, here goes nothing." Tony inched toward the pond.

"Stop!" Olive screamed.

Tony nearly leapt out of his skin. "Gosh, Olive! Calm down a bit, will you? *Jeez*. What is it now?"

"You've already done a test. If you try to start another—"

"Let me guess. Something will—knock my head off?"

"Maybe not that, but you will be killed."

"And what happens if, say, only one or two people get stuck here? They're doomed?"

"No," said Olive. "The island adjusts to however many people 'enter the game.'"

"Oh...well, that isn't disturbing *at all*," Tony quipped.

Amber peered into the gloom that hovered over the next test. "But if we don't know whose skill will be best yet, how are we to pick who will do the test?"

Silence rang in their ears. Even the insects ceased their racket, waiting noiselessly for the answer.

"Didn't the riddle say, '*be light on your feet, as light as a feather*'?" Katherine murmured.

Amber nodded. "Correct."

Katherine exhaled. "Couldn't that mean a kind of dance or at least a test where dance skills would be useful?"

"That makes sense," Isaac stuttered.

"Then I think I should do the test," Katherine said.

"Wait," said Amber. "Why?"

Tony rubbed his eyes. "Because she's a ballerina."

Katherine smiled at her brother's concerned expression. "You've known I'd have to do one eventually. I'll be alright. This is our best guess, and I'm the best candidate."

Dispirited, he handed her the star-in-a-bottle. "Just be careful, alright?"

Katherine approached the bank and, casting an anxious glance at the others, opened the bottle. Its light swelled as if itching to escape its tiny prison. Gingerly, she poured it into the water. After every drop had been drained, there was a small, glowing gem resting at the bottom of the bottle.

Amber's brow furrowed. "*That's* the star?"

"My mistress caused it to die long ago," said Olive. "It melted until it was nothing more than a gem in water. She kept it in the bottle to be used in her games."

"What do I do with it?" Katherine asked.

Amber shrugged. "The gem is a part of the star's remains. *'Pour the power from your hands,'* it said. Drop it in."

Katherine dropped the gem into the water, which lit up like an aurora. The body of water before them was a pond. The huge lily pads floating atop twinkled and blinked like a light show.

Amber stood mesmerized by the breathtaking lights. The pond was like a rooftop on Christmas or the sky on New Year's, and the lapping of the water against the bank was a miniature version of the ocean waves crashing on the shore. Despite the daunting jungle wrapped around them, the scene was beautiful.

Her mother and she once walked along the shore on the night of the Fourth of July. Fireworks could be seen leaping out of civilization and exploding in the air. She had gazed up at them in awe, but her mother had pointed toward the ocean. Red, blue, and green were those waves, painted by the spectacle far away up in the sky.

But the smile that now creased Amber's face was washed away as she stared at the bank. Her mother had been swallowed by the ocean she had treasured. The warmness that memory brought turned to ice. She would never be hurt like that again.

"It's a pattern!" Katherine said after a moment of observation. "It's the ballet, *La Sylphide*. I'm *very* good at this dance."

"Oh my g-g-gosh." Isaac's eyes were as wide as saucers. "Look!"

Amber followed his gaze and saw that Venus flytraps the size of lions lined the bank. They hissed and hungrily snapped at the air.

Katherine gulped. "Ok, it may be a little harder with those things. But I can do this...maybe." She stood at the edge of the pond, watching the lights closely. When the one right in front of her lit up, she leaped onto it and the dance began. An enchanting, inhuman voice accompanied eerie, unseen instruments playing the *La Sylphide* theme. But the music could never compete with Katherine's grace and elegance.

"Woah. She's fantastic," Amber said.

"Yeah," Tony replied, "but I'm afraid those flytraps might get the best of her."

Katherine, however, didn't appear swayed by the vicious plant monsters. She danced as well as any other with an occasional leap or duck to avoid sharp teeth and slithering vines. They snapped and hissed but didn't so much as scratch her. The music ceased as she reached the end, safe and sound.

She stepped onto solid ground. As she reached for the lever, an earsplitting scream cut through the air.

"Katherine!" yelled Tony.

"Oh, no!" shrieked a horrified Olive. "They got her. They got her!"

Katherine collapsed, clutching her left calf. Blood gushed from her leg and ran down her arms. Her face contorted in agony. The flytrap approached for another blow; its bloodied teeth bared.

Amber's pounding heart lodged itself in her throat, but she was able to squeeze out an order. "Kielwein, the lever is right above you! Reach out and pull it, or be that plant's dinner!"

Katherine obeyed, and the Venus flytrap retreated immediately. A large stone plank rolled over the pond. Tony, Amber, Olive, and Isaac rushed over to Katherine. Her brother crashed onto his knees beside her. Through Katherine's fingers, Amber could see the deep, bloody teeth marks on her calf.

"Just hold still," she said soothingly over Katherine's moaning. "Logan, can you hand me the first aid kit out of my backpack?"

"You brought a first aid kit on a cruise?" Tony asked as Isaac handed it to Amber.

She began to doctor Katherine's leg. "I snatched it from the ship before we left." A neat bandage was wrapped around her leg in no time.

"Wow, you do good work," Tony said, failing to hide that he was impressed. "Are you alright, Katherine?"

"Yeah, yeah, I'm fine," she murmured weakly as the last flickering rays of starlight went out, surrounding them in total darkness.

"Oh, *lovely*," Tony grumbled. "How are we going to find our way out?"

"I g-g-got a flashlight," Isaac piped up.

Tony's voice suggested a glower. "Now why in the world did you not mention that before, stutter-boy? You didn't think we might need that when we were completely in the dark back there?"

"I'm s-s-sorry." Isaac brushed Amber's arm in an action she assumed was him putting his hands up in defense, sending an alarming current of goosebumps from that spot all the way to her neck.

"Logan, you're a real pain in the—"

"Tony!" warned Katherine.

"Neck! I was going to say neck."

"Sure you were."

"I'm sorry," Isaac stammered. "This place has me on edge, overwrought. I can't think straight."

Tony scoffed. "Aren't you *always* jittery?"

"Enough teasing, Kielwein. We should find a place to get some sleep," Amber said. "It's getting late."

"I-I-I agree," Isaac said.

Amber's eyes had adjusted enough to see Tony cross his arms as he said, "Hey, wait a minute. Why are you making all the calls? Who put you in charge, anyway?"

"What are we supposed to do?" snapped Amber. "Keep walking till we drop dead from lack of sleep?"

"I don't know, Quill"—Tony threw his arms up—"but I want to get off this island. Maybe we should keep walking. Maybe—"

"Um—hello?" Katherine shouted, lying helpless on the ground. "Whatever you and the missus do, Tony, just help me up, already."

Embarrassed, Amber put one of the girl's arms around her shoulders, and Tony did the same after mockingly gagging at the idea of him and Amber getting hitched. The survivors took Amber's advice and searched for a place to sleep. Isaac followed Olive with his flashlight, while Tony, Amber, and Katherine (hopping along in between them) brought up the rear.

6

WE CAN BE FRIENDS

It would seem logical to think that nighttime would welcome cooler temperatures, but this was not the case on the Island of Thanatos. Soaked with sweat, Amber and Tony helped Katherine hobble through the jungle.

Wiping her forehead, Amber panted, "Stop. Stop! I—I need—I need another break." She unloaded Katherine's full weight onto Tony before bending over to clutch her knees.

"Another one?" whined Olive. "At this rate, we'll never get to the next test!"

"Unless you have a little fairy hospital," Tony growled, "we can't help all these pit stops. Maybe *you* should fly over here and support her weight."

"Oh, don't be—Wait!" Olive gasped; her face was so lit up that Amber was half expecting a tiny lightbulb to poof into existence over the fairy's head. "I just had a spectacular idea. I have some friends that can help. Follow me!" The fairy led them away from the semi-cleared path and through the jungle.

The clearing they soon entered couldn't be described in any other way than a midnight paradise. The flowers were aglow with blue light, and the fireflies twinkled along with the stars. The surrounding trees (looking more like trees of an English wood than a tropical jungle) were ripe with every kind of fruit. Tiny houses sat atop giant mushrooms and hung from tree limbs in the Disney-princess-esque botanical garden. If there were ever a place that caused someone to believe in fairies, this was it.

"Woah." Tony's jaw dropped. "Would you look at that."

"It's beautiful," said Isaac. "Have y-y-you ever seen any-thing like it?"

Amber breathed, "It's *amazing*."

"Understatement of the century," Katherine murmured.

"Rose! River! Missy! I'm back! I need your help with a plant bite. Come out! It's Olive. Hello?" Olive hollered at the top of her lungs, ending the traveler's adoring comments.

"Tell me," Tony whispered to Amber, "who in their right mind would name their kid Missy?"

Amber giggled silently and caught Isaac's eye. He appeared dejected as his gaze shifted from her to Tony. It was almost as if he was *jealous*. A smile tugged at her lips, but she ordered it to stand down. She couldn't harbor such thoughts.

Katherine had just finished saying, "Well, where are they?" when Rose, River, and Missy zoomed into the clearing. Olive let out an overexcited squeal and rushed over to greet her friends. The following conversation made clear which fairy was which. Rose was a pale fairy with bright red, braided hair and a rose-petal dress. White-headed, River wore a knee-length dress that looked like running water. Missy's golden hair was as long as she was, and she had a gold dress that was so shiny it was almost blinding.

"Girls," said Olive breathlessly, "I need you to make some of that pink stuff you use to heal up wounds. My friend has a boo-boo."

Rose puffed out her chest. "You mean our Sarta serum?"

"Yes, please. Will you help us?" Olive pleaded theatrically, and Tony rolled his eyes.

"Of course!" Missy said with a flutter. "Any friend of yours is a friend of ours. Let's hop to it, girls."

With that, they got busy making the healing serum. Rose, River, and Missy zipped here and there, gathering different plants and berries. Then they circled around a small bowl, working in haste.

"Are you sure this is going to work?" Amber asked Olive.

"Oh, yes!" She nodded. "One hundred percent!"

Finally, the fairies fluttered over to Katherine, carrying a bowl full of pink, sparkling liquid.

"Can you remove the wrappings, please?" squeaked Missy.

Gingerly, Amber unwrapped Katherine's leg, and the fairies poured the Sarta serum over her wound. She gasped as it flowed onto her leg. There was a hissing noise and tiny wisps of steam rose, like an ice cube placed onto a hot stove. When River washed the serum off, the bite was gone.

Katherine gaped and ran her fingers across her leg tentatively. "What do you know? Thanks."

"You're welcome," the fairies said in unison.

"Is it alright if we crash here?" Amber asked, rubbing her arms; it was nice and cool in the fairies' clearing. "We need a place to get some rest."

"No problem," said Rose. "We'll build a fire." And the fairies got to work again.

Amber sat down beside Katherine. "How are you feeling?"

"Pretty good," she replied. "It's like nothing ever happened! And I, um—er—thanks for taking care of me back there."

"It was really the fairies that got you fixed up."

"True. But you helped before them."

Amber winced. "You shouldn't be thanking me. I'm afraid I've misjudged you, after our meeting on the ship. That was unfair of me, to judge so soon."

Katherine grew solemn. "I can see how you would think low of me. I'm not the most likable person. And the worst part is, it's by choice."

"What do you mean?"

"After we moved to America, I tried to make new friends at our school, but no one wanted to talk to me. No one liked me. So, I thought, if they were going to treat me nasty, I might as well give them a reason to. I put on an attitude and became the snobbiest girl at school. It was stupid, really."

Amber frowned. "I took you as the popular girl."

Katherine smiled ruefully. "I'm not. It's funny, the popular kids don't behave that much different from me. I guess the only difference is that I'm not considered 'cool,' whatever in the world *that* means."

Amber stared down at her hands. "If it makes any difference, *I* think you're cool. I mean, the girl I'm talking to now, the *real* you. I've seen her in glimpses. She's caring, kind, friendly. She's pretty cool."

"Thanks." A tear fell into Katherine's lap. "Maybe I will try things her way again. Say, when we get back home, maybe we can—"

All the blood rushed from Amber's face. She knew what Katherine was about to say, and she couldn't risk it. "What's that? I think one of the fairies called me. I better, um—" She leapt up and hurried away, leaving a confused Katherine staring after her.

From where she sat on a rock at the edge of the clearing, Amber watched the others build a fire and gather food. Katherine's leg was perfectly fine. She walked around and nagged her brother like she hadn't almost been eaten alive by a plant the size of a rhinoceros. Tony came back at her with wisecracks as per usual, but they had become halfhearted. He wore an expression of pure gratitude that his sister was still breathing, but simultaneously, there was utter terror at how close he'd come to losing her. Amber empathized with both his relief and alarm. By a bizarre turn of events, Isaac and Katherine appeared to be getting along. He said something to her that caused her to burst into giggles. He stood a little straighter, proud of himself that he came up with a decent joke. Envy pecked at Amber, but she caught herself. She averted her eyes from the scene as Tony and Isaac struck up a conversation. Now the boys were getting along. Wait, why did that matter? She was letting them get a foothold in her heart.

I can't do friends. Such things only scar.

A fire sat in the middle of the clearing with the survivors and the fairies gathered around it. The soft hoot of an owl, hiding somewhere in the woods, was heard over the flame's crackling.

Having eaten a fruit dinner, they all settled down to sleep. Amber gazed up at the canvas of stars above, like pinpricks of hope piercing the gloom of their situation. She laid there waiting...waiting for the nightmares to come. She would see her mom again soon. With a tight hold on her locket, she drifted off to sleep, traveling to quite a different time and place, a day that would haunt her forever. It was the one day she wished she would forget...

The boat glided across the perfectly still ocean, smooth as glass. The young girl and her mother stood on the deck, watching the sun drop into the sea. But then, a massive wave crashed over the deck, drenching the girl and her mother. The suddenly restless ocean tossed the boat to and fro without mercy. The girl turned and saw another wave approaching. Something was within it: a woman's sinister, grinning face. The mother pushed the girl down and lifted her hands. The water crashed into some invisible wall overhead and then receded without harming the boat. The girl shouted for her mother, who was gripping the rail in exhaustion, to take cover, but it was too late. Yet another wave, a much fiercer one, collided with the deck, blinding the girl. When the mist cleared, her mother was nowhere in sight. She was simply gone. The young girl screamed in agony, tears pouring down her face. Her mother was dead, lying motionless at the bottom of the sea...

"Quill! Quill, are you alright?" came a man's voice. "Quill! Oh, come on. Amber. Amber!"

Her eyes snapped open. Her heart slammed itself against her ribcage in a futile attempt to escape. She was trembling and soaked in sweat.

Tony Kielwein was hunched over her with concern written on his face. He had a firm grip on her shoulders; it must have been difficult to wake her. Breaking free from his grasp, she sat up and saw that the others were still asleep.

"What is it, Kielwein?" she asked wearily.

"You started screaming in your sleep." His voice was stern but quaking. "So I *think* I have the right to be a bit worried."

"It was just a nightmare."

"A nightmare? From the way you were screaming, I thought you'd seen Dracula, which wouldn't surprise me at this point. *Jeez.* Must've been a downright awful nightmare."

Amber blinked, then looked into the fire. "Yep." The flames wrapped themselves around the log and reached up to the heavens. Living fire, a red glow, coursed through each coal beneath. Together, they whispered about something. They danced and chanted, "Yes, yes, finally!"

Had she lost her mind? What a strange perception to have of mere fire and wood.

She glanced at Tony to find worry in his eyes. He said, "Why do I get the feeling that this is a normal thing for you?"

"Probably because it is."

He shifted uncomfortably. "I don't mean to pry, but you have talked to someone about this, right? I mean, I don't think nightmares that bad are to be kept to yourself."

"What, you mean like a therapist?"

"Not necessarily. Just somebody. A friend?"

She looked away from him. "I don't do friends."

"I heard you say that to Isaac earlier. You mean to say that you have *no* friends."

"Yep."

"Your choice or theirs?"

"Mine."

Why am I telling him this?

"That's bad for your health, you know. People need people." Now he was getting irritating.

"Who made you the king of relationships?" she retorted.

"Look," he said, his words clipped, "I may not be a therapist or doctor or whatever, but it doesn't take a fancy education to realize that we'd lose our heads if it weren't for others. I know at least I would. What on earth caused you to believe friendship was such a negative thing?"

"Would you stop? Just stop!" Amber exploded. "My mom died when I was nine years old, alright? Right in front of me! She was everything to me, and suddenly, she was gone. I watched my dad fall apart, *helpless* to comfort his daughter. My friends weren't around. They didn't care. So, I was determined never to hurt like that again. There, you happy?"

The chirping of crickets and the crackling of fire (unusually loud after the heated conversation) banged against her eardrums as she rubbed a hand across her wet face. *Did I really just say that? I'm losing my senses on this island.*

She risked a glance. The compassion in Tony's face took her aback. Something was on his mind, she could tell. He seemed to wrestle with it, unsure if it should be voiced.

"I am sorry, Quill. I had no idea," he whispered at length. "I am deeply sorry about your mother and everything else. And I know this is not my place to say, but I fear no one else will tell you if I don't. This—this anti-pain system you've developed is, well, it's stupid. Actually, it's downright depressing."

Amber tried to conceal the fact that she was startled by this; she must have succeeded because he continued, "You said you were nine years old when this happened, right? So, first of all, your friends at the time probably weren't the most sensitive in the world. Adults don't know what to do when their friends lose a loved one. Why would you expect nine-year-olds to act any different?"

She froze. *That's a good question.*

A lump formed in her throat. Before she could stop herself, she blurted, "I just can't bear to lose someone else. I can't go through that again."

Tony paused thoughtfully. "And how is this no-friends policy working out for you? How do you think your mother would feel if she knew what her death led you to believe? Tell me, would you have rather not known her at all than go through what you did? I know I wouldn't want that. The four of us, we don't know each other well, but I think it would hurt if—if something were to happen. I can tell you've been keeping us at bay, but do you think that means you're not gonna feel it if one of us dies here? We felt it when people we've never spoken to passed, in the rafts, on the ship. After all we've been through together, you think you can prevent enduring the sting of death?"

She clenched her teeth and balled her fists, holding back the floodgates that threatened to spill over. It was like pushing against the tide.

"Losing people hurts, I know," he went on. "But death is going to touch our lives no matter what we do. It's better to have loved someone and endured the pain of their death than to have lived in isolation. At least then you can look back and smile at the memories, not regret not having known anyone at all. We need each other, Quill. It's as simple as that. You don't have to tell me about the nightmares, if you don't want. But please, for goodness' sake, go make a friend and tell them."

She glared at him, her breath quickening. What did he know? Who was he to tell her what to do, what her problem was? Was he some great philosopher? No, he wasn't. She wanted to scream, to yell in his face and tell him all the ways in which he was wrong. He didn't know what she had gone through, how she felt. He had no idea how deep the wounds were or how high the walls were. He didn't know it was too late. And—she began to sob—he was right.

His words soaked into her skin, became part of her very blood. He was right. Turning her back on everyone was the worst plan. She had insisted it would make it better, meanwhile clinging to her grief and blaming those closest to her for it. She had been holding on too tight, trying to control every outcome, to prevent further pain. But it did the opposite. It was time to let go, for how could someone heal if they were holding their hurt close? The web of lies she had convinced herself was truth had her bound, hands and feet.

How could she be so foolish? What a powerful and dangerous thing fear was, particularly when it convinced you isolation was the cure. That was when it got deadly, because then you had no friends to warn you, "It's lying!"

Amber gripped her arms and stared at the fire in dismay. What had she done?

Tony appeared to have regretted his words. "I'm sorry, Quill. I didn't mean to—"

"You're right," she whispered, sniffling. "I know you're right. I've been torturing myself. But it's too late."

"No, it's not, Amber. Can—can I call you Amber?"

She met his eyes. Could she let someone in after all these years? Her heart quaked at the notion, but the idea of a friend was like the sun hitting clammy skin, like the salty breeze at the seashore. This step was one she should've taken long ago. How could the wounded march on if they didn't allow a friend to support their weight? She didn't have to be alone.

She let out a tearful chuckle. "Ok, Tony. We're—friends?"

He laughed. "*Yes*, Amber! We can be friends."

Hold on, were they on the same page? She shifted her weight. "You do mean *just* friends, right?"

"What do you mean?"

"You don't like—I mean—you don't want us...you know."

It took him a second before he understood. "Oh, no. I don't like you like that. Not on my radar *at all*. Honest! I have a girl back home. Besides, it's quite obvious that your attention in that department is elsewhere." He pointedly looked at Isaac.

The fairies' clearing became very warm. "Shut up."

"Seriously, though"—his amused expression faded—"I do want to apologize. I could've been nicer today. I was just frustrated."

"Well, I wonder why," she jested.

"It's no excuse, though."

"It's alright. So—um—about that nightmare." Amber gulped. "I dream about the day my mother died every night. She was thrown overboard by a wave. We were on my dad's crab boat. He thought it would be cool for us to see his work. The water was very still, so my mother and I went on deck for some fresh air. And...yeah."

"I'm sorry. That's so messed up."

She wasn't listening to him. Something just occurred to her: the water should've never been that calm out on the ocean. It was strange, like right before the wave struck the rafts, like the stillness before the cruise ship was hit.

My dream wasn't the same tonight. Wait, what happened? I can't—my mother pushed me away. I've never dreamed that before. And she...no, that doesn't make any sense.

The most disturbing facts about her new dream resurfaced. There were three waves instead of two. One of them— her stomach lurched—was accompanied by a woman's face, the same face that she saw on the raft. And apparently, by some magical power, her mother had stopped the second wave from hitting.

What the heck? Why would Norcepta attack a crab fishing boat? All the recent excitement must have altered my dreams.

That argument grew weaker by the minute. The more Amber pondered it, the more real it seemed and the more sure she was that these new details were long-forgotten memories.

"Amber?" Tony's voice interrupted her self-interrogation. "You ok? Looks like you got some gears turning in there."

She guffawed. "You've known me a couple of days and can already tell that?"

"You're not that hard to figure out." He shrugged.

The silence that followed was broken by a snickering voice, "Should I set up a romantic candlelit dinner for you two *lovely* people?"

Both Tony and Amber jumped. Katherine, in a frenzy of giggles over her own joke, was propped up on her elbow. Amber heaved a heavy sigh and rolled her eyes.

Tony cocked an eyebrow. "So, who invited the comedian?"

"Oh, you're *so* funny." Katherine sneered. "The question remains."

Tony's nose wrinkled. "Ew. That'd be like going on a date with you."

His sister gagged. "Gross."

"No offense, Amber," he added.

"None taken," Amber said. "I'm glad you cleared it up."

Katherine smirked. "*Of course*, none is taken. We all know who Amber has eyes for."

Amber gritted her teeth. "Would you two just shut up about it?"

"No," the twins said in unison.

"You guys don't even know if it's true."

"Oh, give me a break." Tony folded his arms. "Are you *really* going to try and deny it?"

Amber sighed. "*Anyway*. Katherine, I suppose you're wondering what we're doing up—"

"Oh, I know," said Katherine. "I don't know how Isaac and the fairies slept through your scream. I bet you woke every baby in China! I heard the *whole* conversation."

"Wonderful eavesdropping, double-oh-seven," Tony said, clapping his hands in mocking applause.

Katherine ignored him. "I hear we're doing first names now. So, you wanna be friends after all, Amber?"

Amber blushed as she fiddled with her locket. "Yeah—er—sorry for the way I acted earlier."

"I understand. Like I said, I heard the whole conversation. Oh, and you can call me Katherine."

"Should we wake up stutter-boy and see if he'll let us call him Isaac?" Tony joked.

Amber grunted in frustration. "Call him stutter-boy again and I'll knock your head off."

"As you wish, your *royalness*," he teased with a bow. "You still gonna deny it?"

"You guys," Katherine began to titter, "this conversation is *so* stupid."

They stared at each other for a moment then burst into laughter.

"You g-g-guys are very easily amused," Isaac muttered, rubbing his eyes.

"What!" exclaimed Tony. "You're up too?"

"Yep. 'S-s-stutter-boy' is up, and he too heard the whole conversation."

Amber tensed. *The* whole *conversation? I hope not.*

"Aw, I'm sorry, pal. I don't mean anything by it, and I do apologize for being a little rude to you today. We're friends, yes?"

Isaac blinked. "You want to be m-m-my friend?"

"Of course," Tony said, with the girls nodding in agreement. "We all do."

Eventually, Isaac's straight face broke into a smile. "I s-s-suppose I like you, *bonehead*."

"Oh! *Burn*." Katherine said as Amber stifled her laugh.

Isaac chortled and snorted.

He's got a cute laugh.

Tony grinned. "Ooo, looks like the kid's got a sense of humor after all."

After a lengthy chat about things only slightly less stupid, they went back to sleep. For the first time in years, Amber had no nightmares. She slept in peace.

Sunlight seeped through the leaves to announce that morning had come. Dozens of fairies were out and about, buzzing around to complete their morning chores. It was hard to believe they were on the same dreadful island as the day before.

She rolled over, opened her locket, and studied the Quill family's beaming faces. Her lips curved into a soft smile as she recalled the sweet memories of that day. It had been her mom's birthday, so they had gone to the beach, of course. They had arrived at sunrise and didn't leave until the sky was plastered with stars.

Amber snapped her locket shut, abruptly ending her walk down memory lane. However, unlike in times past, the journey left her feeling uplifted instead of broken. That old wound was finally closing.

After breakfast, they set off through the jungle. Olive bid her friends farewell, and the survivors thanked them for their help. The three fairies' goodbyes followed Amber and the others until they were out of earshot.

7

THE CREATURE WATCHING

Amber trailed behind her friends, reading *The Island of Thanatos*.

"The survivors could not find their way out of the jungle. They would see light through the trees and head for it, but suddenly, they were back where they had started. Even if they had played the game, they could not have gotten out. It was a trick. Only one could pass. The island was not meant to be escaped."

She halted and read the paragraph again. Only one could pass? She walked on as calmly as she could manage, but her mind was in chaos. Something wasn't right.

"Olive. Olive!" she hissed. "Come here a minute."

"Just keep going straight," the fairy told Tony as she zoomed over to Amber. "Whatcha need?"

Amber held up the book. "If I understand this right, the book says that only one person can pass the tests. I don't know if that means only one of us can leave or only one person in the world is able to pass these tests or if it means something else entirely. But it doesn't make sense."

Olive's eyes darted from the book to Amber and back again. "It's just a book."

"I'm starting to get the feeling that there's more truth to the book than we would like...I don't like this, Olive."

The fairy grew tense. "The author probably got his facts mixed up." Olive zipped back to the head of the group and announced, "Ok, we're getting to the middle of the island. This part of the island is even more dangerous, so stay sharp!"

Amber wandered behind the group in a trance. Her dream and the incident on the cruise ship had one too many parallels. The book claimed that escape was impossible, and Olive wasn't very inclined to share information. Amber twisted the hem of her shirt around her finger. Did the book's events actually happen? What was Olive hiding? What did—*SNAP!* She whirled around just in time to see a branch twitch.

She stood, petrified. *Were those—eyes? I know I saw eyes, and they weren't natural. Goodness, none of this is natural.*

"Come on, Ace," Katherine called. "Keep up!"

Amber jogged up to her friend. "Ace?"

"Just a little nickname I made up. You mind?"

"Fine with me...*Kat?*"

"I love it! The boys need nicknames too, and I *do not* care if they like it."

"Yeah." Amber glanced over her shoulder. She couldn't shake the uncanny feeling that someone—or some*thing*—was watching them.

They came upon another clearing. At the opposite end stood a massive, stone gate, heavily guarding the horrors that were sure to lurk behind it. Vines slithered up the crumbling walls that stretched endlessly in both directions as well as circled around the tall, cylindrical table in the middle of the clearing. The tabletop was a foot deep with small, elaborately designed stone pieces set into it. One piece lay discarded on the ground, a foot-long stone spear extending from the bottom of what appeared to be an image of an eye. It was a puzzle.

"Ok." Katherine put her hands on her hips. "By now, we all know there must be some sort of riddle around here."

"Th-there it is." Isaac pointed. On the side of the stone table, framed in vines, was a riddle:

YOU'LL NEED GRACE NOR BRAVERY
FOR THIS TEST.

YOU NEED TO SEE THINGS A DIFFERENT WAY,
THE WAY THAT IS BEST.

OUT OF THIS PILE OF RUBBLE,
FIND THE HIDDEN PUZZLE.

YOU NEED ONLY REMEMBER:
THE PEOPLE WHO NAMED THIS ISLAND
WOULD KNOW NO LOVE WITHOUT HER.

"'The people who named this island would know no love without her'?" Tony cocked his eyebrow. "That makes absolutely no sense. Who in the world is 'her'?"

Amber bit her cheek, glancing down at the stone eye. "Maybe the puzzle is a portrait of this woman."

After a few moments of examination, Isaac mused, "The word Thanatos m-m-means death, right? In what language?"

"Greek," replied Amber.

Isaac's eyes lit up. "'*The people who named this island*' means the G-G-Greeks. Then it said, they '*would know no love without her*,' s-s-so the Greek goddess of love. Th-the puzzle is a picture of the goddess Aphrodite!"

"That makes sense," Amber said. "Impressive."

He turned bright red and pretended to study the riddle.

"The goddess of love on the island of death," said Tony. "Talk about oxymoron."

"So," Katherine chimed in, "which one of you is going to do the puzzle?"

Isaac's face went from red to white insanely fast. He shuffled his feet. "I'm very g-g-good at puzzles...so I-I-I guess that means I'm up."

"I guess so," Katherine mumbled and proceeded to bite her nails.

Tony murmured, "Be careful, man."

"Yeah," Amber was able to squeeze out, "be careful."

It was torture to watch Isaac approach the table. There had to be a catch. One way or another, the puzzle was lethal. Poisoned arrows would shoot out. The ground would open up and swallow him. Tigers would emerge from the jungle and tear him to shreds.

She squeezed her eyes shut and inhaled deeply. *You don't know that.*

There *had* to be a trick to the game. It couldn't be that easy. Her thundering heart would explode any minute. Was she about to lose a friend already? She watched intently as his hands darted from here to there, picking up pieces and placing them elsewhere. But nothing happened. He was fine. He was doing well.

Her tensed muscles relaxed a bit. *Maybe it is just a puzzle.*

All of a sudden, he gasped and then screamed, "No!" At that moment, a ginormous blade fell from the gate and slammed into the ground just inches from where Isaac was standing. An invisible hand socked Amber in the gut, and she braced herself against a tree.

"Oh, sh—" said Tony.

"Tony," Katherine warned.

"—oot."

Isaac's narrow escape from death rattled him pretty good. He stood so perfectly still it was difficult to tell if he was even breathing.

He needs to finish the puzzle. I don't know what happens if you fail one of these tests, and I don't want to find out.

Pushing through her lightheadedness, Amber shouted, "You can do this, Isaac. Don't give up!" Her encouragement snapped him out of it, and he continued the puzzle with more confidence than when he started.

A few minutes later, he cried gleefully, "I g-got it! I did it!"

She heard massive stone gears grinding, and the gate swung open to reveal a straight and creepy pathway. Black, twisted, leafless trees huddled around the path. They leaned in to block the sky from those who dare journey beneath on the ground laid with stones that had long since been broken. However, not much of the path was visible. The murk abruptly cut off her line of sight five yards down.

Katherine said, "That is the darkest and foggiest path I have *ever* seen in my life."

"Yep," Tony agreed. "Definitely haunted."

Amber wasn't concerned about the ghost highway right then. She rushed up to Isaac and threw her arms around his neck but released him quickly. She cleared her throat. "Um, that was amazing. You were awesome."

"Yes," said Tony. "You're a smart cookie."

"Totally brave!" Katherine added.

"I knew you'd do it!" Olive squeaked.

Blushing, Isaac mumbled, "Thanks, g-guys."

"Come on, everybody. We can't wait around all day. This way! This way!" Olive said, leading them through the gate.

"Um, Amber?" Isaac stuttered as Amber was about to go through the gate. "Thanks for—um—the vote of confidence back there. I—er—" Fascinated with his shoelaces, he failed to keep eye contact for longer than three seconds.

Amber replied coyly, "You're welcome, Isaac."

A smile pulling at the corners of his mouth, his eyes flickered to hers then went back to his shoes.

She simpered. "What?"

"N-n-nothing."

"Come on. We'd better catch up with the others."

They turned and headed down the path.

Strolling alongside him made her insides flutter. She hadn't considered this last night. She frowned and glanced at him. How close was she willing to get? Could she afford to take the risk? He had almost died during that test. Was she gambling with her heart, or was she opening up?

She replaced those troublesome thoughts with the words of her novel, like that would be any better. *The island was not meant to be escaped.* That proclamation wasn't exactly comforting.

Amber gulped. *It's just a book—maybe.*

She treaded down the haunted pathway, growing more edgy with each step. The trees reached for her with their gnarled, wooden hands, and she was certain she could hear them breathe. Their leafless limbs twitched with each hollow exhale that wafted down her sweaty neck. Something in the treeline growled at her from the right, then from the left. There was this feeling, a chill in her spine, that something was watching them, that wicked eyes were following them. The fog wound between the trunks like serpents of smoke, obscuring her surroundings and playing games with her eyes. In malefic glee, it snickered at her foolishness. Before the gate was out of sight, she was quivering in dread and battling the urge to grab Isaac's hand.

Then she saw it: a pale, decayed face with what looked like seaweed for hair. Through its blueish-grey skin, she saw its frail bones. Its eyes were nothing more than black holes. She collapsed against a tree, swallowing her breakfast back down as her head went on a Ferris wheel ride.

"Amber?" Isaac knelt beside her. "What's wrong?"

She wrenched her gaze away from the odious thing and looked at him. Locking eyes, his expression morphed from concerned to disturbed.

"What is it?" he asked. "You don't look s-s-so well."

Her only reply was her unsteady breaths. She held his gaze, not wanting to look back at the appalling creature.

"Is everything alrigh—Amber, you ok?" Tony had come over to investigate the holdup. "You look like you've seen Frankenstein."

I did see Frankenstein.

"Amber," whispered Katherine, "what happened?"

Amber finally glanced back to where the ocean mummy had crouched, but it was gone.

"Amber?" Isaac slipped his hand into hers, sending those alarming goosebumps up her arm again. She shivered.

"I'm fine," she lied, rubbing her forehead. "Just—um—stomachache. Bad fruit, I guess."

Despite herself, she got up and continued the journey, her friends seeming to have believed the story about her stomachache. Isaac, however, didn't look convinced.

Hand still tingling from his touch, her mental gears started to turn again. *The eyes—that's what I saw before. What was that thing? I bet I just imagined it. I imagined it...I couldn't have made that up. It was real.*

What gave her the idea that reading *The Island of Thanatos* would help her uneasiness in any way escaped her. But she opened the book and hit another startling paragraph:

"It was said that the island is about fun and games. That it is death's playground. The island, however, is about a goddess's revenge, nothing more. These games are in fact not games. They are a manhunt."

Amber's nausea hit an all-time high. What did it mean, the games were a manhunt? Whatever it meant, it could not be good. Did these eerie comments have anything to do with her new dream? It made no sense that Norcepta would attack a crab fishing boat.

Maybe the where had nothing to do with it. Maybe it was the who.

After her mom had gone overboard, the sea went back to its normal behavior. Then, for the first time in eight years,

Amber had gone out onto the water, and Norcepta sunk the ship. By some miracle, Amber survived to wander around on the Island of Thanatos.

If the island is about revenge, is Norcepta after my family? Was mom...am I—no. No, it can't be.

Her mother had stopped a wave with her bare hands, and Amber was certain that, when water had flooded the bridge, she had still been able to breathe.

None of it made sense. It was impossible. Why would her mom push her away? No matter where she was on deck the wave would've hit her, so her mother wasn't protecting her from the wave. What if she had known who attacked, that it was an attack?

No, it doesn't make sense.

The woods around them only grew thicker and more ghastly as they went on. Amber's brain was drowning in questions, with no answers on the horizon. Actually, an answer was close to shore, but she wouldn't accept it. She couldn't.

She peeked over her shoulder multiple times, catching glimpses of the empty eye sockets before they vanished into the trees. Now and again, the sound of ragged breathing reached her ears. It was as pleasant as a fork raking across bare bone. It sounded hungry, and not for proper food.

A certain rattling exhale caught Tony's attention. He hissed, "What was that?"

"You heard it too?" whispered Amber.

"Yes, I heard it. If I didn't know better, I'd say Gollum was in those woods."

"You don't know better."

"Gee, Amber, thanks for the reassurance. Let's just hope we have Bilbo's luck in getting out of tight spots."

Olive nearly gave Amber a heart attack when she bellowed, "We're here! We're at the last test!"

8

THE LAST DESCENDANT

Another clearing lay before them. A heavy fog hung over the place, and ivy coiled itself around everything. The same vile trees from the pathway surrounded the clearing, and the same wind uttered its ghostly whisper. There was a tall stone table in the center, bearing a rusted dagger propped upon a stand. Six large statues, each a different animal with a gem set into it, stood in a circle as they guarded the weapon. The fiendish statues had life. Their eyes studied Amber's every movement.

"Guys." Katherine shuddered. "Look." Her trembling hand pointed at the next riddle on a pillar of stone at the edge of the clearing. The letters weren't carved into the pillar but written in red ink.

ONLY ONE CAN PASS THE FINAL TEST.

SEIZE THE DAGGER AND FINISH THE QUEST.

IF YOU ARE THE ONE,
DRIVE IT INTO THE STONE

THAT CLAIMS THE NAME SAME AS YOUR OWN.

TAKE THE HAND OF DEATH, LAST DESCENDANT.

IT WOULD BE FUTILE TO RESIST IT.

Amber took a step back. "Is that—*blood?*"

Tony gulped. "It's still wet."

"Last descendant?" Katherine said. "Only one? What's this all about?"

Amber glared at the red letters, blood still oozing down the stone. "Only the last descendant can complete this test."

Tony's head jerked in her direction. "What? Olive, is that true?"

The fairy hugged herself. "It is true. It is my mistress's way of making sure she'd captured the last one."

"I thought the island was some sick game of hers," stuttered Isaac.

"It was," Olive said, "but after that girl stabbed my mistress, the goddess changed its purpose."

"So, you're telling me," Tony said, his words clipped, "that you *dragged* us *all* the way across this island in hopes that we could leave when there was none?"

"It's my job to lead people through the tests, but until you guys, I had never considered any of those people my friends."

Katherine scowled. "Oh, that's better! Now you've led *friends* on a hopeless journey."

"So, the book is a true story?" Amber asked.

"It is not an actual event," the fairy responded. "During my mistress's reign over man, the happenings of each of her games were recorded. The author must have found some of these manuscripts and made them into a story."

"How would he know about the island's new purpose?"

"That was undoubtedly recorded too. See, the dagger trapped my mistress in the sea. That's why it's so important for her to kill every descendant. Revenge isn't her sole motive. The death of all the descendants is the only way to break the curse, so she can return to land and rule once more."

"There's a marvelous thought," Tony quipped.

"The humans hid the girl who cursed her as far from every shore as they could, but..." Olive paused, her expression downcast. "They should have stayed away. Let my mistress be trapped by the curse. But they had lost so much at her hand, and revenge can consume anybody. They set off to destroy the island and kill my mistress. They didn't know the island had become inescapable. Many fairies died to bring news of the island's change to the men, which prevented the siege. Even without the updated test, it would've been a massacre. They were no match for my mistress."

Katherine huffed, "We've just discovered we can't escape this nightmare of an island, and you're talking about that stupid book."

Amber sat down on a nearby rock and hung her head as her companions continued arguing. She, who had encountered Norcepta twice, had landed on the goddess's checkpoint for the last descendent. It had to be more than coincidence.

"Olive," she mumbled, "am I the last descendant?"

The quarrel hushed. The fairy stared at her blankly. "I never knew for sure. But I knew about your mother and the cruise ship. I knew there was only one left, and since no one's been on the island for years...I knew my mistress believed that you were the daughter of the one she thought was the last. Because, in her foul delight at having the last descendant, she didn't put your mother through the test. I knew it was very likely, and I hoped you were. But there's only one way to be sure. I must warn you though, there are some very terrible things that will happen if you can't remove the dagger."

Tony ran a hand through his hair. "This is insane."

"So," Isaac said, "Amber is th-th-the last descendant?"

"Unless there is another out there that we're unaware of, yes. I will be very surprised if she isn't," Olive replied.

Katherine bit her lip. "So, it wasn't *hopeless*. You really thought Amber could get us out of here."

"Yes," said Olive, "but I should have been more open with you. I'm sorry."

"We probably wouldn't have believed it then anyway," Tony admitted.

Amber studied her hands. Could she really be the last descendant? "I have one more question. In my dream last night, I saw my mother stop a wave by merely raising her hands. How is that possible?"

"The dagger," explained Olive, "did more than just curse my mistress. She lost a portion of her power that day. Every descendant has power over the ocean."

Power over the ocean. Amber could breathe underwater. She lifted her head. "It has to be me. Though it doesn't really matter. I'm the only one who hasn't completed a test."

As she stood up, Isaac grabbed her hand. "Amber—"

"It's going to be ok." She squeezed his hand.

"Just be careful."

"You've got this, Ace," Katherine piped up halfheartedly.

Tony's grin seemed forced and anxious. He jested, "Don't do anything stupid."

Amber cocked an eyebrow. "I thought stupid was your department, Tony."

He smirked. "Yeah, whatever."

She turned toward the table, inched up to it, and gripped the dagger's hilt. She tightened her hold on it but did not lift it. What if she wasn't the last descendant? Would she get blown up or eaten alive? What if she was? Would she find answers for that accursed day? She took a deep inhale and yanked the dagger. It came off its stand without a fuss and sent her stumbling backward a couple steps.

"Oh, my goodness." Amber gaped at the weapon in her hand. She could not make sense of what her eyes were seeing. Despite her surety, it was beyond comprehension. It was true. She was the last descendant.

"You *really* are her! You really are *the one!*" Olive squealed as she danced in circles.

Katherine slapped a hand over her heart. "Oh, good. She's not dead."

Tony's jaw dropped. "That's downright awesome! *Insane,* but awesome."

Isaac sprinted to Amber's side. "Are y-you ok?"

"I'm fine. I'm...*relieved.* It all makes some sense now."

"I'm just g-g-glad you're not hurt." He buried his hands in his pockets. "Th-that was nerve-racking."

Amber's cheeks flushed. *Nerve-racking? He really was worried.*

She seized him by the shoulders and planted a kiss on his cheek. Because why not? Maybe it was a gamble, but she didn't much care. He was worth the risk.

"Woah, you two." Tony snickered. "Cool it. You still gotta stab a stone, Amber."

Amber simpered at Isaac as he looked anywhere but her face. "Yeah, yeah. I'm stabbing."

She strolled to the beginning of the line of animals. The first statue was of a snake. It had glimmering green stones for its eyes.

"*Drive it into the stone that claims the name same as your own,*" Amber recited under her breath. "So, I need to find an amber stone, and this one's an emerald." She walked to the next statue, which was a dolphin with a blue stone for an eye instead of green.

"And that's a sapphire."

She went down the line of statues: a snow leopard with a diamond eye, a fox with a ruby, and a lizard with a jade stone. Finally, she came to the last statue, which was a mosquito. An orangish stone hung around its neck on a chain.

She grinned. *Amber.*

Above it, written in blood, was one word: *Thanatos.* She gulped, pulled back the dagger, and jabbed it into the stone. The wind ceased, leaving the atmosphere still, *too* still. Every breath and heartbeat was frightfully loud.

"That's it?" Tony whispered, but then the ground trembled. Four slabs of stone rolled away, leaving four holes circled around the table. Coral-covered swords arose from the blackness. This test had a stage two.

As Amber secured the dagger in her belt, Katherine asked, "What are *these* for?"

"To fight," Olive quivered, aghast. "They are coming."

"*They?* Who in the world are *they?*" said Tony, but his question was soon answered. Four of the ocean mummies appeared in the treeline.

"The Water Demons!" Olive shrieked.

"Level two, then." Tony positioned himself into a combat stance. "Kill ocean zombies."

"Quick! Grab a sword!" ordered Amber.

Swords in hand, they stood back-to-back in a tight circle. Olive pulled her sword out of thin air, though it looked more like a needle.

"What are you going to do with that thing?" mocked Tony. "Fight Water Demon atoms?"

"Focus!" Amber shouted. The armed Water Demons approached, hissing through their coral-encrusted teeth. They stared unwavering—if they could stare with their empty eye sockets—at the survivors. The hair on the back of her neck stood on end. It didn't look good. She and her friends were about to die. It was unlikely that any of them knew how to sword fight.

Olive's words resurfaced from Amber's subconsciousness. *Every descendent has power over the ocean.*

She closed her eyes, concentrating on the sea, willing it to come. A second later, water gushed over her feet. Crouching down, she placed her hand in the water. *We need help. Help us fight.*

The water responded. Tiny rivers defying the laws of gravity slithered up all five of them, soaked into their skin, and—Amber screamed. Agony tore through her body. For a moment, she wished she'd just die, but it was over in a flash.

"Yahoo!" Tony whooped. "*What* a rush! Alright, you nasty ocean zombies! Who wants some?"

Blades crossed, and Amber was suddenly a master with a sword. She didn't think. She just did. She blocked the Water Demon's strikes one after another, but it was time for a little offense. Knocking her opponent's sword out of its hand, she gave it a fatal cut across the chest. It crumpled to the ground.

Her friends had been triumphant too. All enemies were defeated.

Katherine gaped at the dead Water Demon lying at her feet. "*How* did I *do* that? How did *I* do *that!*"

Tony wrinkled his nose. "These things are downright disgusting."

"Let's go, guys. They'll get up soon," Olive warned. "You can't kill something that's already dead. Come on!"

They darted from the scene, heading towards the shoreline now visible through the trees. The monstrous growls at their heels informed them that the Water Demons had already recovered.

Tony peeked over his shoulder. "We have *company!* We have *serious* company! The zombies brought their friends!"

They flew like the wind, but the enemy was faster. One Water Demon clawed at Amber, dangerously close to snagging her hair.

"Amber, look out!" Isaac rammed into her pursuer with surprising force. It crashed into the trees with a sickening CRACK! He staggered and another Water Demon almost had its claws around his ankle.

"Isaac!" shrieked Amber, screeching to a halt.

But he got up at the last minute and shot towards her. "Come on!" He grabbed her hand and pulled her after him.

They ran side by side until they broke free of the jungle's grasp, nearly colliding with the Kielweins. The smell of saltwater greeted them, and the sun gave Amber a warm hug. The monsters halted at the tree line. They snarled and hissed but didn't attack.

"We're safe here," said Olive. "They can't come into the light."

"I'm glad to be out of there," Isaac stammered, breathless.

Amber stuck her sword in the sand and looked around. A sailboat was sitting on the shoreline.

"Is that the boat?" Katherine asked.

"Yes," Olive said, "but there's something you must know. Amber has passed the final test. My mistress will know she has found the last descendant. She will come for you."

With a groan, Tony ran a hand through his hair. "Is there any chance we could outrun Norcepta?"

"It is unlikely," the fairy admitted. "But there is one final piece to this puzzle you do not know. There was a prophecy. It said that the last descendant would be the one to finally kill my mistress, to set free every creature and Water Demon under her reign and control. The prophecy foretold the name. That was another detail making me suspect you as the last descendant. It was said her name would be Amber."

Katherine threw up her hands. "Of course, it did."

"So that's why the test was centered on a name? The last descendant's name was supposed to be Amber," said Tony, and Olive nodded.

"Wait," Isaac quaked, "are y-y-you saying the only way we will escape is by Amber killing Norcepta?"

"That's the only way I see," Olive responded gravely.

Isaac sputtered, refusing to make eye contact with Amber. "There's g-g-got to be another way. S-something else."

"We'll cross that bridge if and when we get to it," said Amber.

"Alright then. Let's go." Tony started towards the boat but stopped in his tracks. Amber shared in his revelation: this was goodbye to their fairy friend.

"Don't worry about me." Olive blinked away tears. "I'll be ok. It's really not that bad here. My mistress can't be on land, remember?"

Nobody spoke for ages. Amber had never dreamed it would be so hard to say goodbye, but the fairy had become her friend. She couldn't help a soft smile as she recalled Tony's words from the previous night. True it was difficult, but the friendship was worth it. She would always hold the fairy dear in her heart.

"Well," Amber choked, "I guess this is goodbye, my friend. Thanks for everything."

After several tears and thank yous, they climbed into the boat. Olive turned and waved at the survivors before disappearing into the trees.

The four of them sat down on the deck, and the boat drifted away on its own accord. It glided across the ocean, as smooth as glass. Soon, the Island of Thanatos veiled itself with sky and cloud.

9

GODDESS OF THE SEA

Amber glared at the water. *It's too calm, too still, just like before.*

She sat cross-legged on the deck with Isaac at her side. Katherine was propped against the mast, and her brother lay on his back next to her, observing the sky. Isaac was not so relaxed, however. He wrung his hands and repeatedly shook his head as though failing to accept some fact.

"Amber," he paused and lowered his voice so the others couldn't hear, "y-y-your not really considering fighting Norcepta, are you?"

Amber refused to take her gaze off the horizon. "If she shows up."

Isaac rubbed his eyes. "Th-that's a death sentence."

"I doubt I'll have much of a choice, Isaac."

"Amber..."

His trailing off made her look at him. She swallowed. Something more than Norcepta was on his mind.

"What is it?"

"I...I just want us to m-m-make it home. All of us."

"And we will."

He met her eyes. "That includes y-y-you."

She heaved a heavy sigh and laced her fingers through his, savoring the tender touch of the breeze across her cheek.

The breeze became a wind that yanked at her hair. A low groan emitted from the deep, sending a chill up her spine. Isaac tightened his grip on her hand. He sensed it too. The goddess was coming.

Katherine bolted upright and craned her neck. "What's that noise?"

The ocean roared as a ginormous wave formed and advanced towards them. Norcepta's baleful face appeared as it started to crest. Thunderous laughter boomed from every direction, a laughter so vile and terrible that it could stop the heart cold.

"Watch out!" Amber yelled, and the wave swallowed the boat. Numerous hands took hold of her, towing her to the ocean's floor. A muffled voice cried, "AMBER! NO!" Deeper and deeper, she was dragged, squirming and thrashing. She had to get back to the surface. She couldn't hold her breath forever.

Every descendent has power over the ocean.

Had she actually breathed underwater on that bridge? She rolled the dice and inhaled. Her lungs filled with oxygen.

I really can breathe underwater.

Slightly comforted by the fact that she would not drown, she glanced over her shoulder. It was Water Demons who were hauling her downward.

Abruptly, they pulled up, restraining her by her arms before a monstrous woman with deathly pale skin and black hair as transparent as smoke. Her scanty top was made of seashells tied together with seaweed, and her enormous, dark green tail extended down until it disappeared into the abyss. Her eyes—oh, those barbaric eyes—danced with wrath and vengeance. Blood red and ablaze, eye contact was almost unbearable.

Amber had the sudden notion that she must do absolutely anything to escape Norcepta's horrific gaze, but her captors held her in place. Still, the remains of the goddess's elegance were visible through this diabolical appearance.

"*Norcepta*," Amber growled. Apparently, she could speak underwater too.

"Yes—*me*. You thought you could escape me?" the goddess howled with bone-chilling laughter. "No, child. No one can escape me."

"And yet, eight years later, here we are."

Norcepta hissed. "Yes, your idiot mother saved you, kept you from my sight with those feeble powers of hers. She thought she could protect you from me. What foolishness! And now, despite her sacrifice, you will die."

"And then what?" Amber retorted. "What then, Norcepta, when your mission is complete?"

"What then?" Norcepta cackled. "I will return to land and reclaim my power from those vermin you call mankind, and I will exterminate all who have the *nerve* to stand up against *my* rule."

Amber scoffed. "Right, good luck with that."

"You doubt my power?" barked Norcepta.

"No, but you've underestimated *this* vermin. It will be quite hard to reclaim your power once I've killed you. You shouldn't have messed with my family—or my friends."

Norcepta's ominous guffaw shook the ocean. "Good luck with that, child." Her gaze greedily dropped to the abyss below. "Bring me her head."

A legion of Water Demons emerged from the blackness and rushed towards Amber. It was time to test the limits of her new abilities.

With the tiniest inflection of her will, gushes of radiant water slammed her captors into the sea floor. She drew the dagger from her belt, but that wasn't going to help much against those undead minions. How was she to fight all the Water Demons at once?

One approached her left flank. She put up her hand and the Water Demon ricocheted off an invisible wall. Three more opponents came up on her right. She sliced through the water with her arm, and the Water Demons were flung backward twenty yards. Still, countless ocean mummies rose from the depths. There was no way she could take them one by one, and she had no clear shot at Norcepta with them in the way. She must wipe them out in one fell swoop.

She closed her eyes and willed the sea to bend, to expand, to charge. There was an explosion, a shock wave that vibrated every single water molecule in the ocean. When she opened her eyes, she and Norcepta were the only living things in sight.

Whoa! Wasn't expecting that.

"No. NO!" the goddess shrieked. "It is impossible. Curse the prophecy!"

Amber raised the dagger overhead and commanded the water to propel her toward Norcepta. In a blink of an eye, the blade pierced Norcepta's heart. She let out an earsplitting scream.

"You're never going to hurt anyone ever again," Amber declared through gritted teeth. The wrath flaming in the goddess's eyes was short-lived. Their light went out, and she sank to the bottom of the sea. The darkness engulfed her as it welcomed its old friend.

The use of Amber's newfound powers had zapped her energy. The Water Demons gathered around her, now tranquil. Their sinister look had left them. Their eyes were more than just blackness; life had returned to them. Humanity had come back to their faces: this one had been an old man, that one had been a young woman, and this one had been a little boy. Their caged spirits set free, they beamed at Amber with tear-stained faces. One by one, they faded into the sea. Their souls were finally at rest.

Her heartbeat grew slower...and slower...and slower. She had no strength to move. Into penetrating cold and crushing blackness, she sank. This was how she died, at the hand of the ocean, but her friends were safe. Tony, Katherine, and Isaac would go on to live full lives, away from the danger of the island, away from the danger of the sea.

She slid further into the murk, to where her mother lay below. *My friends...*

Her trajectory changed. She rose, and her skin soaked up the warmth. But it didn't matter. A shadow soon cast over her vision and everything went black. Everything was gone...

Her spine was flush against a hard, wet floor. Her chest was aching. Someone pressed their lips against hers and blew into her mouth.

A man's voice choked, "Amber? Come on, wake up! Don't do this, Amber."

"Please, Amber, wake up," a second man's voice stuttered with a whimper.

The first man pleaded, "Come on, girl! Wake up!"

"She's gone, Tony," a woman wailed.

"No, she can't be," came the second man's trembling voice. "Th-there has to be s-s-something we can do."

The woman sniffled. "Isaac—"

"No! She can't be—can't be..."

"Isaac, Katherine's right. She's passed on, man," the first man said.

The second man sobbed, "Amber. No." His hand slipped into hers.

The first man placed his head on her shoulder and whispered, "I'm so sorry, Amber. I'm so sorry."

Her brain finally computed what was happening. With effort, Amber opened her eyes and found Tony crying into her hair. Isaac was kneeling beside her, cradling her hand in his lap, as Katherine stood behind. Her chin quivered and her body convulsed in an attempt to muffle her bawling. None of them noticed Amber was awake.

Amber murmured weakly, "Piece of advice Tony: go on a date or two before you start kissing a girl."

Tony jerked away and stared down at her, stunned. "Amber!" he exclaimed, pulling her into a bone-crushing hug. "I thought you were dead."

"I'm alright, Tony." She patted him on the back. "Ow. Can't breathe."

"Oh, sorry!"

After Tony let go, she turned towards Isaac. He wiped the tears off his face and gently wrapped his arms around her neck. "You s-s-scared the life out of m-me."

She blushed, returning his embrace. "Sorry."

Trying to suppress her giggles, Katherine said, "Uh, can I have a turn?"

"I guess," Amber sighed teasingly and stood up to hug Katherine.

"What happened, Ace?" Katherine asked.

"I met Norcepta, and now she's dead." Amber shrugged. "That's the abbreviated version anyway."

Tony chuckled. "You'll have to tell us the story sometime."

"But not now," decided Katherine. "I've had enough of goddesses and curses and the walking dead to last a lifetime. I don't want to think anymore about it today."

With a grin, Amber clapped her friend on the shoulder. "It's fine, Kat. We'll save that story for another time. How'd you get me back on the boat?"

"Y-you just floated to the top," Isaac replied. "Honestly, we were shocked to find you s-s-still had a pulse."

Amber nodded. "It doesn't matter now. We're together. No need to worry."

"Uh, I think there is, Ace," Katherine said. "How do we plan to make it to shore?"

Tony gazed up at the sky. "The accident was only yesterday. Surely the Coast Guard is still looking."

The survivors talked about how they longed for home as the boat rowed itself across the ocean. The sun began melting into the sky in spectacular hues of pink and orange and blue. The waves rocked the boat back and forth as a chill wind hurried past them. Even amidst the endless sea, an air of kinship wrapped itself tightly around them. Their bond would never break.

Amber fingered her locket. *Mom would've loved them.*

She noticed a piece of paper lying on the deck, breaking her chain of thought. She picked it up and burst out, "It's from Olive!"

Dear Amber, Katherine, Tony, and Isaac,

Thank you, Amber, for defeating Norcepta. I know because the curse on the island has lifted, and the Water Demons have left. When you guys finish reading this, make sure you keep it. This is special paper. When you have finished reading it, the words will vanish. Then you can write on the blank paper, and those words will appear on my paper and vice versa. This way we can still talk though we are far apart. I miss you guys already! I hope one day I'll see you again.

Your dear friend,
Olive

"Well, what do you know?" Tony mumbled when the words started to fade.

As Amber pocketed the letter, Isaac asked, "Do you hear th-that?"

She craned her neck and heard the whirring of a helicopter. It soon came into view, and the glorious sight gradually advanced toward them.

"Hey!" Amber hollered, jumping and waving.

Tony joined in and yelled, "Over here! Yo!"

"We see you guys!" boomed a voice from the helicopter. "Hang on!"

"We're saved! We're saved!" shrieked Katherine, dancing in circles.

Tony guffawed. "You look like Olive."

"Oh, shush!" Katherine slapped his arm playfully.

"So, how about dinner at my house Friday?" Amber asked the others.

"That sounds great," Tony said.

"No," Katherine corrected, "it sounds *awesome!*"

"I-I-I'm in," Isaac said.

"Wait"—Katherine furrowed her brow—"what's today?" They all burst out laughing, then she shrugged. "Whatever. *One* thing I *do* know, though, is that you guys are the *best* friends ever." She put one arm around Isaac and the other around Tony.

Amber stood beside Isaac and took his hand. Out of the corner of her eye, she saw his lips curve into a smile.

"We're going home," she whispered.

Amber rested her head on the vibrating wall of the helicopter, relishing the wind ripping through her hair as they flew over the sparkling blue sea. How her life had changed over the past few days, as quick as the ocean shifted moods. That island of torture had set her free.

But that was life, wasn't it? Its worst nightmares could beckon its sweetest gifts. Like the ocean, it was a paradox— beautiful yet horrific, disastrous yet curative. A storm could be a wondrous thing to behold, giving birth to the clearest skies.

Life's going to throw some rogue waves at you, but never—oh, please, whatever you do, *never*—isolate yourself from those who love you. Don't face it alone. We need each other.

Her storm was a battle, lasting eight long years, but it had a most incredible end. Just to think, she would be hugging her father within the next hour and, by Friday night, having dinner with her friends. She wasn't alone anymore. Maybe she never had to be. Maybe she never was...

10

A PROPHECY FULFILLED

"And so, they were rescued and were soon in the arms of their very worried parents. Amber, Isaac, Tony, Katherine, and their families remained friends for all their days. The kids wrote Olive often and relished every letter she wrote back. In later years, they told their children and grandchildren of their adventures. Often those children lay in bed at night, wondering if the stories were true. And they all lived happily ever after. The end," Grandpa Greg finished the second story of the Greenwood's Christmas vacation.

"That was a great story," Jonny said. "But somebody always marries somebody. Let me guess: Amber fell in love with that Tony character."

"No, actually," Greg responded, "the person Amber ended up marrying was—"

"Isn't it obvious?" Rae blurted. "She married Isaac!"

Jonny's jaw dropped. "*Really?*"

"Boys are idiots when it comes to romance," Natasha mumbled lazily.

"We are not!" snapped Jonny.

"Yes, Amber married Isaac seven years later." Grandpa Greg's eyes twinkled with amusement. "Now off to bed."

Natasha clambered into bed. "That was amazing!"

"Yes, it was!" Rae agreed wholeheartedly. She pulled out her journal and began to write.

Dec 21, 1955

Today was Jonny's birthday, and Grandpa Greg told another cool story. It was about a magical island and a bad goddess named Norcepta. I liked this story because it showed how much we need each other. We can't do it alone. In the end, after becoming good friends, the survivors of the boat crash escaped the island and set the creatures on it free. I can't wait for the next story!

Rae put down her journal and settled into her covers.

"I wonder what story Grandpa Greg will tell us next," Jonny spoke into the darkness.

"You said that yesterday," Natasha complained.

"I know. It's just Grandpa can tell all kinds of stories. I just wonder..." Jonny seemed not to want to finish his sentence.

"It's always a mystery with Grandpa Greg, Jonny," Rae replied sleepily, turning over in her bed with a yawn. "Always a mystery."

THE GRIFFIN KEY

1

A RAINY DAY

Tap, tap, tap went the rain, beating against Rae Greenwood's window, waking the little girl to a drowsy winter day. She lay in bed, watching the raindrops collide with the glass as she twirled a lock of her long, brown hair around her finger. She smiled. Today would be a perfect day to curl up with a book and pillow while she listened to the rain play its music.

Jonny sat up in his bed and moaned, "Rain? Oh, come on! It's December. It *should* be snowing."

"What are you whining about now, Jonny?" Natasha asked sleepily while rubbing her eyes.

"It's raining!" Jonny said.

"I can see that," mumbled Natasha. "But every day's a great day here, Jonny—even if it is raining, because Grandpa tells us a story."

"Way to keep a positive attitude, Nat," Rae murmured.

The children headed downstairs for breakfast, dragging their feet and yawning as they went.

"Rain makes me sleepy." Rae yawned.

"I hate rain!" Jonny burst out, stomping his foot.

Natasha groaned loudly, "You're such a baby."

The children entered the dining room where their mother and Grandpa Greg were sitting.

"Well"—Grandpa Greg peered over his reading glasses—"what a sleepy crowd we have today."

Rae smiled. "We *did* just wake up."

While the family was eating breakfast, Jonny asked, "What are we going to do with this rain *pouring* down?"

Natasha scoffed at her brother's whining, but then cowered under her mother's stern look.

Mrs. Greenwood, turning to her son, said, "We could make Christmas cookies. I know you guys wanted to do that sometime."

Rae gasped. "I have an idea! Why don't we make cookies that look like the characters and stuff from the story last night? We can have *Island of Thanatos* cookies."

"I like it!" Jonny declared. "Can we do it, Mom? Please?"

"Yeah, *please*," said Natasha.

"Alright," Mrs. Greenwood said. "We can do that."

The children had a blast making the cookies. After the rolling and cutting was done, they were covered from head to toe in flour, and each tittered at how funny the others looked. They washed off while their mother put the cookies in the oven to bake. The little ones played hide-and-seek as they waited, checking on the cookies' progress so many times that Rae lost count. The cookies seemed to take forever. When they were finally done, the children decorated them with icing and sprinkles. They nibbled on some as they put them into tin boxes. Rae thought the sweets looked awesome.

"Good heavens, look at the time!" Grandpa Greg said. "I believe it's story o'clock, children."

They wasted no time. Jonny, Natasha, and Rae scurried into the sitting room and quickly took their seats. As Grandpa Greg seated himself in his favorite armchair, Mrs. Greenwood strolled into the room holding an envelope.

"It's from Daddy," Natasha announced, pointing at her father's handwriting on the letter. Mrs. Greenwood opened it and read aloud.

Dear Amy, Jonny, Natasha, and Rae,

I hope you all are having a wonderful time. There's a lot of work for me to do here, but I look forward to seeing you all soon. Keep a lookout tomorrow because I will be sending a little surprise package. And no, I'm not going to tell you what it is. You'll just have to wait. I miss you all and am very much looking forward to you telling me about Grandpa Greg's stories. Say "hi" to him for me.

With lots of love,
Dad

"I wonder what the package will be," Rae said eagerly.

"Yeah, I wish he would have told us in the letter." Jonny slumped his shoulders.

"If he had told us"—Natasha grinned—"he wouldn't be Daddy."

"You're right, Nat. Daddy always likes to give us surprises." Rae giggled as memories of those surprises filled her mind. "But now it's story time. I've been waiting all day!"

"Oh yeah!" Jonny cheered up. "What's the story about, Grandpa?"

"Today's story is about a Key. A Key that, if put into the Door it opens, will unleash tremendous dangers and horrors," Grandpa Greg whispered, a mysterious gleam in his eye.

Rae felt that familiar pull, that familiar call into a world that would take her on another adventure far away yet right there. Excitement for the upcoming journey tugged at the calm of the house. Anticipation killing her, she exploded, "Oh, I can't wait any longer! *Please* start the story now."

"Ok, ok." Grandpa Greg put his hand up in a pacifying manner. "Just giving you a tease."

At last, he began in a hushed voice, "Once upon a time, there were seven elves. These elves came together and, with their magic, made a Weapon of immense power, but the elves did not truly understand what they had done. They had created a most horrible evil, a Weapon that could think for itself. Centuries later, the Weapon fell into the hands of a human king. This king used it to win many wars, but soon, its malice consumed him, and he died. His son was afraid of the Weapon, so he built a dungeon deep in the ground from where it came to hide it.

"However, a strange thing happened: no key was able to lock this dungeon's Door. They cast dozens of keys. They changed the lock over and over. Nothing worked until a Key rose from a Pool of mercury, from whose waters the Weapon was forged. A guard snatched the Key from where it floated in midair and successfully locked the Door. After that, the young king kept the Key tucked away, and it was passed down through the generations.

"But soon, a new power arose. A being named Levian stole the Key and took the Weapon. She ruled over the kingdom cruelly for many generations. The true royal bloodline lived as peasants until one day, the rightful king escaped with his son. He hid his son and went back for the Key. Oh yes, he went back for it, and he was very brave to do so. It was a miracle, indeed, that he was able to take it. Since it also originated from the Pool, the Weapon could not be controlled without the Key. Levian losing her Weapon was the only chance the people had at overthrowing her. But the king had to ensure that, should Levian be deposed, she could never come back into power, so he needed to destroy the Key. However, there was a problem: how was he to destroy it? It was a magical Key, and mortal weapons could not harm it.

"If the Key could not be destroyed, the king risked Levian reclaiming it and regaining her power. Despite knowing this, he clung to hope that his people's freedom could still be secured. In the distant future, the Key would fall into the hands of two sisters from London..."

2

AND SO IT BEGINS

King Orion dashed through the woods, Levian's Key bouncing on his chest as he ran. He glanced behind him; the Shatari were gaining. The horrifying, deformed faces of those unholy creatures sneered at him, eyes dancing with malicious glee. The trees ordered the king to halt with their long, unyielding limbs, and their roots attempted to trip him as though it was humorous to do so. With a quick sprint, he got away from the Shatari. He leaned up against a tree to catch his breath, and his heart rate slowed. The beats his heart had remaining were few, but the fear of death was drowned out by desperation. He had to save his people.

"Father!" his son's voice sounded in the night. Orion peered in between the trees and spotted the prince.

"Luca!" the king rasped, rushing up to his son. "What are you doing? I told you to hide!"

"I'm sorry, Father." The boy stared at his shoes. "I was worried about you."

Orion knelt beside Luca. "I'm ok, my son."

The thunder of Shatari feet reached the king's ears. He froze. They would soon be in the Shatari's custody, and the

Key would be back in Levian's hands. It would be the doom of the kingdom. He could not let that happen, but what was he to do? They would have to flee until they fell dead from exhaustion. Poor Luca would grow weary long before he would. His son could not manage under such haste. No matter, it would change nothing. The Shatari were relentless. Capture was inevitable, but he would not see the Key returned to that witch. He would not see Luca at her mercy. He could not.

As Orion gazed into the blue eyes of his son, an idea struck him. This was the kingdom's last hope. It was a perilous gamble, but he had little choice. Be it folly or not, this was his only option.

Cupping the prince's face in his hands, Orion's voice quivered, "Luca, I need you to do something for me. I need you to take the Key. Destroy it, however you are able. Find a way. Never let it leave your bloodline. Do you understand?"

"But what about you? I'm not leaving you." Luca whimpered as his father placed the Key around his neck.

The king fought back tears. "We would never outrun them, but your small size may conceal you from their sight. Hide until they leave. Do as I say, son. Everything will be ok. Just survive. Promise me you'll keep the Key safe. Promise."

"I promise, Father," Luca choked.

The prince hurried away, tears stinging his eyes. He settled into a cranny between two trees. The surrounding bushes hid him well. He pushed a branch back a little. Levian's army had captured his father. They were talking, but Luca could not hear what about.

Outraged, the largest Shatari suddenly roared and drew his sword. The lightning-fast movement was accompanied by a slashing sound. The king collapsed. The boy gasped and slapped his hand over his mouth to keep from screaming. Tears dripped down his chin as the reality of what had occurred stabbed him like a sharp blade, over and over. His father was dead. What hope did he have now? What hope was there for his people? He looked down at the Key around his neck and took a deep breath. It wasn't over yet; he had to be brave.

The Shatari searched the grounds, but did not discover the prince. At dawn, they headed towards the village, which, the prince prayed, was being liberated from Levian's iron fist. Luca slipped away, escaping to a distant land. The Key was out of the wicked queen's grasp, and he intended to keep it that way. He intended to keep his promise. He would find a way to destroy this Key that had cost him his father, no matter how long it took.

Standing on a ledge that overlooked the working mines, Levian's cold gaze swept over her army as they dug deeper into the earth, diligently searching for the Door.

Her eyes narrowed. *The Door.*

Where could it have gone? The Door that concealed her beloved Weapon had changed locations on its own accord that fateful day, the day Orion had stolen her Key. Sunlight had become unendurable, forcing her and her army to crawl into the deep caverns of the earth, restless to find her Key.

She raised her hand, gazing at it as she rippled her fingers. The cool of her Weapon's metal still chilled her palm.

The undeniable weightlessness as it disintegrated from her grasp, returning to its prison, still haunted her every waking hour. She needed it. She scraped her fingernails down her face and neck. She must have it. The scorching of the sun and the sting of arrows and daggers lingered on her skin. The riotous cries of the villagers plagued her dreams. She growled; the insufferable infection of humanity would pay for what they did to her.

"I need it," she breathed. "I must find it...*Beloved.*"

Centuries she had sought her Key but could never find it. So, she had turned her attention towards the Door, but to hope that it could be opened without her Key was foolishness. Her Key was the only way to unlock the Door, and it stayed in the possession of thieves. She must reclaim it to rescue her beloved.

Orion's kin—the Griffins—were her greatest adversary. If they succeeded, her Weapon would be forever lost. If her Key was destroyed, vengeance would remain outside her reach for all of eternity.

Levian gritted her teeth. *Griffin.*

That name was detestable, the name by which Orion's bloodline had become known. By some cruel irony, her Key had been renamed the Griffin Key, according to human legend. She scoffed. Legend was simply a term the human cowards used for things that frightened them, for magic and immortal beings.

The Griffins must be annihilated. They brought their demise upon themselves, for she had been corrupted by their hand. Levian had been a sight to adore—the fairest maiden in all the world. Tall and graceful with eyes like black diamonds, lips the color of wine, skin forged from copper, she had had a face of elegance and wisdom, framed in long, flawless hair black as tar. What a terror she had been to behold in her bronze armor with its underlying strips of violet fabric. But Orion's kin had ruined her. Along with her power, they had bled her dry of her splendor. She was now marred with scars and burns, and the Griffins were to blame.

Driving her fingernails into her palms until she drew blood, she glared at her toiling soldiers. The Griffins would pay. She would watch them burn as she had burned.

As her army hopelessly picked at the earth's unforgiving rock, unwavering eyes focused on the back of Levian's head.

"What is it, Vitus?" she lazily asked her captain of the guard. Not being nearly as misshaped as the rest, Vitus was much more pleasing to the eye. His intelligence far outmatched his fellow Shatari. He could reason and make logical observations, a skill the others lacked. He had even been seen with emotional expressions, a rarity among Levian's soldiers. These facts somewhat frightened her, but she could never let Vitus get wind of her fear. That would be dangerous. She couldn't have him growing a mind of his own.

"My queen"—Vitus bowed—"the Griffin Key has resurfaced. The last known living descendant of Prince Luca has been located."

She slowly turned to face him. "*What?*" She let out a shuddering exhale. "You have found it?"

"Yes, your majesty."

"Very well." She reached up and grasped her chest for her Key that was still gone. Her jaw clenched. "Then go and *slaughter* that *horrid* Griffin and BRING—ME—MY—KEY!"

Squeezing her eyelids shut, she sucked in a breath through her bared teeth then whispered, "*Yes*. Bring it to me." Her lips twitched upward. Brief fits of giggles escaped her before morphing into full-blown laughter.

"As you wish, my queen." Vitus smirked and departed to complete his task as Levian's cackling echoed through the caves. She had them in her clutches at last. The Griffins would learn the meaning of death.

3

MURDER ON THE THIRD FLOOR

Twenty-seven-year-old Diana Griffin awoke to another busy, clamorous day in the city of London. Sunbeams scattered across her room, their orange light dyed grey by the lens of clouds. Brown eyes fixated on the ceiling, she absorbed all the noise floating in from the street. London sounded rather dejected in the decline of the holiday festivities.

With a yawn, she sat up and stretched before pulling her wavy, brown hair into a ponytail. She rolled out of bed and staggered over to her window. Chilled by winter's bitter wind, the glass cooled her forehead and left arm as she leaned against it. Outside, cars zoomed by and visible trails of breath followed each hurried worker. A couple strolled hand-in-hand down the street—newlyweds, no doubt, or on their way to becoming so. The man kissed his girl on the cheek. A sweet gesture to her, but a miserable reminder to Diana. Such a thing would never happen to her. She averted her watery eyes and went downstairs for breakfast.

Upon entering the kitchen, she saw that her mother, Tara, and her sister, Anne, were already at the table.

"Slept in a little late, didn't you?" twenty-four-year-old Anne Griffin teased as Diana took her place at the table, peering at the spread of bacon, eggs, grilled tomatoes, and beans.

Diana shrugged as she helped herself to some eggs. "Firstly, it's Joan's turn to help Mrs. Brown at the library, so I don't need to work today. Secondly, I was up late last night folding *your* laundry. Terribly large pile, I might add."

"Oh, right. Cheers for that."

Diana clicked her tongue. "Do not pretend like you *forgot* them."

"Now, loves," Tara said calmly, "let's not get in a fuss so early in the morning." She glanced out the window, her demeanor uneasy.

Diana studied her mother. "Are you alright, Mum?"

Tara turned back to her daughter and smiled. "Of course, love. Why wouldn't I be?"

"No reason. Just asking."

After a lengthy silence, Anne piped up, "I can't wait for the New Year's fireworks. I hear they're to be absolutely brilliant!"

"You and your fireworks, sis." Diana chuckled. "Blimey, I can't believe the year's nearly up. We're just days away from 1930."

Tara propped her chin in her palm. "How time flies."

The family finished eating breakfast, cleared the table, and tidied the kitchen. Over the next couple of hours, Tara grew more and more overwrought. She constantly looked over her shoulder and spoke in a hushed voice. Something had set her on edge, but Diana dared not continue to inquire for fear of agitating her further.

What had upset her so? Were they in financial trouble? Had she been threatened? Was someone stalking her? Or was she hallucinating, seeing an unreal threat? Diana bit her lip. None of these explanations were reasonable.

"How about going to the market today, loves?" Tara said. "We haven't had a girl's day out in a long while."

"Yes!" Blue eyes sparkling, Anne leapt from the sofa. "Lovely day to shop."

"It's always a lovely day to shop for you, sis," Diana pointed out, amused.

Anne ignored her. "I'll call Maggie and ask her to take my shift at the salon."

At the marketplace, the women browsed the different food, jewelry, and knickknacks the merchants were selling. However, Tara was not at ease. She clutched her purse and scanned the crowd as if expecting to spot some unsavory character. Had someone once mugged her, leading to paranoia? Attempting to keep the observation of her mother unnoticed, Diana absentmindedly grabbed a silk shawl and pretended to admire it.

"Yes, Diana, perfect!" Anne bounded up to her. "That will look positively gorgeous on you!"

Diana turned her attention to the item in hand. It was deep brown, the faces of wolves embroidered into the fabric with silver thread. Each wolf had red gems for eyes.

She frowned. "You think so?"

"I know so," Anne insisted. "The color really brings out your eyes."

"It's not exactly my department, but the wolves?"

Anne seized the shawl and draped it over her sister's shoulders. "Makes it even better. Yes, very...mysterious. *Elegant*, but with the air of strength."

Diana giggled. "Alright, sis. Your fashion sense has always been reliable." She turned to the merchant and said, "I would like to purchase this, please."

Their mother, tense as a soldier on the eve of battle, made a distracted comment about Diana's purchase but continued to study the passersby suspiciously.

After leaving the market, the three women went window shopping at a few of the nicer stores. They wandered over to an excellent Italian restaurant when evening arrived, and then sat on a park bench, watching the sun sink behind London's buildings. Though Tara relaxed under the glow of the sunset, she returned to her distressed state once they were back home.

"Thanks for the day out, Mum." Anne took off her coat and slung it over the living room sofa.

"Yes, I had a marvelous time." Diana, exhausted from the long day, yawned.

Tara smiled at her daughters then, once again, glanced over her shoulder.

What was the matter?

"I think I will turn in for the night," Tara said. "Good night, loves."

"Good night."

"Night, Mum."

Tara trudged upstairs to her bedroom on the third floor.

"I guess we should get to bed too." Diana rubbed her eyes.

"Yeah, come on." Anne went up the stairs dawdlingly, followed by her sister.

Once in her room, Diana snuggled into the covers and drifted off to sleep...

It was green as far as the eye could see. The sun was melting into the rolling hills as the dandelions swayed in the wind. The gentle breeze hugged her tight, and the smell of the air was glorious after the fresh rain. The world seemed perfect in a place like this. But then, an ear-piercing scream shattered the peaceful evening...

She jerked awake to discover a bloodcurdling reality: the cry had journeyed from her dream into the real world. She threw off the covers and glanced at the clock. It was 3:00 a.m. She zipped into the hall and collided into Anne.

"Mind yourself, Diana!"

"My apologies. Have I gone mad, or did I just hear someone scream?"

"I heard it too."

"It must be Mum!"

The sisters scrambled up the stairs and yanked the door open. Diana stumbled backward at the sight: their mother's bedroom had been ransacked. The drawers stood open, the furniture turned over, things scattered everywhere, and the large, circular window had been broken.

Anne quaked. "That's a sizable hole."

"It looks like"—Diana gulped—"like a person could fit through there."

The women inched toward the window and peered over the broken glass.

All the blood drained from Diana's face. *It can't be.*

At the foot of the Griffin house lay her mother, beautiful brown hair matted with blood. Her body in a painfully awkward position, a scarlet river flowed from her head onto the sidewalk. Her white nightgown had been dyed red by the knife protruding from the center of her chest.

Anne sucked in a sharp breath and leaned against the window frame for support. She sobbed, "No...*Mum.*"

It couldn't be real. It had to be some heinous nightmare. Diana turned away and plopped onto the bed, dumbfounded. The image of her mother was burned into her eyes. Staring at the bedroom floor, she could still see Tara lying before her. Her eyes snapped shut, but still there lay the phantom body of her mother, bloody and broken.

Sorrow's blade sank deep, carving out all joy. The world was cold, as cold as the fires of war. Like when a battle explodes in a peaceful town, darkness suddenly veiled the path to the future. Her hope was vanquished, her desire to press on stifled. The world was cruel and rotten. Tears escaped the tightly closed gates of her eyes, then, with a wail, she slipped off the bed and collapsed onto the floor, trembling.

"First Dad in the war," whimpered Anne, "now Mum? For what? For nothing? No reason? No cause? Just gone."

After a few deep breaths, Diana opened her eyes and whispered, "We should...call the police."

Her gaze fell upon her sister. Anne had curled up on the floor, hand pressed against her mouth as a river of tears rushed down her cheeks. There was nothing Diana could do. What words could she speak? What comfort could she give? How could she ease another's heartache when her own was so severe?

Without a word, she rose and called the police. They arrived soon after. A man in uniform approached the women, who were waiting at the front door.

"I'm Commissioner Williams," the man, standing a head above Diana, introduced himself flatly as five other men made their way to her mother's bedroom.

Anne did not shake the hand the commissioner had offered. She stood, eyes fixed on the ground, hugging herself with an expression of utter horror. She was completely oblivious to the world's existence.

"I'm sorry, Commissioner," Diana murmured, extending her hand. "We're not exactly ourselves tonight."

"Don't apologize. I understand," Commissioner Williams said, a hint of compassion on his stone face. "I'm terribly sorry for your loss."

"Thank you," choked Diana.

The commissioner attempted to take Anne's statement, but she was so in shock that little of what she said was intelligible. One of the men from upstairs interrupted, pulling the commissioner aside to have a whispered conversation. Diana observed them from her seat in the living room. After a few moments, the commissioner heaved a sigh and rubbed a hand across his face. He wore a grave expression as he approached her. Passing Anne, who was staring absentmindedly out the door, he paused as if he wished to console her. Seeming to think better of it, he continued toward the living room.

"Miss Griffin, I'm sorry to have to tell you this, but it looks like homicide."

Diana closed her eyes. "I expected that, but I still don't understand."

He shifted his weight. "I am sorry to pry, Miss Griffin, but I need to take your statement."

Diana looked at him blankly. "I'm afraid there's not much to tell."

"That's alright," he sat down next to her, "whatever you can tell me will help."

"Very well. I heard a scream at 3:00 a.m., then Anne and I ran upstairs. We found the room torn apart. When we looked out the window—I'm sorry." She squeezed her eyelids shut but failed to erase the image from her mind. She could not unsee the blood. It didn't make sense. Who would want to harm her mother? Fear had fled at her word and anxiety had melted at her touch. She had been the kindest woman one could meet. What enemies could her mother have possibly had?

Diana buried her face in her hands and sobbed. The commissioner squirmed in his seat. It was a long while before a hand rested ever so cautiously on her shoulder. She peeked between her fingers. The commissioner's stone face had given way to empathy. His duty was to justice not solace, but there he was attempting to numb the ache. A sudden cool washed over the burn of her wound. However brief the moment, he had brought relief by his small yet significant act of kindness.

Her hands fell from her face, and she took a shuddering inhale. Composing herself, she dried her eyes with her sleeve and said, "I'm alright."

He removed his hand from her shoulder. "If you need anything, Miss Griffin, just give me a call."

"Thank you, Commissioner." She sniffed.

Commissioner Williams and the other policemen left.

"What do we do now?" Anne questioned the still house.

It seemed like ages before Diana replied, "Go back to bed, I suppose."

The sisters sat in silence on the sofa, the surreal event consuming Diana's mind. This must be a fiction, a fragment of ghastly imagination, a play to which she was the audience. It was far away on a small stage, closed off and untouchable by the real world. Nevertheless, as fiction often did, it caged her soul in utter terror and drowned it in undefeatable desolation.

But this naive game of hide-and-seek with reality did not last. Comprehension came in intervals. A moment here, a second there, she could truly grasp that it wasn't some horrid nightmare. It was not confined to the stage. It had managed to come to life, to reach out and take hold of the real world. She was not watching a play. She was in the play, and the plot was murder. There was no audience, no twist, no curtain closing. This was it. This was all there was. This was reality.

Face wet, eyes weary, and soul drained of life, she absorbed the details of the home about her with an uncanny certainty: things would never be the same. A glance in Anne's direction revealed that she was undergoing the same revelation. There was no going back. Now and again, a sob would emit from Anne's lips; and though Diana remained noiseless, the frequency of her tears was no less.

With a heavy heart, she went back to bed, her sister at her heels. Would they have enough strength to face the next day? Would they tarry on in cold nothingness, or would a battlecry for freedom ring out? Would the curtain ever close on this act, or were they locked in this moment of their story for eternity?

4

THREE MONTHS LATER

Drumming her fingers against the sofa's armrest, Diana stared at a phone atop the end table. Should she call Commissioner Williams to check on how the investigation was coming along? She had called numerous times, though. To do so again would be shameful. Besides, every call brought unwelcome news.

The criminal was truly ingenious, she had to admit. In all their weeks of searching, the police had found no leads and no clues.

The killer had vanished into thin air, and she didn't want to hear it again. Yet she deeply desired to talk with the commissioner. Truthfully, he was the only person that could numb her ache and silence her loneliness. The war around her would step into the background as she lay on the sofa listening to his voice floating through the receiver to her yearning ear.

Perhaps she should call him, just for a talk, to get her mind off things. A rueful smile touched her lips. She always savored their lengthy conversations.

Though she hadn't seen him face to face since their somber meeting, affection swelled in her heart with each phone call. She wished the relationship would go further, but this was a childish fantasy. An attempt at such a thing would indefinitely result in failure. Likely, he only engaged in their conversations to pacify a grieving daughter. He would never notice, much less be fond of, a woman like her. Nevertheless, she called him two or three times a week, seeking consolation in his affable words.

"I'm back," Anne announced as she stumbled through the door, arms full of groceries. "I had a beastly trip to the market. It was packed. Some kid tried to nick my purse, and, to top it off, this git nearly collided with my car! Stepped right out onto the street. Didn't even look. Crikey! How thick can you be?" She closed the door with her foot and stumbled into the kitchen. After the thud of bags being dumped onto the counter, she entered the living room. "Oh, don't trouble yourself. I'm fine, thanks."

"Hmm?" Diana continued to stare at the phone.

"*Well.*" Anne put her hands on her hips, flipping her blonde hair over her shoulder. "I thought you would come and help me carry all those bags into the kitchen, so I wouldn't nearly break my back."

Diana glanced at her, "Don't you think you're overreacting?"

"*Overreacting?*" Anne sputtered. "I've worked *endlessly* to keep this house running. You haven't done a thing!"

"What rubbish! I haven't done anything? Really?" fumed Diana, turning in her seat to look at Anne. "Do you think all those bills take care of themselves?"

"Oh, *marvelous.* You shuffle papers around."

"'Shuffle papers around'? There's more to it than that, you daft girl."

"Whatever. But what were you doing when I walked in? Nothing! *Literally* nothing."

"I only work every other day, remember?"

"Exactly!" Anne threw her hands up. "You couldn't have gone to the market? I had to work today."

"I didn't even *know* you were going to the market. I can't read your mind. If you need something, you must *tell me!*" Diana said, slamming her fist on the chair's armrest.

"Don't give me that. This isn't just about your indifference to errands. You hardly leave the house at all. Why do you stay shut up? Do *something!*"

"What if I like being shut up?"

"Why? To think on—on *it* until it's torture?"

Diana jabbed a finger at her. "Maybe you should think on it more."

"Maybe you should think on it less. You're not even trying to move on."

"And you've moved on too quickly!"

Anne stared at her a moment. She took a step back, and her jaw slackened. "You think I've...you think it doesn't... Oh, bother it! Don't talk to me—*ever!*" She stomped out of the room.

"Fine!"

"Brilliant!"

A door slammed upstairs. Diana began to snivel. Elbow propped on her knee, she rested her forehead in her palm. Teardrops slid down her arm and pooled in her lap. All the sisters did these days was quarrel. She was losing the only family she had left, the only person who still loved her. Well, Anne once did; she once loved her.

Misery, rage, strife—it was a never-ending war. Battle after battle, her life raged on with no sign of triumph, and her will to fight had been murdered.

Anne once did. She once loved me.

Diana was defeated.

Once she had drained herself dry of tears, she slumped into the sofa and began toying with her necklace, a silver chain that bore a small key. Her mother had given one to each of the sisters in her will, but they hadn't a clue as to what the keys unlocked. Other than the necklaces, her mother left them the house and all within it, a sizable fortune in the bank, and some oak box the women were unable to find.

Diana sighed. Her mother had willed them everything. Why point out the box? Why point out the key necklaces? What was so special about them? Did the contents of the box—

Diana sat bolt upright. A ghostly whisper filled her ears:

> *You hold the key*
> *to this box that hides itself from thee.*
> *She left to you this journey.*
> *You must find out why your key exists.*
> *Your mother's dying wish was this:*
> *destroy what's in the old oak box to live.*

Heart thundering, she clutched the edge of the sofa. "Hello?" she said to the still evening, her breath ragged. "Who's there?"

She gasped. Someone was coming down the stairs. The shadow of the intruder neared. She told her body to flee, but her muscles refused to act. She was frozen to her seat. The footsteps grew louder. Then a figure came into view.

"Oh, it's just you." Diana sighed in relief, placing a hand on her chest.

Anne scanned the room. "Were you talking to your—?" Her eyes widened. "Crikey, Diana! You look as if you've seen a ghost."

Diana quavered, gaze darting around the room. "I heard a voice, as clearly as I hear yours now. It spoke of that box and our keys. It said Mum wanted us to destroy it or—no. Oh, I don't know. It gave me such a fright!"

Anne crossed her arms. "Making up stories now? What are you playing at?"

"What? No! It really happened!"

Anne scoffed and went back upstairs.

Diana started pacing the floor. That voice had felt so real, but her sister didn't believe her. To her credit, the tale wasn't very sound. Diana bit her lip. She must have imagined it.

Oh, dear. I'm going mad.

She went about the remainder of her day, but the voice's words constantly replayed in her mind. Her attempts to silence them were in vain. Not being able to shake a feeling of urgency, she went up to her mother's room to search for the box but was unsuccessful.

That night, all was tranquil in the house, all except Diana as she wrestled with sleep. The clock sounded its rhythmic tick as she stared unseeing into the blackness. When sleep at last took hold, she found her dreams polluted with missing boxes and strange voices.

Suddenly, the voice shook the bedroom walls, waking Diana with a start.

Wake up! WAKE UP!
You cannot give up!
You must find this hidden thing,
but not alone, or endure failure's sting.
Remember, your mother's dying wish was this:
destroy what's in the old oak box so all can live.

Eyes as wide as saucers, she forced herself to breathe steadily and craned her neck. There was complete silence in the Griffin residence.

One thing was for certain: the voice was real. And the contents of the box were obviously important. She listened and waited...listened and waited. Nothing—quiet's siren screeched in her ears.

What had it said about failure? *But not alone?* Who could help her?

Then she knew. "Anne."

Releasing her tight grip on the mattress, she jumped out of bed, darted down the hall, and burst into her sister's room.

"Anne! Anne! Please wake up!"

"*What?*" Anne whined.

"I heard the voice again. I know it seems dodgy, but I'm telling you, it's not a lie. It wants us to find the box. It said I needed your help. I don't know what's going on, but I *do* know that I need answers—for all this. If that means following this voice and finding this mysterious box, then so be it."

Anne sighed and pinched the bridge of her nose. "You've always been trustworthy, so either you're being honest, or you're deranged. Either way, I need to help you. And...I need answers too. You really think it's related to Mum's death?"

"It seems to be." Diana knelt beside her sister's bed. "Thanks, Anne."

"Yeah, no problem. It is curious, though," Anne said, setting her feet on the floor, "that this voice would want you to find this box so bad yet not coax me to search as well. I mean, why can't I hear it? It was left to the both of us."

The silence that followed was shattered by the booming voice, causing the vase on Anne's nightstand to rattle.

> *Don't give up,*
> *or she will reign, she who is unjust.*
> *Your mother's dying wish, remember.*
> *Find where she hid the treasure.*
> *Turn the house upside down if you must,*
> *to find what is cursed,*
> *and return Levian eternally to the earth.*

Anne whimpered. "That was dreadful."

"You hear it?"

"Yes. I'm—I'm sorry, Diana."

"It's all right, sis."

For a long time, the women sat and listened, but nothing happened. Eventually, they returned to bed. Diana clutched her blanket to her chest, scanning the darkness as if she might spot the voice's owner. Something wicked was afoot, and they were caught in the middle of it.

The Griffin sisters looked for the box everywhere. They hunted for weeks, in fact. Every inch of wall and floor, every nook and cranny, was searched in each and every room.

They even looked outside the house and peered up at the roof, but they came up empty.

"Oh, bother it all! This is *hopeless!*" Anne exploded a month later.

"Yes," said Diana, "maybe we're *both* going mad."

They abandoned their search, making the following days gloomy and quite dull. Diana waited in angst for another speech, but no such speech ever came.

I never heard any voice. That must be it. I made it up.

Unfortunately, this resolution did not settle well with her.

It was late into the afternoon a week later. The top of the sky was painted black, and Anne still wasn't home. Her shift had ended over an hour ago, and calls to friends and coworkers offered no clues. Where was she?

Diana peeked out the window for the hundredth time. Should she go search for Anne? What if her sister returned home while she was out?

Diana began to pace again, wringing her hands. *What if...*

She stopped cold, staring in horror at the mental scene formulating. What if the worst had happened? Had she lost Anne too?

She strode over to the phone. She must call the commissioner. He would know what to do. The moment she placed the receiver to her ear, the door opened. Anne walked in.

Diana slammed the receiver onto the base. "Where the blazes have you been?"

Anne furrowed her eyebrows. "What?"

"Don't *what* me! You are *royally* late. *Where* were you?"

Anne scoffed. "I don't see how that's any of your business." She walked into the living room and dropped her purse onto the tea table.

"None of my business?" Diana huffed. "Anne, after what has happened, you disappearing with no explanation does not welcome pleasant thoughts."

Anne seemed to consider this. "If you must know, I was on a date."

"A date?" Diana combed her fingers through her hair. "Why didn't you let me know you'd be going out for dinner?"

"You don't mind me when I'm here. Why should you mind if I'm gone?"

"What nonsense are you going on—"

"His name is Walter, and we had a pleasant time. Thanks for asking." Anne plopped onto the sofa, folding her arms.

Diana opened her mouth but didn't say anything. She took a deep breath and murmured, "I'm glad you had a good time."

There was a silence, an eerie silence, as questions lingered in the air. Would they tarry on in cold nothingness, or would a battlecry for freedom ring out?

The sun's dying light cast a warm glow into the Griffin residence, the serene winding down of the city in stark contrast to the tension of the house. Meekly, Diana glanced at her sister, whose melancholic eyes were fixed on the floor. Would the curtain ever close on this act, or were they locked in this moment of their story for eternity?

Anne took a trembling inhale. "This isn't working."

Shoulders drooping, Diana averted her wet face. Was their relationship recoverable?

"Well," she mumbled, "I haven't had any dinner."

Anne sniffed. "Right. Go on."

As Diana trudged into the kitchen, the voice shattered the composure of London.

> *Follow me! Follow me!*
> *Follow me to find your Key!*
> *Before I spoke in riddles,*
> *now I speak to you plainly.*
> *Follow me to find the Key that hides.*
> *Do what your mother couldn't achieve in her time.*
> *Destroy the Key that's cursed*
> *to save the world from Levian's worst.*

"There's that ghastly voice again!" Anne said, springing from the sofa.

"Where's it coming from?"

"Upstairs! What does it sound like?"

The women darted up the stairs. At last, something to distract from their disharmony. Diana couldn't help but be relieved. The mystery of the box was the only topic that appeased their strife.

They followed the voice to the second floor, then the third. They bumped into each other so many times, it was a wonder one didn't send the other tumbling back down.

"What's this about another Key?" Diana panted.

Anne shook her head. "Dunno."

After what felt like ages, the sisters entered their mother's bedroom.

Diana gasped in bewilderment, "Good heavens!"

Before them, in the center of the room, hovered the ghost of a blonde-haired, blue-eyed little boy. Appearing to be from medieval times, he was about nine years old, wore peasant clothes, and had three parallel gashes on the side of his neck. They were still red—no doubt from the moment of his death. His legs melted into a waterfall of fog, his feet nonexistent.

"Hello!" the ghost chirped. "My name is Cirrus, and I'm the one who called you up here."

"*You're* the dreadful voice we've been hearing?" Anne tittered.

"Don't be so surprised," the ghost said in a sing-song manner. "It is true. It was I who has been speaking. Watch."

Cirrus cleared his throat and then, as the women slapped their hands over their ears, roared, "Follow me to find your Key!"

Diana shushed him. "Alright, alright, so you're the voice. But since you are the voice, you have a whole lot of explaining to do."

"No, no, no, that is not my job," Cirrus declined hastily. "I am here to show you where the box is hidden." He pointed to the floorboard beneath him.

Diana crouched and ran her hand over the floorboard. "It's a different color. How did we miss this?"

"I know, right!" Cirrus said, but then got hilariously serious and, making a motion with his hand, added, "Just under there."

"It isn't *overly* obvious." Anne knelt down beside Diana. "Just a slightly different shade."

"But we were so careful in our search."

"We weren't exactly looking for color variations in the floor, were we?"

"True. The wood feels different also."

"Different how?"

"It feels—it feels like paint! Get me a knife."

Anne knit her eyebrows. "Get your own knife."

"Anne!"

"*Fine.* I'll get your bloody knife."

Anne scurried out of the room and soon reappeared, knife in hand. Diana began scraping the blade over the floorboard. Color peeled away to reveal a floorboard identical to the rest. Diana kept scraping, eventually uncovering a message carved into the wood accompanied by a symbol of a key.

YOUR DESTINY AWAITS.

"Well, fancy that," Anne said.

The Griffin sisters pried the floorboard up. In the space underneath sat a weathered oak box. A rose was carved onto the lid. Vines, decorated with leaves and buds, extended in every direction from the flower, covering the box. The corners were protected by bronze engraved with tiny roses. A hefty, two-keyhole lock guarded its entrance. Molded to resemble the head of a wolf, the elaborate lock boasted a name: *Griffin.*

"Have you ever seen anything like it?" Diana breathed as she lifted the box from the floor and set it on her lap.

Anne gazed at it in awe. "It is gorgeous."

Diana fingered the lock, the keyholes hidden in the wolf's fur on either side. "Two keys for two keyholes. '*But not alone, or endure failure's sting.'* That's why you wanted the both of us."

"Question," Anne said. "What's with all the riddles?"

"I was fearful that an uninvited guest might be listening." Cirrus glanced over his shoulder. "Go on! What are you waiting for? Open it!"

The Griffin sisters took off their necklaces, fit the keys into the lock, then turned them in unison. The box clicked open. Diana, hands shaking, lifted the lid while Anne held her breath. Inside was a sizable, ancient-looking brass Key, two rings (one made of crystal and the other of iron), and what appeared to be a rather freshly written letter.

Diana's shoulders slumped. "Is that it? What's so special about this stuff?"

"The letter will explain, of course," Cirrus said as though it was the most obvious thing in the world. "But first, put on the rings."

"Why?" Anne asked.

"Once the elves discovered Prince Luca's mission, they made the rings to aid the Griffins," Cirrus explained. "The rings will help you defeat Levian."

Diana bit her lip. *Elves? Prince Luca? Levian? What is he going on about?*

Anne eyed the rings and shrugged. "What's the harm?"

"We're talking to a ghost," said Diana. "There could be a lot of harm."

Anne rolled her eyes. "It's jewelry, Diana." She slipped on the iron ring. Diana followed suit with the crystal.

"Is something supposed to happen?" Diana asked after a few moments of silence.

"Oh, bother it!" Anne threw her hands up and strode toward Cirrus. "Just tell us. What are you playing at?" With another wild hand motion, her palm burst into flame. The curtain ignited, the nightstand candle melted, and sparks sprinkled the floor.

"Blimey!" Diana yelped. Her hands flew up to shield her face as the sparks rained on her. Tiny beads of ice, not fire, shattered against the ground as ice crystals flew from her fingers, striking the curtain. Smooth, sparkling ice encased the curtains and spread over the window. Her trembling arms remained outstretched as Anne stood, petrified, staring at the stiff pieces of fabric.

Diana rubbed her eyes. "Did you see that?"

"Of course I saw it," said Anne. "That was barmy."

"Destroy the Key!" the ghost cried. "Defeat Levian! It's the world's only hope. Cheerio!" Cirrus vanished, and it was as if he had never been there. The women and their frozen curtain stood in the quiet.

Anne huffed. "That was bloody confusing. I feel more lost now than when we started."

"Perhaps this will help." Diana picked up the letter. Her sister peered over her shoulder as she read it aloud.

Dear Diana and Anne,

If you are reading this, it means that I'm no longer with you. I regret having to give you this terrible burden, but the Key must be destroyed. It is the mission of the Griffin family. The good news is I have found a clue. Whatever is capable of destroying the Key sits right in front of the Door it opens. What sits in front of the

*Door and where it is located, well, your guess is as
good as mine.*

*At this point, I'm sure you two are quite confused. I
never wished to pass down this mission, but my time
is near. I opened the box and brought the Key into the
open. I'm certain I saw a Shatari, soldiers that Levian
sends in search of the Key, in my window, and he
saw the Key. I gave into temptation. I failed to keep
it hidden. And now I depend on you girls to succeed
where I failed. It is crucial to get rid of this Key. It
unlocks the Door, and the Door holds horrors greater
than you or I could imagine. I don't know what's
behind the Door, but whatever it is will enable Levian
to regain her power. Find the Key's weakness. Look
for the clues. Be swift about it, for she will never stop
searching for her precious Key.*

*Please know, my daughters, that I love you dearly and
always will.*

Your loving mother,
Tara

"This is maddening." Anne pinched the bridge of her nose.

Diana gazed at her mother's flawless pen strokes, the
paper her hand once rested upon. How ordinary it appeared,
as if nothing was out of place. But everything was out of
place. Diana pressed the letter to her chest.

Something wicked was afoot indeed, and they were des-
tined to stop it.

"So," Diana whispered, "the Key must be destroyed."

Anne's head jerked up, eyes wide. "You're actually considering this?"

"Anne, we have to."

"Oh, so you're going to save the world now?"

"This is what Mum died for," choked Diana.

Anne stared at her, the hardness of her face softening. "We're only a couple of women. What are *we* going to do?"

"I don't know. But this was Mum's life, and evidently, the lives of everyone else depends on it. We have to try."

Anne sank onto the bed with a nod. "Where do we start?"

Diana studied the letter. "Levian...that name sounds familiar. I believe I read it in a book somewhere. And this Shatari name too."

"Brilliant. Which book?"

"That's the problem." She rubbed the back of her neck. "I read so many books, I can't remember."

Anne groaned. "You're a bookworm if there ever was one. We ought to take a trip to the library tomorrow and see if we can jog your memory."

"Very well."

"Probably best to put that elsewhere"—Anne gestured toward the Key—"in case one of those—Shatari, was it?—decides to come snooping."

Diana placed the Key in her bedside table before turning in for the night. She lay staring at the drawer's handle. Where would this uncanny path end?

5

THE CLUES OF LONDON

The next morning, Anne strolled down to the London Library with Diana. The air was cool and crisp. People scurried about in coats, some weary of use and others undoubtedly a collection of many worn once a year. The early morning fog drifted through the streets, and the sun peeked curiously between the buildings to see what the sisters were up to.

Once at the library, they split up and began their search. Anne went down aisle after book-crammed aisle, which varied from horse-and-buggy wide to narrow alleyways one could hardly squeeze through. The towering shelves were filled with goodness-knew-how-many volumes of history texts to tiny children's books about talking rabbits. There were new, decent-sized books with fresh binding to hefty, dusty old copies whose names had long since vanished. She flipped through several of them with no success. The one thing the library seemed not to have was a book that boasted of cursed keys.

Not one of these bloody books says anything about Levian, the Shatari, or our Key.

She came to the end of a narrow aisle. A wall with a faint marking stood there, so she turned back the way she came. Halfway down the aisle, she halted. What was that marking? She returned to the wall and studied it. Her fingers hovered over it. It looked oddly like a key.

A key!

She excitedly began running her hands all over the wall. There had to be some sort of secret compartment. Right above the symbol, her fingers slid in between the bricks. She gasped, moved her fingers along the groove, then hit a dead end that directed her downward. Suddenly, there was a click, and a little door, one foot wide and six inches high, swung open. She removed the sizable book from within. It had gold lettering on the spine: *The Legend of Prince Luca's Key.*

Anne gaped at it. *I found it.*

"I found it," she repeated aloud. She took off down the aisle to find her sister. Over the clopping of her hurried footsteps and the shushing of the librarian, she shouted, "Diana! I found it!"

She finally arrived at the end of the aisle that Diana was in and said breathlessly, "I found something. This book has information about Prince Luca, the prince Cirrus mentioned."

Diana snapped the book she had been examining shut. "Brilliant. I was starting to lose hope."

Anne nodded to the book Diana held. "Is that the book you read before?"

"Yes, but there isn't much information. It simply mentions a few horror stories about Levian and her army of monsters."

"Army of monsters? How *pleasant*."

"Let's see what clues your book offers."

The library had a reading area set up with sofas and tables. The sisters sat side by side and set the book on a table in front of them. Tugging it open, they began to search for clues.

The book had a lot to say for itself, none of which was quite useful to the sisters' quest. It took some time before Anne found anything noteworthy. "Look! It's a picture of the Key."

Diana peered at the page. She took the Key from her purse and compared it to the picture. It matched the one depicted in the book.

"You had that *thing* in your purse?" Anne asked, raising her eyebrows.

"I didn't feel comfortable leaving it at the house."

"But you feel comfortable lugging it around town in a bag?"

Diana sighed. "In an empty house or in my purse on the street. Take your pick."

Anne turned her attention back to the book. "Let's just continue reading."

The next fifty pages held nothing but dull information. Prince Luca's lengthy genealogy, a timeline of different places the family lived and when, maps speculating about the layout of his original kingdom—that sort of hogwash. They finally came across something more interesting: legend told of a boiling, ancient Pool of mercury, from which the Weapon and the Key came from. Rumor had it that every soul taken by the Weapon is trapped in the Pool, and the victim's screams emanate from its silver waters. Because of this freakish detail, the Pool was given the name Pool of Spirits.

"Mum said the thing that can destroy the Key is in front of the Door," Anne mused. "What if this Pool is in front of the Door? It made this Weapon, whatever it is, and the Key. Could it unmake them?"

"That's a nice theory." Diana rubbed her chin. "Though I wish we had harder evidence for that conclusion."

"I doubt we'll find something that says, 'Go to this place, at this time, and do this to destroy the Key.'"

"I'm only saying it's not much to go by." Anne's jaw clenched, and Diana quickly added, "Perhaps we'll find more clues."

The sisters kept reading and came across a passage that had been inked in.

"In 1859, an elderly Griffin fell ill and could not make the journey to the Door himself. Not trusting such delicate information to something so vulnerable as paper and ink, he placed clues all around London that led directly to the Door. He had to be discreet so Levian wouldn't find her way to the Door. Having no children of his own, the Griffin Key was left to his nephew, who didn't put much credence in the ghost stories his uncle had told him and was unlikely to have told his children of the mission or of London's clues."

"Fancy that," Anne murmured. "There are directions."

Diana said, "Why hasn't anyone figured this out before, with the information so out in the open like this?"

"I didn't exactly find the book sitting on a shelf," admitted Anne.

Diana blinked. "Where—where did you find it then?"

"I noticed a key symbol etched into the wall. It was quite faded, hardly noticeable. It marked a secret compartment, which I opened, and there was the book."

"The book itself is the first clue," whispered Diana.

"So...now we go find the rest?"

"Looks like it." Diana's eyebrows furrowed as she looked at the current page. "Hold on, what's this mean?"

Anne leaned in and read the paragraph her sister was pointing at.

"*The Key was known to 'whisper' to people close by, due to it trying to get back to its former master, Levian. The whispers of the Key would drive people to insanity and turn them against each other. The Weapon is persistent on breaking free from its prison.*"

"Rather unsettling, that," Diana murmured.

The Key was eerily alluring. Anne's eyes locked onto it. There it was, resting innocently on the table. It sat in the open, so...*takable.* She swallowed hard and stammered, "Who—uh—is this Levian person—do you think?"

Though she seemed disturbed by her sister's sudden fascination with the Key, Diana turned back to the book. "According to this, she subjugated a kingdom for years with the Weapon. She needs it back to regain control."

"Lovely. A psychopathic dictator is now our likely enemy."

"Pretty much."

For the life of her, Anne could not take her eyes off the Key. The voice sounded so sweet in its coaxing whisper, "*Anne...Anne...I can give you control, control over death itself. Why destroy a harmless Key? You need my power to turn back death, to stop it. You shall never suffer its sting again. Oh, poor little lonely Anne. Your sister has left you alone. She doesn't care.*

You need your mother back, I know, and you can have her. You can have her back. Anne...Anne...Anne..."

Her hand hovered over the Key. Just this once she could use it to turn back time. Surely such a powerful object as this Weapon could bring her mother back.

Tears stung her eyes. *Mum.*

Diana had pushed her away; she had no idea what she was going through. Their friendship was dead. Anne needed this. What else was she to do? Her heart couldn't bear it anymore. She needed her mom back. But her mother had wanted the Key gone. It was evil, wasn't it?

As Anne held the Key's gaze with rapacity, its whisper grew louder and its pull grew stronger. She forced her eyes shut and took a deep breath. This was going against her mother's wishes, but her mom would understand. She needed her family back.

Someone took hold of her arm. She jerked it away and snapped it back for a punch, breathing heavily in rage. A smirk danced across her lips. How mighty she would be. Death itself would bow. Nothing, no living soul, would stand in her way. The spear of death would turn outward. As for those who opposed her, their bones would rot in the streets.

The alarmed eyes staring back at her broke the trance. With Anne's right hand holding her down and the other pulled back for a blow, Diana gazed up at her sister, hands outstretched to protect herself. Anne immediately backed off and plopped unto the sofa. Her body wouldn't stop shivering. Horrid images of blood and murder ran rampant in her mind. Quickly did the line between right and wrong blur.

Her stomach squirmed and bile bubbled up in her throat. She whispered, "Carry the Key, Diana, at all times. Out of my sight."

Diana continued to stare at her, daunted. "Al—alright. I will." She concealed the Key within her purse.

Anne began to sob.

Diana looked over the last paragraph again. "I guess they weren't joking about the Key's whisper."

Anne chuckled half-heartedly, tears streaming down her face. "Yeah."

The Griffin sisters left the library. When they got home, Diana replaced the key on her necklace with the Griffin Key. Anne having recovered from her episode, the sisters practiced their newfound skills, which came quite naturally to them.

Knowing a long and exhausting day was ahead, she went to bed early. She blew out the candle, and all was darkness—a vivid depiction of what her world had become. Tears escaped her eyes, slipped down her temples, and soaked into her hairline. Joy was a cold corpse.

Alone—she was fighting the monsters alone in bed at night. Little had she known that there was a monster within herself, whispering into her mind.

She pressed her hand against her lips, trapping a wail inside. Blackness coaxed the ache, which had been allowed to stay within her, rotting her soul. Allowed to stay for Diana had grown indifferent to her. Where had the family gone?

A mournful sleep captured her, her dreams memories, cruelly reminding her of the preciousness of that which had been stolen.

At noon the next day, she was getting ready in her bedroom. She strolled over to the mirror and evaluated her outfit. Her polka-dotted dress hugged her neck and ended just below her knees; a tight strip of fabric was wrapped around the waist. The dress was accompanied by a half-sleeve white leather jacket, black gloves, a small purse, a black cloche hat, and white closed-toe high heels. She gave her reflection an approving nod and went downstairs to meet her sister.

Anne paused on the steps. "You look smashing, Diana."

The oldest Griffin sister wore a beige tweed suit with buttons down the front of both the top and skirt, a fedora hat, and black pump heels with a strap. She looked down at herself. "You think so?"

"Yes. Lovely."

"Thanks...you look rather dashing yourself."

"Cheers. And I should for what I paid! Pricey, this."

Diana offered a weak smile. "Shall we get on with it, then?"

"Where should we start?" Anne asked.

"Didn't the book say he attended Westminster Abbey?"

"I believe it did."

"Then that's our first stop."

The Griffins set out in their car to Westminster Abbey. They searched the grounds and then journeyed inside. The ceiling arched high above them, massive pillars holding it in place. Light reached through the stained glass windows depicting Biblical characters, splashing brilliant colors across the floor. And somewhere amidst the elaborate design hid a clue. How would they find it?

An hour into their search, Anne groaned and leaned up against one of the pillars. What a pointless search it was.

There was no way they'd find anything in that enormous place. The clues probably didn't even exist.

Something shifted under Anne's weight. She turned. There was a loose brick in the pillar. She glanced behind her to ensure no one was watching and carefully removed the brick.

She peered inside. "Crikey! And there it is."

In the empty space, a key symbol had been carved into the stone with a message above it.

THE GRIFFIN KEY MUST BE DESTROYED, TIME IS OF THE ESSENCE.

Anne pinched the bridge of her nose. "That's not overwhelmingly helpful." She scanned the room, spotted her sister, and called, "Diana, I've found one!"

Diana rushed over and examined the message. "Indeed you have."

"That old geezer must think the Griffins are *really* thick to tell us what we already know."

"I don't think we're supposed to take this literally."

"What?"

"I think he's playing with words."

"Playing with our brains, rather."

"*Time is of the essence,*" Diana repeated under her breath. "Time...time...what's connected to time? A clock. Time is important. A clock is important. A clock...Big Ben. He's talking about Big Ben. It has to be."

Anne read the message again. "That makes sense."

"To Big Ben, then?"

"Right. Let's crack on!"

The women arrived at Big Ben and began their search, looking thoroughly at every brick. There was nothing on the outside, so they went in.

They hiked the gray stairs up to the top, checking each step and inch of wall as they went. They journeyed through the belfry and examined all four clock faces. An hour, then two, then three passed, but they discovered nothing.

Anne stood, glaring at one of the clock faces from within the tower. She inwardly demanded that some marking would appear. It didn't.

Diana joined her in the ridicule of the clock face. "Perhaps we missed something."

"Thanks for stating the obvious," Anne retorted. "We didn't look at the bells closely enough. I'm going to check it again."

Anne ascended the steps and walked around the room. There wasn't a mark on the walls or on the floor. She started studying the bells.

When she came to the final one, her jaw dropped. "Well, I never." She took off down the steps shouting, "Diana! Diana! I found something!"

Diana bumped into her halfway down the stairs. "What are you going on about?"

"I found a clue in the belfry," Anne said. "It's on a bell."

"You're joking. On the Great Bell?"

"No, on one of the quarter bells."

Anne showed her sister what she had found. Etched into the interior metal of one of the bells was another clue.

PRINCE LUCA TOOK THE KEY,
YOU SHALL FIND THE ANSWER WITH ROYALTY.

Diana was stunned. "How'd he manage that?"

"Any bright ideas?" asked Anne.

"*With royalty,*" Diana mumbled to herself. "Buckingham Palace, perhaps?"

"Seems about right."

The sisters drove to the castle. Anne strolled in front of the gate and scanned the bars. Two thin horizontal lines ran across one of them. She pushed on the section in between them. It squeaked as it began to turn. When she had twisted it all the way around, the section popped off.

"Gracious me!" hissed Diana. "Did you just break part of the gate off?"

"Clearly, it's *supposed* to come off," Anne muttered as she turned the piece of metal over in her hand. There was another clue on the bottom.

ACROSS AND DOWN.

"That's bloody vague," Anne huffed.

"Across and down," Diana said. "Sounds like directions."

"I know they're directions," snapped Anne. "But across *where* and down *where*?"

"Maybe in the park over there? Across the street and on the ground?"

They crossed the street and looked around in the park, but no clue was to be found.

"You'd have to be a dim bloke to put the clue out here for all to see," Anne said.

"Or a genius."

"Yes, he's bloody brilliant." Anne rolled her eyes, but something caught her attention. At the foot of a tree was a grassy bulge. Her eyes narrowed. "Does that look curious to you?"

Diana followed her gaze. "It does indeed."

They approached the bulge, and Diana's fingers began searching blindly through the long grass. "There's stone underneath." She was able to push the greenery back enough to reveal a keyhole nestled in the grass. She traced the keyhole with her fingers. "Could it be..."

"Are you going to finish that thought?"

"What if he designed this keyhole for the Griffin Key?"

"Try it, then."

Diana slid the Key into the hole and turned it. The stone slab rolled away to reveal a message: directions to another location.

"Those lead out of the city," Anne said.

Diana nodded and pulled out a paper and pen. "Best write them down."

Once the directions were recorded and the clue again concealed, they drove to their far-off destination. They arrived an hour later at a fog-covered wood blocked off by a husky gate that gave the warning: DO NOT ENTER.

Anne heaved a loud, irritated sigh. "Blast! This place was blocked by the police a few years back. Something about ghastly happenings around here. A solid story never came about, but there's been a lot of talk. Let's just say that anyone who went into that wood was doomed for a bloody awful day. People disappeared. Cars pulled off the road like metal to a magnet, only to be found empty by the police. Strange noises sent people fleeing in terror." She shook her head. "Odd, that."

"It's not odd at all," Diana countered. "If the Door and the Pool of Spirits are truly in that wood, it's reasonable that it would be a dodgy place."

"That's it, then? Game over?"

"No, we have to get in there."

"By climbing over the gate and trespassing? I don't fancy breaking the law today."

"Nor do I. We need to figure out how to get in there— *legally*. At the very least, we discovered where we must go next. That's more knowledge than I expected to gain today. Nothing more we can do at the moment."

On the drive home, an unnerving notion passed through Anne's mind. If they couldn't find a legal way in, they'd have no choice but to break the law. To save the world, to answer questions, they would have to, and they'd be criminals.

She sighed and pinched the bridge of her nose. It didn't paint a pretty picture: her and her sister behind bars for trying to protect humanity from an all-powerful psychopath.

6

ANOTHER JOINS THE HUNT

Glaring at her wardrobe on the opposite end of the room, Diana lay in bed. She disliked it, the thought that had presented itself so enthusiastically—a cringeworthy solution to their gate problem.

She jerked the blanket rudely as she turned over. In all honesty, she fancied the thought, and she despised herself for it. The idea of going to the commissioner for help was disquieting, but he was the only lawman she knew and the only apparent solution to the locked gate.

The difficulty was this: he wouldn't do such a favor for her, much less believe her story. There wasn't a chance. Nonetheless, she had to try, for they desperately needed past that gate.

"See you tomorrow, Commissioner Williams," she whispered, anxiety and delight in a waltz upon her chest.

Early the next morning, she slipped out of bed and tiptoed around the house. Anne was a light sleeper. The slightest sound could wake her.

Diana made it to the bathroom with the noiselessness of a mouse. Once she finished brushing her teeth, she reached for the hair brush and knocked it off the counter. It clattered on the floor. Footfalls sounded in the hall.

"Diana, you klutz," she scolded herself. Soon her sister staggered into the bathroom, rubbing her eyes.

"Why are you up so early?" she whined, glaring at Diana through the slight crack between her eyelids. "It's Saturday."

"I'm going to meet a friend," Diana said brightly and proceeded to brush her hair, trying to keep the commissioner out of her thoughts.

Anne's eyebrows furrowed. "You haven't been out with a 'friend' since...I didn't even know you had friends anymore."

"Don't be daft, Anne. Of course, I have friends," said Diana.

Anne muttered something along the lines of "Well, when you stay shut up," which Diana elected to ignore.

Anne leaned against the doorframe as Diana finished brushing her hair. When she began pinning it up, Anne asked with a yawn, "It's not a man, is it?"

Diana tensed. "No."

The weariness in Anne's eyes evaporated. "Crikey, it is! I didn't know you fancied anyone."

"I *don't*."

Yes, you do.

"Is that so? Why are you blushing, then?"

"I'm *not* in a relationship."

Anne was miserably failing to suppress her grin. "You must *really* fancy him. Is this a date?"

I wish.

Diana scoffed. "Me have a fellow? You actually think someone would fancy *me*?"

Anne threw one hand up. "*Yes*, Diana, I do. Just because that one git treated you like rubbish doesn't mean another can't take a liking to you. You are aware that you're *allowed* to date, right? You know, you're not getting any younger."

"Put a sock in it, Anne!"

"*Alright*," said Anne, her playful tone officially dead. "You're single."

Diana couldn't help the rising warm feeling upon her sister's banter—a thing so rare those days. To her sorrow, it typically ended in genuine bickering now. She blinked rapidly to keep the tears at bay as she pretended to adjust her hair.

"But you are seeing a *he*," said Anne. "Is it that detective bloke?"

"He's the police commissioner. And yes, I am. I thought he might be able to help us get into the wood."

Anne considered this a moment. The corners of her mouth twitched upward. "That will work." She turned and disappeared down the hall.

"Wait, what makes you so sure?" Diana sputtered, but all she got in response was the bang of a shutting door.

Riding the Tube, Diana gazed unseeing at her hand clasping the bar. "*I'm not in a relationship.*" The words stung. They were accurate, of course, but she disliked the fact—particularly the fact it wasn't Commissioner Williams.

With each phone call, his words had grown increasingly welcoming:

Regretfully, we have no leads, Miss Griffin, he had told her at first. *I'm deeply sorry.*

I know this is hard, he had said. *Feel free to call anytime.*

A month in, he'd said, *There's been nothing new, but I won't give up. I promise.*

It will get better. I believe that, he had told her a couple weeks ago. *I know it doesn't seem that way now, but it will.*

And with each word, she permitted her affection to grow deeper.

She had gotten too close. What had she been thinking?

Her uneasiness prevented any excitement of seeing him from solidifying. Conversations over the phone were easy; she couldn't see his expressions. But in person—she tightened her grip on the bar. She wouldn't be able to bear the slightest gleam of disappointment or disinterest in his eyes.

The absence of such a bond made her chest ache. Her last relationship had ended many years prior, and it had ended brutally. What he had said to her at their parting was true. She didn't measure up. No one would ever want her.

Diana walked through the front door of the London Police Department with a sigh. The commissioner wouldn't help her. There was no way.

She strolled up to the receptionist's desk and told her she had come to see Commissioner Williams. The receptionist asked her to wait a moment then left the room. Diana used the vague reflection in the window to adjust her hair and straighten her clothes.

"A Diana Griffin is here to see you, Commissioner," she heard the receptionist say.

"Really?" His voice sounded taken aback. "Let her in." The receptionist reappeared and escorted Diana into his office.

"Good morning, Miss Griffin," he said, beaming as he stood to greet her. "What a lovely surprise."

Diana shook the hand he offered. He was exactly as she remembered him.

The commissioner was an attractive, brawny fellow with neat brown hair. He had a calm demeanor, the kind of man who would address a raving lunatic with quiet words. A vertical scar, next to his right ear, ran the length of his face—a mark from the Great War, no doubt. And, Diana's favorite part, he had the world's most vibrant blue eyes.

There was something about the look they held, something wise yet mystifying. The weight of their insight was almost unnerving as it mixed with tenderness. Though they certainly guarded mysterious tales behind their gates, their warmth was unmatched.

She fought against her smile in vain. Indeed, he seemed the perfect man.

She seated herself in one of the chairs that sat in front of his large, elegant desk. There was a sizable window to the left and a few awards hanging to the right. A massive bookshelf covering the whole wall stood behind his desk. Her gaze lingered there for a second. He must have had hundreds of books on that shelf. A majority dealt with subjects of history and law, but a handful of fiction works stood out boldly from the rest. Sir Arthur Conan Doyle's *The Adventures of Sherlock Homes* and Agatha Christie's *The Murder on the Links* obviously struck his fancy due to professional parallels. Additionally, Edger Allen Poe and Shakespeare, a bit out of place in the assembly of titles, perched upon the shelf.

"That's quite a collection of books you've got, Commissioner Williams," Diana said.

"Yes, well"—he glanced back at his bookshelf then leaned forward—"I haven't read most of them. They're just to make me *look* clever." A broad smile spread across his face at her giggle.

"I didn't take you as a reader of frightful tales," she said.

"Ah, you noted Poe's penmanship amidst my collection. He is dark, yes, but nonetheless tasteful."

"Agreed. I spied Shakespeare as well. Poe outdoes him in fearsome topics, but I can't deny that *Hamlet* is a true masterpiece."

"I didn't assign such writing to you either, Miss Griffin."

"I love it." Diana twirled a strip of hair around her index finger. "Dark, yes, but tasteful. Although not my preferred type of book."

"What do you prefer, Miss Griffin?"

Her cheeks burned. "*Romeo and Juliet.*"

The commissioner gave a charming side grin, allowing for a long pause before saying, "Besides this lovely conversation of the arts, to what do I owe this pleasure?"

"Oh—er." Diana did not have a plan on how to approach this as she should have had. She needed an excuse for wanting through the gate. How does one go about telling the bizarre story of the Griffin Key?

"I—er—was just curious about—um—how Mum's case is going." She bit her lip, kicking herself for the unconvincing motive of her visit.

"Oh." He sighed and took his eyes off her for the first time. "I wish I could give you better news, Miss Griffin, but we still have no leads. You usually *call* me for such information. Is there something else troubling you?"

"Um." She twisted her left cuff. "Actually, there *is* something I wanted to ask you about."

"Yes?"

"There was a box that our mother left us in her will."

"Oh, yes. The mysterious box."

"We found it a few days ago."

"Brilliant! What was in it?"

"A Key."

"A Key? A Key to what?"

"That's the difficult part. You wouldn't believe me if I told you."

He leaned back in his chair, clearly intrigued. "Try me."

"Well..." Diana gulped. "The Key is—"

No matter how strong her will was, she could not force herself to say it. He would think she was insane, then he'd never talk to her again.

"It'll be easier if I show you. Is it possible you could come to my house? Now?"

He rested his chin in his hand, studying her, but he said nothing.

She shifted in her chair. "You're still working my mum's case, correct?"

"Correct."

"This is related to her murder, so it's your duty to investigate this. Correct?"

He chuckled. "You are astute, Miss Griffin. Alright, I will go to your house and see what all this is about."

Diana allowed herself to let go of the breath she had been holding. "Thank you, Commissioner."

"After all this time, Miss Griffin, first names seem permissible. 'Harry' will do just fine."

"*Harry.*" She blushed, tucking a wayward strand behind her ear. "Then I suppose Diana would suffice."

He smiled, strolled to the door, and held it open. "After you, Diana."

As they drove Harry's car to the Griffin residence, he asked, "Why did you not simply call me about this matter? What prompted you to come to the station?"

"This Key is related to a request I felt better asked in person," she replied.

"What request?"

She didn't answer right way. "I need to pass some gates that guard a wood. It's about an hour from here."

He cast an unsettled glance at her. "The Ghost's Wood?"

"The what?"

"That's what people call it, because of all the abnormal happenings that took place there. Diana, I don't think you want to go in there. People say it's haunted."

Her breath caught in her throat. *Haunted? Does he believe in ghosts?*

"Do you? Believe it's haunted, I mean."

"I would like to think I don't, but there is simply no explanation for all the odd things that happened to trespassers."

Maybe this won't be so difficult after all.

"Why do you want in there?" Harry asked.

"Um...I can't really tell you until I explain this whole Key business."

He looked over at her with a smirk. "So I'll just have to trust you then?"

"I guest so.... Do you trust me?"

He took a deep breath and gazed at the road for a long while, then smiled softly. "Yes, I believe I do."

Why would he trust me?

He changed the subject. "If you don't mind me asking, how are you and your sister? I'm sorry I haven't inquired about it before."

Diana hesitated to reply, yet she hushed her wary instincts. She was in dire need of listening ears. "It's been hard," she choked, her throat tightening. "Anne and I...we're not good. There are moments, but—we can hardly go a day without a quarrel. This whole business seems the only thing that brings any peace. I fear our relationship will never be as it once was."

Harry stayed silent, like he knew there was more.

"She's not the same—Anne," she went on, the words no longer voluntary. "She's angry *all* the time. She used to be so full of life, so bright, so joyous. She isn't the sa—"

She had to pause to keep her tears in check. "That murderer did more than take Mum. He killed something in us both that night. Something died in her. Something died in me. I...I wasn't there for her, Harry. Her broken spirit is my fault. I'm afraid it's too late to fix it. How am I supposed to help my sister walk when I can't hold my own head up?"

She covered her face with her left hand. How, indeed?

So why try?

She felt the warmth of his hand as he took hers and whispered, "I'm so sorry, Diana."

He said no more. What more could he say? But he was there, like on the night of the murder. There was great power in simply being there.

Diana laced her fingers through his as a tear squeezed between her palm and cheek. It was too late—was it not?—to fix what she had done. What if Anne yelled at her? What if she wished to be left alone? What if Diana wouldn't be able to comfort her? She couldn't help her, and she wasn't sure Anne wanted her to. She could see it in her eyes: "I've had enough of you!"

Absentmindedly, Diana began fidgeting with the Key. It's enticing whisper floated up to her ears: *Diana, you will do great things with the Weapon. All will adore you. With its power, you will be enough. You will be extraordinary. Your sister will love you again. The man will too. You will have what you have always wanted. A ring of love. All you have to do is take. Take the Weapon. Let the Key live. Diana...Diana...Diana...*

Diana dropped the Key back in her shirt with a shudder. Anne's reaction in the library made sense now. The Key's whisper was maddening.

"You alright?" Harry asked at her shiver.

"Yes." She couldn't help mulling over what the Key had said as he pulled the car into the driveway. Could she really repair her relationship with Anne? Could she really change enough, be good enough for Harry? And all that was required of her was the theft of the Weapon?

They walked up the stairs to the front door. *No. If the Key is evil, the Weapon must be evil. We have to destroy the Key.*

They entered the house, and Anne, who had put on a cute yellow dress, emerged from upstairs to greet them.

"Commissioner Williams," she said with delight, a wide grin on her face. "What a surprise."

"Morning, Miss Griffin. Lovely to make your acquaintance again."

"Pleasure's mine." Anne shook his hand with a flip of her hair.

A needle pricked Diana's heart. Friendliness never tasted so bitter.

"Diana has informed me I need to investigate something regarding her mother's will and a Key," said Harry.

Anne glanced at her sister. "Yes, yes, *that*. This way."

As the trio climbed the stairs to their mother's room, Anne whispered to Diana, "So he doesn't know?"

"Of course not," hissed Diana.

"*Alright*. It was just a question." Anne surveyed her sister for the next few steps. "You know, I was only being friendly."

"Sure you were." Diana pursed her lips.

Anne huffed. "Be that way then."

Diana kicked herself. *Brilliant, Diana. Go on and make matters worse, will you?*

She mumbled, "I thought it best he see it with his own eyes."

Anne didn't seem to want to drop the subject, but she replied, "Agreed. It is difficult to stomach."

Entering their mother's bedroom, the Griffin sisters called out to Cirrus, and he appeared out of thin air. "Hello, girls! Wha—oh, gracious me—a new guy!"

Harry didn't recoil but became white as a sheet. His mouth opened then closed without a word.

"That's—that's a ghost," he stated blankly.

"Oh, you haven't seen the half of it yet." Anne blew the nearby candlestick a kiss. The wick burst into flame, and the little ball of fire danced atop the wax.

Diana froze the candlestick with a snap of her fingers, then life-sized ice ballet dancers rose from the floor. They performed a number from *The Nutcracker* before disappearing in an icy mist.

"Ok, ok," Harry pleaded. "I get the point. Now, someone *please* tell me what this is all about?"

Between the three of them, Harry was told the whole story. His expression rarely changed. He never gasped nor flinched nor stared in astonishment—or disbelief. His gaze simply traveled from one person to another as he thoughtfully listened to each and every word they said.

"So, you think the answer to destroying this Key lies in the Ghost's Wood?" he asked.

Diana nodded. "That's what we've been able to deduce from our—" There was a tremendous shift in the expression on Harry's face. What was he staring at? "Harry? Are you alright?"

She looked down. The Griffin Key was no longer hidden in her shirt, and Harry's eyes were locked onto it. He had the same look that Anne had in the library. The Key was calling to him. Diana inched towards him.

"Harry?" she cooed, resting her hand on his shoulder.

He wavered. "Wha—what was that?" His eyes at last focusing on her, he slowly removed her hand from his shoulder. "I'm alright..."

She couldn't quite place the look in his eyes. Something from the deep caverns of his soul had surfaced. It had about a million meanings, none of them evident, only growing in intensity as the seconds ticked by. Her cheeks began to burn. He hadn't let go of her hand. Why hadn't he let go of her hand? She wasn't breathing. She reminded her lungs to inhale.

"Diana," he whispered.

The corners of her mouth teased a smile. She loved the sound of her name on his lips.

"Uh—hello? I'm still here." Anne's voice cut in between them.

Diana blinked. She jerked her hand away as if from a scorching stovetop.

Harry averted his gaze and looked at the ground.

Diana cleared her throat. "We were doing something important—um..."

"The Key, Diana, the Key." Anne tittered. "You know, all-powerful maniacs, evil monsters, the end of the world."

"Right," Diana muttered. "The wood."

"I can get you in there," said Harry. "We will leave at nightfall."

"Oh, this is *so exciting*," Cirrus squealed. "It is crucial to destroy the Key. Follow the clues!"

Diana sighed. "Cirrus—"

"Take down Levian!"

"Cirr—"

"Save the world from—"

"Cirrus!"

"Yes?"

"We understand. This is important. Now be a dear and put a sock in it."

"Yes, ma'am!"

"Ok, then. We're back in business," said Anne, rubbing her hands together. "To the—uh, what did you call it, Commissioner?"

"The Ghost's Wood, but we're—"

"To the Ghost's Wood! Crack on." She marched out of the room.

"—not leaving until nightfall." Harry chuckled. "Is this the liveliness you mentioned?"

A rueful smile touched Diana's lips. "A glimpse of it."

Anne's head reappeared in the doorway. "Well, come along. Let's not wait around for the next century."

Led by a Shatari soldier, Vitus glided down the fire-lit tunnel. The soldier was jubilant over something, so much so he could not formulate words. It was obvious what the Shatari had found for it to thrill them so, but it would not do them any good without the Key.

Vitus and the soldier entered a dome-shaped room. The ceiling was composed of never-ending blackness. Flickering torches pushed back with all their might, yet the dark still prevailed. Dozens of Shatari darted to and fro, delighted by their new find. In the middle of the room sat the Pool of boiling quicksilver. Whispers escaped from its depths, faces of spirits appearing then vanishing in the blink of an eye. From behind it, the Door stood proud and menacing, in Levian's spirit. Towering over the Pool, it was arched and its reddish wood weathered. Metal bands and studs fortified it, and its hinges and ring handles were made of tarnished bronze. Then there was the keyhole, the access point to the deadliest power. Under the right handle, it was decorated with the elaborate crest of Prince Luca's family. However, its bronze was without blemish, somehow unaffected by time.

"We can't open it without the Key, Captain," a nearby Shatari grumbled. "It's impossible."

"Where—"

A whisper: "Callum."

Vitus froze. A voice drifted from the Door. He could hear her: a woman weeping.

"Callum."

"Her majesty must know that we need the Key," the Shatari went on.

Vitus, ignoring the comment, trod around the Pool and to the Door. He drew close.

The woman continued, "Callum, does she know? She has come for us. This can't—NO! Callum! Help me! *Please!*"

A second voice sounded, that of a little boy, "Papa, it hurts. Papa!"

The voice of a man cried out, "Don't! Leave them be. They are unarmed. Fight me, coward. Fight me!"

His fingertips grazed the Door as he lifted his hand. He could feel it breathe. He laid his palm flat against its ice-cold surface.

The Door disdained his touch. A force pressed against his hand, but he held it fast to the surface.

"Callum."

He gasped. With the swift stroke of an invisible blade, his mind tore. Something broke. It was as if his soul melted. He refused to permit his knees to buckle.

There was some illusion he was seemingly wrapped in. The thick fog that clouded his mind shifted just enough for him to capture a glimpse of something beyond. He knew, yet he did not know. He had forgotten, but forgotten what? He longed for something, but what could that possibly be?

He drew closer yet. "Hello?"

A terrorizing, ear-splitting scream slashed the atmosphere. The Door rattled violently, causing Vitus to jerk away as every Shatari soldier cowered against the walls. The rattle and the scream ceased with an abrupt boom from the Door.

"Call Levian," Vitus ordered in a hushed voice, then turned to find that no one had obeyed him. "Are you deaf? Now!"

All the Shatari staggered out of the room, rushing to obey his command.

Vitus collapsed onto the floor, shaking. Victim after victim after victim flashed through his mind, all blood spilled by his hands.

A certain night, a certain mission came into focus— the Griffins.

He stood concealed behind a tree on the sidewalk. The full moon was draped with strips of cloud, its light glistening in a blood puddle. Tara Griffin lay crumpled at the foot of the house. Up by the broken window, a woman wept. She gave him an odd feeling—familiarity. He dismissed the notion, turned his back on the scene, and walked down the street, returning to the cave empty-handed...

The memory melted.

The woman reminded him of someone, a nameless shadow lurking in the back of his mind. He had refrained from telling Levian about her, though his motive for such an action escaped him.

He had killed that night. He had been told to.

Levian was cruel. So many deaths she had caused, and he had taken those lives for her.

This isn't right.

His face was wet. Trembling fingers cautiously touched his cheek. As he stared, water drops slid down his index finger, coming to a rest in his palm—*tears*. He dared to lift his gaze to the Door.

The whisper again: "Callum."

He was still shaking. He could not stop. Death, death, and more death—it was the definition of him.

This remorse—was it a newfound thing within him or something forgotten? These feelings—he'd had them for years, but they had been mere whispers, pricks in the soul, proclaiming that something was amiss. He had been able to ignore them. Now they were thunderous battle cries.

Why had he ever pushed them away and denied them a chance to speak? For Levian's sake? Why did he ever choose to follow someone as vile as her? He raked his nails through his hair. He did not recall ever choosing to follow Levian. He just always had.

For that matter, he did not recall anything before Levian. He had never been more than a dagger in her merciless hand. Right and wrong, good and evil—these words had not occurred to him until now. Memory—he had never missed it before tonight. He hadn't realized there was something to be missed.

"It's gone," he whimpered. "There's nothing. Only murder."

He studied his surroundings in disgust. His underground dwelling was misery. What he would give for light, for fresh air—to live out of the shadows.

He hung his head and sobbed. What was happening to him? Whatever it was, he knew in the depths of his soul that it was not wicked. Wicked was what he had been. This was a good thing.

7

LAND OF THE CURSED

The darkened streets zipped past Diana's window as the trio drove to the Ghost's Wood. City transformed into countryside, buildings into trees, citizens into stars. The car zoomed through an area otherwise untouched by mankind. All the nothingness provided a lot of room to think. The mind seemed to relish the quiet and the night.

Why had Harry reacted the way he had at the house? Not his reaction to the Key. That was understandable. But to her? What did it mean, the way he had looked at her? Why had he been hesitant to relinquish her hand?

The answer paced in the back of her mind. She allowed it to present itself for a brief second, then immediately scolded herself for doing so. She took a measured breath, firmly clasping her hands in her lap. Hoping was a hazardous game. It wouldn't happen, no matter how desperately she wanted it too.

Harry does not want me.

They drove in silence. Anne slept in the backseat.

Harry glanced over his shoulder before saying, "When this is all over, Diana, fancy dinner with me sometime?"

Diana's head jerked in his direction, and she stared at him. "What?"

"I—um—I just." Harry tightened his grip on the steering wheel. "I'm inviting you to dinner."

"Just the two of us?"

"Yes."

"As in...a *date*?"

"Yes." He swallowed.

She sputtered. "You—you fancy me?"

With a stunned expression, he blinked multiple times before saying, "I thought it'd be obvious by now, as much as we talk."

A smile pulled at her lips, but she refused it. *No, no. Not possible.*

"I just—I'd never dreamed...I thought you wouldn't want to court me."

Eyes on the road, Harry tilted his head. "Whatever gave you that notion?" He inhaled deeply. "I have to say, I'm perplexed. I thought I was being very—"

"Oi! You passed the gate!"

Harry swerved at Anne's abrupt exclamation.

"Oops." Anne gritted her teeth. "Sorry about that."

Diana glanced in the rearview mirror. "How long have you been awake?"

Anne's reflection simply shrugged.

Harry turned the car around and parked in front of the gate. A fog blanketed the ominous woods. With limbs outstretched, the trees coaxed them to journey in, but a nearby owl warned them with its call.

He leaned closer to the windshield. "That's rather alarming." He got out and opened the door for Diana then turned to get Anne's, but she had just slammed hers shut.

"I got it, Commissioner."

They approached the gate, and, after a moment's hesitation, Harry unlocked it. It swung open silently. Diana's blood turned ice cold as the hair on her arms stood on end. The vague outline of a path bore gashes in the dirt, the evidence of victims being dragged away.

Had she gone insane? Surely, the wind wasn't saying, *Flee...flee, traveler...flee.*

The haunted path lay before them, but no one moved. Nothing blocked them, but they stood transfixed as though frozen to the ground.

"Why aren't you moving?" whispered Diana.

"Why aren't *I* moving?" Anne rasped. "Why aren't *you* moving?"

Harry gulped. "Did anyone else feel that the moment I opened the gate, they had this sudden, unexplained urge to run and hide?"

Anne nodded and quivered. "It's like the wood has cast some terror-hex on me."

Diana clutched her stomach. "I don't feel so good. I think I'm going to be sick."

Harry grabbed Diana's arm to steady her. "Should we come back another day?"

"No. We'll never be able to bring ourselves to come back if we leave." She scanned the woods. "Anne's right. There's a curse on this place."

"Diana," Anne said slowly, "I just had a rather disturbing thought."

"What?"

"What if it's not the wood? What if it's the Key?"

Diana looked at her sister. "Disturbing, but not unlikely."

They inched into the woods. With each step, horror's grip tightened, clouding her judgment, making her weak.

It was the birthplace of fear itself.

The gloom and wrongness of the place increased the further they ventured. A wall of blackness and fog opposed Diana's sight. She could not see but a few feet ahead. With each breath, a puff of smoke was added to the dense fog. The cold pierced her bones; the very marrow felt frozen. Every slight crunch of the leaves beneath her feet threatened her life, and, over the booming beat of her heart, she heard the trees jeer at them. She flinched at this tree, but it hadn't spoken, and shrank back from that tree, but it hadn't said a word. She hadn't heard anything, for the woods were still, in a deathly silence.

The wind whispered, *Flee, traveler...flee...flee.*

Anne groaned. "Bloody dreadful, this place."

The motionlessness of their surroundings felt unearthly. How could there be nothing, no life? It was all dead. Diana wiped her clammy hands on her skirt, trying to ignore the wetness of the hair at her nape.

Fear was alive.

She took a labored breath. *This curse is purposeful. Something doesn't want us here.*

Harry abruptly halted, attentive as a deer upon the snap of a twig.

"Stop," he said in a hushed voice.

She looked about and peered through the trees, but the fog wouldn't permit her to see any threat—if one was indeed there.

"What is it, Harry?" she whispered. When he didn't answer, she approached him. He grasped her shoulder to prevent her from going further. There was an anxious gleam in his eyes.

"I heard something," he insisted. "Listen." He moved forward a few steps, craning his neck. Several moments of noiselessness elapsed.

"Listen to what?" asked Anne.

His body slackened. "I guess I was imag—"

A howl cut through the quietness.

"W-w-what was that?" Anne whimpered, but Diana was focused on Harry. He had whirled around at the cry, and, looking aghast, his eyes were now fixed on something behind them.

Diana looked over her shoulder and gasped. A pair of yellow eyes pierced through the murk.

"Run!" he bellowed. The three of them cut through the woods at top speed as the gnarled branches clawed at them. No matter how fast they ran, the growls stayed close behind them. The wolf's blood-stained teeth were far too close to Diana's heels. It finally managed a scratch, and she stumbled. She flipped over, gasping as it pounced on her. But Harry appeared by her side and kicked the beast away. As he pulled her into a run, a blur of gray fur and talons appeared on her left, then another on her right. The first wolf had recovered and resumed his chase from behind.

Three. There's three of them!

The trees began to huddle together, forcing them into a zigzag pattern as they fled. The fog materialized and draped itself between the trees to the right. Harry darted into the drapes and the women followed. The tangible fog, made of some sticky substance, clung to Diana as she sped through.

Cobwebs.

The webs were not very transparent. Harry was attempting to obstruct the wolves' view of them. To the left, a boulder loomed. He directed the women towards it, and they slipped behind it. Crouching there, Diana flinched as the wolves zipped past them, further into the cobweb curtains.

Harry beckoned the sisters to go in the other direction. They hastened after him and stumbled into a small clearing.

A wolf howled, and barking neared. The beasts had caught their scent.

"In the trees. Quick!" he said. He was lifting Diana onto a limb when a woman shrieked behind them.

Anne, who had already managed to climb up a tree on the opposite side of the clearing, had wolves leaping up and nipping at her dangling legs.

Diana attempted to dart towards her sister, but Harry held her back. "Her powers," she said. "She's forgotten her powers! What do we do?"

He pulled out a pistol. "Kill them."

"Wait!" She grabbed his wrist. "It appears these aren't your everyday wolves. A bullet might not be good enough. I don't wish to risk it. I have a better idea." She explained her plan. After his nod of approval, she sprinted to the other side of the clearing and waited.

Over Anne's screaming, Harry yelled, "Oi! Over here, you mutts!"

They ceased their assault on Anne and slowly turned to face the new threat. They bolted in Harry's direction, and he took off. When they had nearly caught up with him, Diana pointed his pistol at the sky and pulled the trigger. The boom of the gunshot rumbled through the cursed woods.

"Hey, this way," she hollered. "Come and get me!"

The wolves rounded, growling ominously. They darted toward her. She stood her ground. She almost had—SNAP!

Oh, no. Oh, goodness no.

A branch had broken underfoot as Harry climbed up to help Anne. The wolves halted and changed course again, racing towards them. Diana raised the gun into the air. BANG! BANG! BANG! Three shots into the sky, but the wolves didn't fall for it this time. The next scene was a blur: a wolf leaping up to an incredible height, a cry of agony, and a lot of blood.

Diana screamed, "No! HARRY!"

The beast sunk its teeth into Harry's left leg. Blood trickled down into its jaw, its wild eyes dancing wickedly in triumph.

"Let go of him, you mutt!" The attack on Harry appeared to bring Anne to her senses. Fire roared from her palms and pushed the beasts back.

Diana glanced up at the ice cage she had created in midair. She ordered it to make a quick dash towards the momentarily bewildered wolves. With a snap of her fingers, the cage dropped, imprisoning the whining beasts within.

She rushed over to Anne and Harry who were now at the foot of the tree.

"Harry!" Diana exclaimed, dropping to her knees. "Are you alright?"

"I've been better," he moaned, "but alive nonetheless."

She bent down and studied his leg. The lacerations were deep—bloody teeth marks started from his ankle and proceeded upward. Her stomach churned.

Anne averted her gaze and coughed. "That's—that's really bad."

Diana brushed his hair back to its proper place. "It's going to be alright. This should stop the bleeding." With a ripple of her fingers, the wound froze shut, the ice-cast sparkling in the moonlight. "Any better?"

"Yes," he answered, surprised. "I hardly feel a thing."

She wiped her eyes, sniffling. "Can you stand?"

He got up and tested his leg. "There's hardly any pain at all. Amazing."

"Now I wish I would've taken the crystal ring." Anne folded her arms.

Diana said, "That should do until we can get you to a hospital."

"*Until we can?*" Anne repeated. "Did you see his leg? We need to go now."

"No," Harry said. "Your sister is right. I don't believe we could work up the nerve to come back here. We have to keep going."

They continued their journey with Anne leading the way. Harry and Diana trailed behind.

"You sure you're ok," Diana whispered.

"I'm fine...thank you, Diana."

"You're welcome."

As they went on, Harry brushed her hand with his. Her arm exploded with goosebumps. What had he said in the car? She flushed, taking his hand yet still feeling hesitant. Risking a glance at Harry, she nearly started. What a buoyant expression he wore. It wasn't really possible that he fancied her, was it?

After a long while, he stopped in his tracks. "Look." He nodded towards something ahead of them. She squinted. The fog permitted her to see an upcoming cave with a pitch-black opening. There was no indication of how far onward or downward it went.

"You think that leads to the Door?" Anne asked, regarding the gaping stone mouth.

"I don't know," Diana replied.

"There's only one way to find out," Harry said.

Anne gulped. "This is not a good idea."

Staring into the abyss, Diana ran her finger along the Key's chain. "We haven't a choice."

Anne raised her eyebrows. "Do you think it's smart to wander into a random cave in a haunted wood?"

"No," said Diana, "but if the Door is in this wood, which I'm certain now that it is, I don't see a more likely place for it to be."

Anne squared her shoulders. "Let's get on with it then and find this bloody Door."

Diana crossed the threshold, flinching at the ground's sudden hardness. Even through her shoes, the coldness of the stone floor stung her soles. Gloom engulfed them before they were three steps in. The void was a little too eager to welcome them.

"How are we going to find the Door if we can't see anything?" Anne grumbled.

"There's a torch mounted on the wall," Harry said to the nothingness.

Diana heard the *click click* of a lighter, and soon the flame's light pierced the dark.

"Ah"—Anne grinned—"now that's much better."

They were in a sort of underground hall twelve feet wide. The rock walls—without a trace of moss, water, or insect—reached up seven feet and arched over them. Their torch only allowed a three-foot notice, and a curtain of blackness was flush against their backs. Neither the origin nor the destination was clear.

Even with the torch's light, Diana was suspicious of every crack in the wall and every rock on the ground. The air reeked of foulness. On her next step, she almost lost her balance. A grinding noise echoed. Did she push a stone into the floor?

Suddenly, Harry shouted, "Watch out!" He grabbed her wrist and yanked her towards him. A ginormous ax swung from the ceiling and sliced through the space where she had been standing.

"Oh!" Anne shrieked, stomping her foot. "I *hate* this ghastly place."

"Thank you," Diana breathed, trembling in his arms.

He sighed in relief, resting his chin on her head. "You are most welcome."

Once recovered from Diana's near death, they continued on their journey, all the more on edge. Each breath, each footstep, each hushed murmur threatened to awake some ferocious monster within. But they went on and on and on without danger rearing its head. The stillness was unsettling.

The further they went, the more weary Diana grew. The Key absorbed her strength. *Diana, why fight it? Why harm such a meaningless, helpless little Key? It won't hurt anyone. The man doesn't* really *love you, but you can change that. Diana... Diana...DON'T!*

Chills crawled up her spine. *It knows its end is near.*

A sudden scream snapped her out of her trance. Their path had ended, and Anne had fallen into the gap.

"ANNE!" Diana lunged forward and caught her sister by the hands. Her arms trembled beneath the strain. Anne started to slip. Diana's heart skipped a beat. Harry appeared and grabbed Anne's arm. Together, they pulled her to safety. Diana held her shaking sister in her arms, bawling.

"I thought I lost you. *Oh*, I thought I lost you."

Anne sat up, pushing her away. "Stop, Diana."

"What?" Diana searched her sister frantically for sign of injury. "What's the matter?"

"You say you almost lost me, but you lost me a long time ago, didn't you?"

An icepick to the heart. A lump formed in Diana's throat. She did not reply. Would they tarry on in cold nothingness or would a battlecry for freedom ring out?

Is our relationship recoverable?

She said nothing.

Anne said nothing.

Would the curtain ever close on this act, or were they locked in this moment of their story for eternity?

Is it too late?

Anne's whisper felt like an explosion. "Or did you give me away?"

"Wha...*what*?"

Face contorted in anguish and fury, Anne's eyes met Diana's. "We haven't been sisters since Mum died—*real* sisters. Did you realize how much I needed you? You closed yourself off. You didn't say a word. I was so alone. I...How can you act as if I'm the most important thing in your life when you *left me*?"

Diana stooped. Her vision blurred. "I didn't mean to. Anne, you *are* the most important thing in my life. I just—I didn't know what to do. I didn't know how to comfort you when my own heart had been ripped open, and the bleeding wouldn't stop. I couldn't fix it. I—"

"I didn't *want* you to fix it! I just wanted you to *be there*!"

Diana's breath hitched—the power of being there. Had it not been just hours prior that she was consoled by Harry's mere presence? Why hadn't this simple act occurred to her before?

Anne bawled. "We *never* talked about it. Never! Didn't you need to talk about it?"

"Yes, but I thought—I thought you didn't want to."

"*What*? Why—why did you think that?"

"You were so angry. I thought you hated me for not helping you. I thought you didn't love me, that it was too late. I had messed up too bad. I had ruined it. So, I didn't try.

I'm not enough, so I didn't try. Not enough to take your pain away."

The sorrow on Anne's face deepened, making the previous anguish appear joyous. "Diana, you're a human being. You *can't* take that sort of pain away. I never, *ever* hated you. I wasn't angry at—well, I *was* angry with you, but I didn't hate you. I was angry at—at life, at everything. I didn't know how to handle anything anymore, and it came out as anger. I—I thought you were indifferent towards me...that you were the one who didn't care."

"Indifferent?" Diana sniffled. "Oh, Anne, of course, I care. I let my own problems get in the way when I should've been there for you. I wanted to."

"We should have been there for each other." Anne pinched her nose, a tear sliding down her thumb. "But instead we threw pity parties."

Diana's lips cracked into a smile. "I'll be there, Anne. *Always*. It won't happen again. Forgive me."

Watery eyes glued to the ceiling, Anne swallowed. "No, forgive me. I listened to these lies when the truth should have been obvious. I still had a family. I have you, and I gave up on you. I'm so sorry."

"We both gave up," murmured Diana, "but I've done you a *greater* disservice."

Anne cupped her sister's face in her hands, forcing eye contact. "We've both committed great disservices to each other. And it's lasted this long all because we were too stubborn to speak up and reveal the darkness. The most absurd lies can sound so logical when one doesn't open one's mouth and bring them into the light. I see that now."

"You're starting to sound like Mum." Diana laughed through her tears.

Anne laughed somberly. "Diana, you've always been enough for me. You don't have to measure up. You keep trying to be this perfect person, when all any of us ever wanted was you. You, Diana. I've always looked up to you. *I've* been trying to measure up to *you* since we were kids. I love you so much. Forgive me for believing you didn't care."

"I love you too." Diana embraced her sister, sobbing. "I forgive you."

"I forgive you too."

The curtain closed. The act ended. The battlecry rang out, and they won.

The two women sat on the floor, weeping. Arms secure around her sister's ribcage, Diana clung to Anne, whose tears watered her scalp. She soaked her sister's sleeve with muffled sniveling. In a bone-crushing grip, Anne held her up—the little sister who proved mightier than soldiers.

There was great power in simply being there.

"We're in this together," whispered Anne.

Together.

They were half-dead, but they were together—two soldiers in grief's trenches. Anne was, despite everything, the bunker that deflected bullets and muted the boom of grenades, a canteen's tea that warmed the bitter chill of No Man's Land.

In that moment, Diana was strong.

Could she be such a fortress for Anne? Perhaps not, but she would be the gentle hand continuously lifting her from the floor.

Was their relationship recoverable? Yes, it was.

Anne had never hated her. She deemed Diana worthy of her affection, and if she was the only one in the world who would, so be it. Diana could live with that.

However, the question had to be asked. What if she had been thinking falsely all this time? Could Harry truly fall in love with her?

The Griffin sisters rose from the floor, attempting to compose themselves.

Harry spoke, reminding the sisters of his presence. "I'm sorry you two had to go through so much."

"I'm not," said Diana. "We're better for it."

Anne swatted at the air, as if shooing away the conversation's thick emotion. "Enough of this mushy stuff. We'd better get on with it."

"Right. We need across the gap." Diana looked over the edge, and her eyes widened. "Goodness, gracious me!"

Beneath the deadly, abrupt end of their path was a pool of black water and bloodthirsty sharks.

Harry peered down and gulped. "I don't believe sharks are supposed to behave like that."

The animals were restless, flipping and turning violently. Their razor-sharp, blood-stained teeth chomped at some invisible feast, their barbarous eyes searching desperately for an actual victim.

Diana crouched. "Those wolves. These sharks. They're— they're—"

"Incomparably and absolutely barking mad?" her sister suggested.

"Yes. They act like they've been starving all their lives. It doesn't feel right."

"Nothing feels right in this place," murmured Harry. "How are we going to cross?"

Diana placed her hand on the ground and spears of ice reached across the gap. When she stood up, there was a sturdy ice bridge to the other side.

Harry chuckled. "Of course."

She gingerly stepped onto her ice bridge and walked forward a bit—no cracks or groans. She glanced down. The sharks' greedy eyes glared up at her. Her gaze snapped back up, and she continued onto the other side.

"It holds," she announced. "Come on."

Harry's voice reached across the gap. "Alright, Anne. Your turn."

"No," she stuttered, peering at the sharks. "You go first."

"Your sister made it across fine."

"I would feel b-b-better if you went first."

"You won't fall, Anne," Diana said. "Come on. It's ok."

Anne would not step onto the bridge.

Harry moved to block Anne's view of the gap. "How about we go together?"

After a moment's hesitation, she nodded. Harry took her hands and stepped backward onto the bridge. Inch by inch, they made their way across. He ordered her to keep her eyes on him and take deep breaths. The rest of his coaxing words, though inaudible, were evidently a great comfort. They stepped off the bridge.

Diana touched her sister's arm. "You alright?"

"Yeah, yeah. I'm fine," she said. "Thanks, Commissioner."

"Don't mention it."

As they went on, they faced numerous hazards, including blades, poisonous snakes, and trap doors, among others. The path went on and on and on. There was no sign of an end.

Diana shivered. The piece of biting cold metal pressing on her chest stung her skin. With trembling fingers, she pulled the Key out of her shirt. It was glazed in frost. Her teeth chattered.

"Diana?" said Harry. "Are you alright? You're shaking something horrible."

"I-I'm f-free-z-zing."

He touched her hand. "Gosh! You're cold as ice!"

Anne fell into step beside them and observed her sister. "I didn't think it was *that* cold in here."

"I-I-It's the Key. It's-s-s like it is in a sort of p-pan-n-nic. It really does-s-sn't want to be here."

"Well, of course not." Harry hastily relinquished his coat and draped it over her shoulders, rubbing her arms against the chill of both cave and Key.

"Do you—need me to take it off your hands?" Anne said, her voice hesitant.

"N-no. You t-t-told me to carry i-i-it for a reason. I-I-I'm ok."

They walked on, Harry's arm around Diana, continuing his attempts to warm her. Though his efforts improved her condition, the Key still kept her shivering.

After what seemed like years in the vile cave, Anne halted and doubled over. "Hold up a minute. Oh, I'm exhausted," she heaved. "Bother it. We'll drop dead before we get there."

Harry's weary eyes stared into the gloom. "Where *is* this Door?"

Diana let out a quivering exhale. "I d-don't know, b-b-but we can't turn back n-now."

They went on. Anne asked a few minutes later, "Does the hallway appear to be getting bigger to you?"

"It does. Wait—look!" Harry pointed. "Do you see that light ahead?"

Diana squinted. A tiny speck of light had appeared amidst the dark. They quickened their pace. At last, a sign of the end.

Their jog soon turned into a run. As they ran, the tunnel brightened. Firelight washed over them—the sweet warmth latching onto Diana—as they darted into a large room.

Her breath hitched. "The Door."

8

I WANT MY KEY

Diana's muscles became gooey. She shook off the bitter cold like shackles. The Key, however, remained as ice, and she fancied it began to quake. A sudden yank of the chain dug into her neck. She winced.

That will bruise, no doubt.

The ancient, hefty Door loomed over the Pool of Spirits, from which whispers arose and ghostly faces appeared then disappeared. The mercury boiled noiselessly. Torches lined the circular room, but they failed to reveal the ceiling, if indeed there was one beyond the pitch black above.

"Lovely," Anne quipped.

"Um." Harry swallowed, eyeing the Pool. "Are you seeing those faces as well?"

Diana removed the necklace.

"So, that Pool can destroy the Key?" he asked.

"Mum said the thing capable of destroying the Key was in front of the Door," said Anne. "The Key came from the Pool. That's why we concluded it must be the way to rid ourselves of the beastly thing. And since the Pool is obviously in front of the Door, it has to be right."

Diana fingered the Key. "So I just—throw it in?"

Anne shrugged.

Diana straightened her posture and strode to the Pool's edge. She planted herself there with a wide stance and raised her arm. The Key dangled from its chain.

Let go, she ordered herself. *Let go.*

But the Key resisted. The necklace remained glued to her fingers. Phantom chains entangled her, holding her hostage, locking her hand shut. Her muscles twitched and flexed, straining to obey her commands to move, but no limb budged. The messages her brain sent to her hand only came halfway down her arm. The Key held her prisoner as it began to drain her energy. Her knees wobbled, and her body felt three times its usual weight.

It knew its death was near.

Let go.

Diana...Diana...Diana, the Key whispered to her.

She couldn't move—even if she wanted to.

Diana...Diana...Diana.

Squeezing her eyelids shut, she shook her head. *Be quiet.*

It was relentless. *Diana...Diana...Diana.*

She glared at the Key and clenched her jaw. *Stop!*

But it wouldn't stop, would it? It was fighting for survival. The longer she stared at it, the louder the voice became. It boomed in her ears. It begged for its life:

Diana, Diana, why do you fight? You know it is no use destroying a harmless little Key. Why do you believe such lies? Do you think it'll make a difference? Do you think you're doing a good deed? Saving the world?

Diana, Diana, this will not change anything. Now what would change something is what's behind that Door. Take it, child, and then you can stop all wars, all pain, and all suffering. There would be no more death, no widows or orphans. You will be worth something. You will be enough. You will be beautiful. Your mother didn't really mean what she wrote. This is just a misunderstanding.

"You lie," she hissed. "That Weapon is evil."

Fine, don't use it to save lives. But you would be good enough, good enough to be loved.

"You lied before; you lie now. Anne never stopped loving me, and Harry—"

You really think that man wants you? Foolishness, child. I say foolishness! You know full well that he could never love you. The only way is the Weapon, Diana...Diana...Diana...

A lump formed in her throat. Her gaze drifted to the Door. She yearned, not for the Weapon, but for the notion that it might cause Harry to love her. With a wobbling inhale, her heart plummeted. Nothing, no matter how powerful, could accomplish such a feat. Perhaps the appearance of it, but it would not be real. She acknowledged that fact solemnly and welcomed it into her heart, which shattered on impact.

"Maybe he doesn't love me." Her voice cracked. "Maybe he never will. But wielding that vile Weapon is a price I'm not willing to pay."

Please, Diana, enough of this evil talk. He—

"You know what, I just had a revelation." A chuckle escaped her lips. "I've been taking love advice from a Key."

Straining against the phantom bonds, she forced her grip to loosen, and the chain slipped through her fingers.

Immediately, she collapsed to the ground. The Key seemed to hover in midair for a split second before falling to its death. It hit the mercury and stayed afloat for a moment before the Pool was set ablaze. The Key slipped beneath the silvery liquid.

A blood-curdling wail emitted from the Door, which rattled so harshly Diana feared its hinges would snap. It had lost. With a deep boom, stillness seized the cursed place again.

Her strength began seeping back into her body, and she breathed with ease. The Weapon was forever beyond reach. The world was safe from its power.

"I'm glad that *beastly* thing is gone," Anne, arriving at her sister's side, said as she looked into the flaming Pool.

"Yeah, me too," Diana mumbled, getting to her feet.

"So," asked Harry, joining the sisters in the observation of the fire, "now what?"

"Good question. We just leave, I guess," Diana said.

"Not so fast, thief," growled a foul voice behind them.

She whirled around, coming face to face with about four dozen malformed monsters dressed in medieval armor.

"The Shatari," Anne rasped.

More and more of them appeared at every side. Soon they were surrounded. The trio moved into a back-to-back position.

"You won't be leaving, girlie. *Ever!*" sneered a Shatari to Diana's right.

"Oh, it's been *such* a long time since I've tasted girl!" another said and cackled.

The soldiers kept inching forward, the sight of their elated and revolting faces almost more unnerving than the threat of battle.

Anne's voice wobbled as she said, "We're going to have to fight our way out, aren't we?"

"Appears that way." Diana pushed her ring further unto her finger. Her heart rate quickened as adrenaline released into her veins. "You alright, Harry?"

He grunted. "Define alright."

She gulped. "Please tell me you've been in a fight before."

He shifted his weight. "More than I'd like to count."

"So, you know what you're doing?"

"I don't know about that. I have to say I've never fought Shatari before. But"—he glanced at Diana with a smirk and unholstered his pistol—"I'm ready to teach these ruddy ugly goblins some manners."

To his left, a Shatari took advantage of Harry's momentary loss of focus. He attacked, and Harry shot him. The monster crumpled to the floor, but soon staggered back to his feet.

Harry winced. "Of course bullets don't kill them."

The multitude of Shatari charged, and Diana erected a circular ice wall between them. An unrhythmic thumping sounded as several bodies rammed into the wall. Then there was the *clink clink* of axes against ice. Pieces of the wall broke off, and the repugnant eyes of their enemies peered hungrily through the gaps.

"Oh, dear." Diana moved closer to Harry.

"This igloo's not gonna hold them," Anne warned.

"We need a new plan," Harry said as he shot a clawing hand on his right. It slithered back into the hole. "They're almost through!"

Anne raised her hands and said, "If ice doesn't work...." A ring of fire ignited around them, disintegrating what was left of the wall.

The soldiers shrieked. Some shrank back, but the majority pushed through, trembling. Once inside the fire circle, they shuddered as though it was the most horrendous thing. The sound of their deep, rattling inhales made Diana's skin crawl. Growling through corroded teeth, the Shatari drew their swords.

"I don't believe they appreciated your fire," she said.

"Noted," Anne declared before kicking a crawling Shatari in the face.

The flames did not stop them, but it slowed them down. Though bullets hardly phased them, Harry shot as many Shatari as he could. Diana froze them solid. However, it was Anne's fireballs that did the real damage. It didn't even have to be a direct hit. A miss by a couple of feet would still send the soldiers screeching, "The light! The light! It burns! It burns!" Even the ones who fought through the apparently odious light appeared greatly disturbed by the increasing flames.

And the fire would have worked if it weren't for the constant flow of Shatari from the room's entryway. They needed an army of their own. Diana stomped and an army of ice soldiers rose from the floor, advancing against the influx of monsters. But coldness did not sway the Shatari at all. With little effort, they busted her ice men into pieces. The trio were outnumbered, and despite the effectiveness of Anne's powers, they were losing the battle.

"There's too many," Anne shouted.

"You can say that again," Harry yelled back as he struck one of the creatures with the butt of his gun.

Diana struggled with a Shatari as he attempted to bite her shoulder. An ice blade arose from her palm. She stabbed her opponent, and he fell.

A growl emitted from behind. Claws dug into her back.

"AHHH!"

"DIANA!" Harry cried.

On her knees, Diana glanced over her shoulder just in time to see him seize the blade from the back of the resurrecting Shatari and drive it through her new attacker. He hurried over and lifted her off the floor. Pain pulsed through her back, and blood oozed down until it pooled at her feet. Grimacing, she reached behind her and froze the wound shut.

"We can't hold them off. We have to run," Harry said then ordered her sister, "Run, Anne!"

Fleeing the scene, they darted down the hallway, but it didn't lead to the mouth of the cave. They stumbled into another sizable, dome-shaped room, this one empty.

Gulping down air, Anne looked around frantically. "I don't remember coming through here on the way in!"

Diana grabbed two fistfuls of hair. "That's because it wasn't here. The pathway has changed."

"Look. There's a way out." Harry pointed to a doorway on the right.

"We don't know where it will lead," protested Anne.

The echoing snarls were getting louder. Clamorous footsteps neared.

"We don't have a choice," Diana said.

They sprinted through the right doorway, down another hall much wider and higher than the previous one. Diana ran with all her might, but the Shatari were still gaining ground. She risked a peek over her shoulder, nearly stumbling at the close proximity of the fastest Shatari. Turning her gaze ahead, she found Anne had stopped. Diana skidded to a halt, a quarter of an inch away from colliding with her sister.

"Anne, what are—" But her eyes already found the answer. A sinister woman blocked their path. Behind her was a Shatari, more civilized and human-like than the others. The army came up from behind, trapping the trio between them and the woman.

"Well, well, look what we have here." Her nefarious cackle stung Diana's eardrums.

Levian.

"Now, let's see," Levian mused, her calm obviously artificial. "What do you have that I want—*oh*, I know—MY KEY!" She sucked in a deep, quivering breath. "It's simple, dear. Give me my Key, or you all die."

Diana's fingers tenderly traced the blossoming bruise on her neck. What would Levian do once she realized they didn't have her Key? Bluffing wouldn't help the situation. She knew they wouldn't have come there without the Key. There wasn't a lie she would believe, and the truth would get them killed. In the end, she'd murder them regardless of the answer.

With a shaky exhale, Diana whispered, "It's gone."

Levian flinched as though the words had burned her. A look of denial filling them, her eyes desperately searched the ground for some clarity as her chest rose and fell in rapid breaths. Her gaze snapped up, and she demanded, "What do you mean, 'It's gone'?"

"It's gone," Diana repeated, firmly this time. "Destroyed, in the Pool of Spirits."

Levian's mild panic evolved into fury. She clenched her fists. A gray light emitted from her eyes. The very atmosphere shared her rage. Frost crawled up the walls. The temperature dropped several degrees, cutting Diana's lungs. An unnatural shadow descended in the hall. And then came dread—immense dread. Any flicker of hope was put out. They could not fight her in all her power and glory. They would not win. Every cell in Diana howled for surrender, to submit.

She blinked. It was but a moment, scampering away like a rabbit upon a fox's approach. The frost and shadow shrank back, the temperature normalized, and the dread dissipated. Had it indeed happened, or had it only took place in her mind?

Through gritted teeth, Levian whispered, "Take them."

Like lightning, two Shatari had Diana by the arms and slipped off her ring. She struggled to free herself as Harry and Anne were disarmed. Fighting against her captors' iron-like grip was like fighting a stone wall. Diana wasn't escaping, not when their focus was on her. She stilled and caught sight of the Shatari that stood with Levian. Hiding in the shadows, he wore a conflicted expression. Levian's face expressed disgust that far outweighed her distress. She had seen her soldier's doubt too.

"Come with me, Vitus," she said curtly, and he hastened to follow.

What would happen to that Shatari? Levian was clearly displeased. For reasons she couldn't quite identify, Diana almost felt sorry for him.

The iron grip loosened. With a jerk of her arm, she broke free and kicked one of the Shatari down. However, a violent blow was dealt to the back of her head. She heard Anne scream "Diana!" before everything went black. The terror of her new reality disappeared.

Back on the ledge overlooking the Shatari work mines, Vitus watched his queen slouched in the corner—knees curled up, left elbow propped on them, and face buried in that hand. This posture declared one emotion—forlorn wrath. She was deeply disturbed, and it would make her all the more insane. She was deeply infuriated, and it would make the weight of her outrage more taxing on the world. She was deeply wounded, and it would make every death she inflicted more excruciating.

Vitus knew his queen well.

Another emotion made itself known. Fear?

He closed his eyes and took a controlled breath. The Key was lost, so Levian could never reclaim her Weapon. Though the prisoners might receive an intensified dose, the world would not feel her fury. She could not punish it for her injuries in her weakened state. Thus he tried to reason with himself. But still—*fear*.

"They must be Tara's children," Levian murmured. "Why didn't you kill them?"

"I did not know of them," he said.

Liar, he scolded himself. *You saw that woman at the window—the youngest of the two female prisoners. You knew better than to dismiss her as a possible heir that night.*

"And the Key?" she asked, her voice dangerous. "How did you miss the Key?"

"Truthfully, my queen, I searched thoroughly. I did not find a trace of it."

Liar again. You didn't search the whole house.

Levian elapsed into quietness.

The young captive—the woman from the window—is still so familiar.

That young lady's scream rung in his ears—"Diana!" It was so like the woman's cries from the Door—a nameless shadow lurking in the back of his mind.

"Callum."

Vitus fought to keep the voice at bay, simultaneously concealing external signals of conflict from Levian. He asked, "Why keep them captive? They are no longer of any use to us."

"I wish to kill them," Levian replied smoothly, rising from the floor with a tear-stained face. "I *need* revenge."

"Why linger?"

She glided to the ledge's brink and scanned over the mines. "To let them tarry in horror a while. Then I'll kill them. Slowly. For my *amusement*, Vitus." Her lips twitched, and she released gasps that morphed into psychotic cackling which echoed throughout the cave.

That laugh—it had never troubled him as much as it did now. It was a repulsive sound, causing his muscles to go taut, his skin to crawl. He turned and left, her vile laughter haunting him as he wandered the dingy hallways. The woman from the window reminded him of—*love*. She reminded him of someone he had loved.

Who is she?

Something was missing. He was not who he believed himself to be.

The woman's voice from the Door refused to leave his mind—*Callum*. There she skulked, an outline, a shadow, waiting inside him. A memory? No matter how hard he concentrated, how much he tried, the shadow would not lighten and the outline would not solidify.

What was he missing?

The woman from the window—her face looked so familiar, her voice so similar to the one he heard from the Door.

"Callum."

He stopped walking.

There was a day, a day of blood and screams when other innocents like the Griffins died. Levian had cackled with glee.

That scream..."Callum!"

She emerged. The nameless shadow emerged from the muck of his soul—black hair like a cloak around her dainty frame, brown eyes formed from the very stuff of kindness.

"Callum!"

He gasped and collapsed in great agony, trembling, "*Althaia.*"

9

THE HALF-CURSED

During the tyranny of Levian over King Orion's domain, a man strolled through the village, rubbing his arms against the cold. The sun was barely peering over the horizon; some stars were still in view. Not many other villagers were awake. He spotted just a few in his passing, the wish to go back to sleep evident in their half-closed eyes.

He blew a puff of warm breath into his cupped hands and rubbed them together. This new day was resistant to begin. The only living thing seemingly energized and ready for another morning was a cheerful, chirping bird fluttering above the houses.

The man regarded the little creature. At last, someone who could match the energy of his son. He chuckled to himself. *Crazy boy.*

The man entered his place of work. Flames roared in the stone fireplace, buckets of water dotted the floor, hammers and other tools were scattered on the table, and their metal creations were organized neatly against the wall.

"Good morning, Callum," his young apprentice greeted him brightly.

"Good morning, Petros." Callum shed his tattered coat. "I see you cleaned up. The place has been a mess recently."

"It has," Petros admitted, shoving his hands in his pockets. "I will try to keep it tidy from now on."

"Please do so."

Another friend pushed open the door and stumbled in. Pale and sweaty, his eyes gleamed with uneasiness.

"Janus," Callum approached him, "you look as if you have witches on your tail."

Collapsing into a chair, Janus attempted to conceal his angst with a half-hearted grin. "Times are tough, are they not?"

Callum sat down with his friend and, leaning over the table, whispered, "Are Orion and his son safe? I was beginning to worry that you would not return."

"I helped them escape, yes, but the king has come back."

"*What?* Why would he do that?"

"The Key."

Callum sat back in his chair. "Then he wishes to die."

"Him returning is not the issue." Janus massaged his temples. "Callum, he succeeded. Orion has the Key."

Callum's body went rigid. The Key had been stolen from Levian? He tugged at his collar, then said doubtfully, "If that is true, then this is good news...yes?"

"Not for us. Maybe for our grandchildren, if our children survive what comes next." Janus wiped the condensation from his forehead, looking over his shoulder more than at his friend. "Levian's wrath has never been greater, I tell you. Her power is beginning to fade and—if she does not retrieve the Key soon—will disappear entirely. She will be weak enough to overthrow in a matter of hours. This knowledge has made her especially savage. I have just come from a meeting with my inside source from the castle. He says she's coming *here*. She wants to know where the king plans to flee in the event that her army fails to capture him. Only two people know the specifics of his plans."

Callum's breath hitched. His lungs feared the oxygen, lest it bear ill will upon Levian's command. "You and me." He combed a trembling hand through his hair.

"I should've never told you of it. Forgive me. You must get your family out *now* before—" The sound of hurried footsteps and screams penetrated the quiet of the room. Janus's head snapped in that direction, unblinking eyes glued to the door. "Oh, no. She's here. She's already here. That *murderess* has come."

Petros inched towards the door. "We're being attacked?"

Callum rose. "We must leave—now."

The men stepped into the chaos suffocating their village. Shatari were everywhere, demanding the identity of the traitors from every man, woman, and child. Homes were aflame, and families were being ripped apart. People covered in ash and blood hid in dark corners and pleaded with the soldiers.

Callum's heart raced. Janus and he knew the details, but there were others who assisted in the escape that could disclose his name and the fact that he knew the king's destination. Without a doubt, the Shatari would soon be at his door. He had to get home to his family.

Though witless, the Shatari were thorough. It was all the men could do to keep out of their sight. They shuffled, bent over, from one hiding place to another. Crouching behind a cluster of tall, grain-filled baskets, they peered in between the gaps and watched the Shatari terrorize the villagers.

"They're coming upon my house," Petros hissed. "I have to fetch my family before it's too late."

Callum nodded. "Go. *Discretely.*"

Petros broke off from the group and darted toward his home, hunching low to the ground as he crossed the street. He closed in on the door and reached for the handle.

Callum's gut twisted; something was wrong. Two doors down, a company of soldiers stormed a house. A Shatari flung a woman from the house prior. Flames painted a building on the other side black. Petros's home sat motionless in between. Why would they leave it be? They wouldn't. The window was cracked open. Callum squinted. A sliver of a malformed face passed by.

"They're already in the house," Callum said, alarmed.

"What?" Janus rasped.

"Petros!" Callum warned, as loud as he dared. "Don't!"

The door flung open, smacking Petros's hand away. A soldier burst forth, turned, and cast a torch into the door as shrieks spilled out. The house was set ablaze. Petros yelled and attacked him. The Shatari plunged a sword into his stomach, and he collapsed at the soldier's feet.

"No! Petros!" Callum struggled to reach his friend, but Janus held him back.

"He's gone, Callum."

"He was just a boy!"

"There's nothing you can do for him! You must get home. Your family, Callum, your family."

He stopped resisting. In the relative stillness, he heard the wails tumbling from Petros's window—an elderly woman and a young girl.

The wails ceased. The fire roared on.

Callum's eyes closed, his fingers digging into the weaves of the basket.

"You can't save them." Though Janus's voice quivered, his grip was firm on Callum's shoulders. "But you can still save your family."

Callum inhaled deeply through his nose to steady himself. After exchanging affirmative nods, they split up to find their families. He ran and ran and ran, threading between buildings and staying in the shadows as much as possible. He was going to beat the enemy to his home. He had to. His speed increased as his front door loomed into view.

He slammed open the door to find his wife, Althaia, hurriedly packing food.

"Callum." She threw her arms around her husband's neck. "You're ok."

He held her tight and kissed her forehead, the smell of the rose she had incorporated into her braid wafting up his nose. "We must leave. Right now. Where is Matías?"

"I'm here, Papa." A five-year-old boy rounded the corner.

Callum sighed with relief and embraced his son. "Everything's going to be alright."

"Are we going on an adventure, Papa?"

Callum refused to let his tears show. "Yes. We're going on a grand adventure in a faraway land. Get your shoes on and come quickly."

"Yes, Papa!"

While Callum concealed a knife in his belt, Althaia whispered, "Callum, does she know? Does she know you have information about the king?"

"She will soon."

Shaking, Althaia lowered herself into a chair. "Then she has come for us. She will kill us all. She will kill our Matías."

"No, Althaia, listen to me." Callum, kneeling down, cupped his wife's tear-stained face in his hands. "We *will* escape. She won't get here in time, and she certainly will not have Matías."

She shook her head, eyes pressed shut. "This can't—"

There was a bang on the door followed by the crack of splintering wood. He rose and whirled around. Five Shatari soldiers had intruded into his home. Before he could draw his knife, one soldier kicked him square in the chest. He crashed into the wall and crumpled onto his hands and knees.

"Callum!"

A boot collided with his ribs and a club struck his face. He tipped over onto his side, pain swallowing his body. Black spots obscured his vision as a high-pitched whine stopped his ears.

Amidst the floating spots, Althaia stood over him, tugging at the soldier's armor to get him away from her husband. The Shatari backhanded her. She broke her fall with her elbows, her assaulter holding her at sword point. Another grabbed Matías. The boy began hitting his captor, but his struggles did not deter the Shatari.

Callum gritted his teeth. *Get up. Do something. Get. Up.*

"Help me," his wife screamed. "*Please!*"

One soldier cut his son's face.

"Papa, it hurts. Papa!"

Ignoring his throbbing head, Callum pulled himself back onto his hands and knees then staggered to his feet. "Don't!" he pleaded. "Leave them be. They are unarmed."

The Shatari paid him no mind. Two of them yanked Althaia off the floor.

Callum pulled his knife and growled, "Fight me, coward. Fight me!"

The head Shatari who had kicked him drew his sword. Callum took a blow to the stomach but managed to cut his opponent's face. With a howl, the Shatari slashed his chest. Callum dropped to his knees, blood flowing down his front from the gash.

"NO! Callum!"

"Papa! Papa, no!"

"Stupid peasant," berated the captain. "We were sent here to fetch you for the queen, not kill you. But these other two, we have no use for. Kill the boy."

Fresh adrenaline ignited in Callum. He sprung to his feet. "No, wait—"

Another Shatari drove his sword into Matías's chest.

"Matías!"

Two soldiers restrained Callum before he could attack the offender.

"NO!" Althaia wailed. "My boy! My baby boy!"

The Shatari captain grunted, "Shut her up."

Callum begged, "Wait! Just, please—"

With one strike to the throat, Althaia was dead.

"NO!" He bawled, kicking and shoving, but the soldiers wrestled him back from their captain. "My Althaia. My Matías. No. You *murderer*! I'll kill you! I'LL KILL YOU ALL!"

However, his chest continued to bleed, and he was weak. When his eyes locked on his beautiful wife and son lying on the floor, any remaining strength dissipated. He stopped struggling and allowed his captors to force him onto his knees.

His shoulders convulsed from tearful gasps that sent lighting bolts of pain across his chest. He gazed into Althaia's eyes. Those enchanting brown eyes, once so full of life, were now still and dull. A ghost of her kindness lingered in them, stinging like salt in his wound. Her neck and chest were dyed red as the flower adorning her hair. She had smelled like roses. She always did, and now that scent would fade... fade...fade...and vanish. He let out a sob.

Despite himself, his gaze shifted to his son, an expression of utter terror forever frozen on that merry boy's face, hardly the age to comprehend death. The sight of Matías's body blurred into a watery painting.

Callum hung his head, his teardrops splattering on the ground. The world spun around him. An army of grief approached, coming in waves.

In the first assault, it was a trance, nightmarish and numb. He felt nothing. Simply nothing. His brain refused to believe his eyes. They couldn't be gone. When the sword had been driven into his son's chest, it had carved out Callum's soul as well. Of course, he was numb. One could not feel without a soul. They were his soul, and now they were dead.

In the second assault, reality's claws dug in deep to release an unendurable agony, an affliction far deeper than his flesh wound. No, his soul was not gone. It was very much there, and it was crushed—repeatedly crushed and torn and cut open. Upon this sensation, he yearned for the numbness. Perhaps his captors would have mercy and finish the job—to carve out his soul so he would feel no more.

These waves kept coming in turn...again...and again... and again. In the numbness, he longed for the anguish. In the anguish, he longed for the numbness. Again...and again...and again.

My Althaia...my Matías. No...No!

He didn't much care what happened next. They had already done their worst. The heartache was more torturous than any misery the Shatari could inflict on him. What was the point in resisting? What was there left to fight for? His family had died for information they did not know, for an action they did not commit. His family had died because of him.

A gnarled hand clutched his collar and drug him out of his house. Unhinged laughter pierced his eardrums. Dirt scraped against his body, and he was thrown at silver clad feet—boots too lavish for one of those creatures. He tilted his bruised face upward to find the diabolical queen herself towering above him.

Levian's eyes narrowed. "I said bring him alive, Captain. Half-dead is not the same thing as alive."

"It was only one stroke, your majesty," said the captain.

Ignoring him, she pulled Callum up by his hair. "I will only ask you this once, scum. Where is Orion running too, hmm? Where is he taking *my Key?*"

Though speaking felt like grating knives across his lungs, he locked eyes with her and wheezed, "I will never tell you."

"Hmm." A taunting smile touched Levian's lips. "Bring me his son," she ordered the captain.

He shuffled his feet. "Um, they are already dead, your majesty."

She groaned in frustration. "*Idiots.* We'll never get the information now."

"What about the one they call Janus?"

"I've tried him already! He's dead."

Callum exhaled sharply and dropped his head. "Janus..."

"Shut up," the Shatari captain scowled and kicked him in his wound.

Callum flopped onto his back and grimaced. He swallowed the lump in his throat.

He didn't make it. My best friend.

Another Shatari jogged up, halting at Levian's shoulder. He bent over and took several rattling inhales before grumbling, "Orion is dead, but he did not have the Key."

Hand on the hilt of her sword, she turned menacingly to face the newcomer. "And the boy?"

"We—the boy has vanished, your majesty. Apparently with the Key."

"NOOO!" Levian shrieked and cut off the messenger's head. Her soldiers began whining and cowering. Heaving like a madwoman, she searched frantically for something else to slaughter. Her gaze settled on Callum, and she plunged her scepter—now slightly transparent—into his cut.

He clasped the pole protruding from his torso and gagged. Every tendon tremored. Poison attacked each member of his body—like cockroaches feasting on his spine and innards, like acid sizzling in his veins. The pain was unspeakable. And there was an atrociousness, a living filth, originating from the scepter and proceeding outward, that began coiling itself around vital organs, muscles, and bones until it had its talons in every part of him. It reached up and grasped his vocal cords. He choked in silent agony, unable to scream. He couldn't breathe. The world grew dim.

The vile thing then tangled itself around his mind and soul, the intangible part of him somehow tangible. That was where it sunk its fangs in and began to suck, began to draw out. Images from his life appeared then melted away.

Where was he? How did he get here—on the ground and covered in blood? Who was the woman standing over him, face stained with rage? Why was he so melancholy?

Who am I? What is my name?

The confused man watched a scepter disappear from the woman's hand—the transparent object suddenly empty space.

"No!" The woman bellowed. "It's gone. My power is gone! *Fools.* You have lost my Key. I cannot control my Weapon or this kingdom without my Key, you idiots!"

"My queen," a monster said. "The villager you've poisoned. Why does he not look like us?"

The woman gasped, her eyes dancing with dread. The confused man heard her whisper to herself, "My Weapon left me before the curse was complete. He is only half-cursed, not fully erased. He may have the mind to overthrow me. Yet he may be cleverer than the rest. I could use that to my advantage. Nevertheless, I must be wary of him."

She barked at the others, "Get him up! Welcome... Vitus, your new brother." She turned to the monster and added, "Your new captain." Then she killed that monster where he stood.

Another groaned. "My queen, the sun is burning us. What is happening?"

"My power," she muttered. "We must return to the castle—quickly! And have every window covered!"

A breathing murk engulfed the confused man's mind, and malice consumed his heart. Though he grappled, he could not take hold of a single memory. He could not remember. What did "remember" mean? He must follow this woman. He must satisfy his bloodlust. But he could not. She was evil. What was the definition of this descriptor, "evil"? Who was he?

He was the captain of her army, Vitus, who must serve his queen.

Someone lifted him to his feet, and his mind submerged into unconsciousness.

10

WHEN EYES ARE OPENED

"Leave him alone!" Diana recognized her sister's voice over the Shatari's whooping. The cold, stone floor beneath her pressed her spine into an awkward position. She rolled over with a wince and gripped the back of her throbbing head. She opened her eyes sluggishly. In the blurry scene at a cell door, a man was on his hands and knees, blood dripping from his chin.

She concentrated to bring the image into focus. *Harry...*

"Get up, scum," a Shatari growled, yanking Harry to his feet. The soldiers threw him and a struggling Anne into Diana's cell. As the door shut with a loud bang, they scrambled over to her.

"Diana, are you alright?" Harry's fingertips slid across her forehead as he brushed the hair from her eyes.

She groaned. "I feel awful."

"What hurts?" he asked as he and Anne propped her up against the wall.

"My back," said Diana, grimacing, "and my head. *Ow*—it's mostly my head."

Misty-eyed, Anne quivered, "We're all going to die, aren't we?"

Diana glanced at her sister but didn't have the heart to reply. The Key was gone. The mission was successful, but the escape had been a disaster. Her very breath mocked their failure, and the angst for their future refused to leave her alone. She had led her little sister and the man she loved—who hadn't even been involved until she dragged him into it—to their deaths.

She slumped against the left wall of their dark, damp prison. Anne sat closer to the middle of the small room, legs crossed, rocking back and forth. Harry rested against the back wall, one knee propped up with his arm atop it. Diana sensed his gaze on her and lifted her eyes to meet his. They were about to die. What harm could a little sentiment do?

What is he thinking?

Harry got up from his seat and sank down next to her. He remained stiff and motionless for a while, she watching his profile. Hesitantly, he wrapped his arms around her and held her tight.

She tensed. *He does not love...he does* not...

Her feeble objections were no match for his closeness. She let herself relax, laying her head on his shoulder. He gently stroked her hair—a desperate attempt to comfort her when he could find no words. A helpless tear dripped onto her scalp, like he thought it wasn't enough. But it was enough, if only he knew how great a comfort his actions were.

Diana twisted her left cuff. "I suppose we won't have our dinner after all...if you were indeed genuine in your asking."

"I was...Diana—" Harry faltered. "Now seems like an inopportune time, but you never answered my question in the car."

"Now's the only time, I'd imagine."

When she did not offer a response, he whispered in her ear, "Why did you think I couldn't fancy you?"

She bit her lip. "The end to my last relationship was—unpleasant. It made me realize no one could ever fall in love with me. I wasn't enough, so I never tried again. And I had accepted that fact, for the most part. But when you came along—what did you mean by what you said in the car?"

"I meant exactly what I said," he stated plainly. "So, I'm assuming the breakup was rather ugly, and this bloke said some proper nasty things. And because of this, you decided you can't be loved by another man—ever?"

She stared down at her hands. "Pretty much."

"He sounds like any other bully to me, Diana."

"I suppose he was, but that doesn't make him wrong."

"Except he *was* wrong." He grasped her hand and elapsed into contemplative silence as he searched for the right words. "You can't let hateful words—or actions—define you. It's dangerous. Letting lies like that get a foothold can destroy us. I've seen gorgeous girls sink into self-hatred because people have told them their appearances don't meet the 'standards' and amazing women *strive* needlessly for the approval of others. It leads them down a dreadful path. All because the lies they have come to believe, they get themselves into loads of trouble and do things they would've never done before."

"I haven't done anything—*rash*."

"You closed yourself off, resisting any chance of love that you encountered. You still believed the lies, which may well lead to a horrible decision one day."

"If his statements were untrue," her voice cracked, "why did he leave?"

"If that man was daft enough to give you up, then that's his problem, not yours." An edge of disdain was in those words. "It doesn't mean no one could ever love you."

"What are you trying to say?"

"I...I'm saying—" he stammered, pulling back slightly to gaze down at her with his brilliant blue eyes. "I'm saying you *are* lovable."

Diana's heart fluttered, and her mouth became dry. Tears falling against her will, she choked, "How do you know that?"

His thumb wiped a tear from her cheek. "Because I..."

"Yes?" she breathed. "Because?"

His eyes flickered to her lips, the words barely audible as he admitted, "I'm in love with you, Diana Griffin." He captured her lips in a tender kiss.

A brilliant light—his resounding confession—exploded in her mind, exposing each grisly lie that had thrived there for a decade and combating them.

I'm in love with you, Diana Griffin. He punched that lie square in the jaw. He wrestled it to the ground.

She could finally see the truth, and the truth was glorious.

All this time she believed herself to be less than, unfit, rubbish, incapable of being loved. When all around her, she had people who loved her—Anne, her mum, and now Harry—waiting for her to realize that she was never unloved. It had never been impossible for someone to fall for her.

Diana broke away, her eyes darting between his. "You truly love me?"

"Yes, Diana. I love you," He tucked a strand of hair behind her ear. "Very much. I don't know how it happened or when it started, but talking with you each week was a joy. Eventually, I found myself hoping you'd call and missing it when you didn't. And then—" The broadest grin spread across his face.

"I don't believe it. I never—I barely thought you fancied me. I—" Her mouth moved without sound, wordless. "I've wasted so much time. Though, if I hadn't believed him, maybe I would have never fallen for you."

Harry blushed, rubbing her arm. "This has taken a painfully long while for me also, but I think it was worth the wait."

She simpered. "Absolutely." Hand on the back of his head, she coaxed his face downward and planted a firm kiss on his lips. "I love you too, Harry. It's taken me a while to admit, but I do."

She laid her head on his shoulder. Anne continued to rock, shut-eyed, though an involuntary smirk peeked through. She cracked one eye open and shot Diana a glance with the unmistakable message of "It's about time!"

Diana took Harry's wrist and pulled his arm tighter around her, feeling the steady rise and fall of his chest. He hummed a laugh. Memories returned to her of moments where his affection had been so apparent—his doting words over the phone, his playful behavior at the station, his soft eyes when she had interrupted the Key's whisper. She had been too blind to see it, or perhaps too frightened to accept it. Only at death's doorstep did she realize it. If only this conversation could have occurred sooner.

Diana jumped at a clang from the door, causing Harry's head to jerk up. A Shatari stood there, the same one who had come with Levian and hid in the shadows.

Anne stopped swaying. "You're the one they call Vitus, aren't you?"

"I am he, miss," the newcomer said.

Her nose wrinkled, an abhorring gleam in her eye. "The other Shatari mentioned you had something to do with my mother's death."

"Yes," he confessed with a downcast aura. "I—I killed her."

Diana's nails bit into her palms. *He's the murderer?*

"How could you?" Anne demanded, words clipped and nostrils flaring. "How could you serve such a *barbarous* woman?"

Vitus's watery eyes flickered to the floor. He placed his forehead on the cell bars before saying, "Levian had me under a curse, like all the Shatari. I have not been myself, a man I previously could not even recall. Then I touched the Door, and the curse began to dissolve. Yet it was only now, when you cried out your sister's name and Levian found humor in your torment, that I—I truly remembered..."

Anne's expression softened. She whispered, "She—she wiped your memory?"

"Yes, and another conscience, a depraved conscience, took its place."

He's a prisoner here. Diana lifted her fingertips to her lips. *Same as us.*

She asked, "Why have you come, Vitus?"

"I've come to help you escape."

Immediately, all contempt in Anne's face dissipated. "*Help* us? Why?"

"It is as I said, I now remember whose side I'm on, and it's not Levian's."

Diana said, "I doubt Levian is a forgiving person. What will she do to you if she realizes you've betrayed her?"

"She will likely take my life, but if that be my end, so be it. I've done so many horrid things under Levian, not in my right mind though I was, I still did them. I wish to do one good deed, one more honorable act, before I die."

Anne said faintly, "Shatari cannot be killed, from what we've seen."

"Levian is the source of those creatures," Vitus explained. "Thus she can also be the end of them."

They sat in somber quiet for a moment before he said, "I know a way out. We must hurry before the Shatari come to take you. I have retrieved your rings and pistol." He unlocked the door and held out their weapons.

When Diana moved to recover her ring, Anne seized her wrist and hissed, "What if he's playing us? He's a Shatari. He killed Mum."

"It sounds to me that his mind was not his own," Diana said.

"I know," Anne faltered, "but can we *trust* him?"

"Mum would."

Anne stared at her sister for a moment before releasing her. "You're right. She would."

Diana turned to Vitus. "Show us the way out."

They tiptoed away, following him down a row of cells. Diana attempted not to dwell on the blood streaks smeared across the floor. The narrow tunnel opened up into a dimly lit room a hundred times larger than the room with the Door. Jagged rocks jutted out from everywhere as if the roof, floor, and ceiling were mini mountain ranges. Wooden ledges were mounted in random places on the walls, creating midair working stations littered with various mining tools. Rope and pulley systems were scattered far and wide, lifting and lowering buckets or platforms on which workers stood. At least, that was their apparent purpose. The place was deserted now—not a Shatari in sight.

"This is the primary mining area," said Vitus. "Work ceased when they found the Door."

Anne squinted. "How can they work with so little light?"

"Shatari cannot be in sunlight. It will burn them to death," he replied. "Fire has a similar effect, though not to that extent. The glow or touch of flame is excruciating, but not fatal. Even this low, a torchlight is irritating. Still, they need to see to dig effectively."

Diana frowned. "Can they not see in the dark?"

"No," he said. "Though, their eyes have adjusted to seeing clearly with minimal light."

They descended onto the floor of the mine, where channels had been dug like a maze. There, they encountered more mining tools and buckets filled with rocks and the occasional basket overflowing with precious jewels.

Vitus navigated the maze without pause or doubtful countenance. How many times had he weaved his way through here? It must have taken years to memorize this place, years of being robbed of his identity. Diana's chest felt weighed down at the thought.

He made one final right turn before the group came up upon an arched doorway. The inside was pitch black. He plunged into the abyss. Diana slipped her hand into Harry's, and he laced his fingers through hers before stepping into the murk.

The only light came from the torch Vitus carried. It appeared they were in another vast hall. She hugged Harry's arm as they journeyed down the hall. The solitude of their company was not a comfort. She scrutinized the gloom about them, paranoid. Where was the Shatari? Where was Levian?

Anne's eyes followed Vitus. Not a speck of contempt remained in her gaze. Were the same sobering questions about their guide in her mind as in Diana's?

Quickening her pace to walk alongside him, Anne asked, "Vitus, could you explain some of this to us? What is the Weapon?"

"The Weapon is a scepter made of iron and crystal. It is a cursed Weapon. After a king locked it away, Levian stole the Key from one of his descendants. With the scepter, she ruled over my homeland for many generations," he replied.

"What about the Shatari?" Anne prompted. "You said Levian was the 'source.'"

"Levian's kiss and touch, if she desired it, were poison," he explained, "transforming their victim into a Shatari. Once a man became a Shatari, they too could turn others into Shatari by their bite. Like the plague, they spread rapidly, and soon, she had a massive army. Her Weapon could create Shatari as well. As long as she commanded it, the

Weapon had her power, and she had its. However, she did not know it was *absorbing* her power. So when the Key was taken from her, Levian's power dwindled. One needs the Key to control the Weapon, and by that time, without the Weapon, she hardly had any power at all."

"What about the energy we felt when I told her we had destroyed the Key?" asked Diana.

"That was the Weapon's power. What is left of it. Traces of its power remained with her after its disappearance, but not enough to be of use. It seems the transfer of energy went both ways, be it ever so slightly."

"And Levian was overthrown after the Weapon evaporated?" Anne asked.

"Correct."

"How did the people fight an unkillable army?"

"Nothing is unkillable," Vitus said. "Levian can destroy them and, since she lost her power, so can the sun. In addition to these two fatalities, there is only one way a human can kill a Shatari—beheading. The villagers knew this, and that is how they conquered Levian's army."

"I suppose it would be difficult to resurrect without a head," Harry quipped.

After a lengthy period of wordlessness, Anne asked slowly, "What about you? What's your story?"

"Her army raided my village the dawn of the day the Key was taken. Though fading, her strength wasn't gone yet." A shadow passed over his face as he recounted in a hoarse tone, "My family...was murdered. Killed—by the Shatari. Just before the Weapon vanished, Levian pierced my heart with it. It disappeared before the curse was complete, thus fragments of my true self were left behind. During my time as captain, there have been moments, mere whispers, that protested what we did. Sometimes, I didn't do my duty to the fullest. I never understood why, but now I believe it was what remained of my soul fighting back. But alas, only when I touched the Door did the fog of her spell shift enough for me to see through it. I was only half-cursed, yes, but I still had no memory."

Face contorted with empathy, Anne touched his upper arm. "I'm so sorry."

"It was not your doing," he murmured, halting and looking down at her hand. His gaze snapped up to meet hers. "It is I who should be apologizing to you. I have committed an unforgivable sin against you. I wish I could fix it."

"You didn't know what you were doing, Vitus. *Levian* killed my mother. It wasn't your fault," she said.

"She's right," Diana echoed.

"I still carried out the order. And my—" he hesitated. "My true name is Callum."

"Callum," Anne repeated quietly.

As a soft smile creased his face, the flesh on his left cheekbone began lacing together, erasing any evidence of a scar. Diana's throat ached as she blinked against the blurriness. How dreadful it must have been to break free from such a hex and behold all that blood on his hands.

"What about *their* names?" Anne whispered.

"Whose?"

"Your family. What were their names?"

"My son was called Matías, and my wife..." He rubbed the heel of his palm against his chest, as if trying to massage the ache out, and exhaled the final name, "Althaia."

"Those are beautiful names," Anne said gently. "What were they like?"

They hiked on and on through the tenebrous hall, the torch only revealing the next couple of steps, as Callum told of his family's lives during the Middle Ages. The memories that tormented him seemed to become memories that soothed him as he related multiple precious stories of his wife and son to Anne.

Too perturbed to enjoy his tales, Diana glanced over her shoulder again. She couldn't shake the unnerving questions that kept pacing in her mind. Where was Levian? Would she come after them?

"Look!" Anne cried out jubilantly. "There's a light at the end of the tunnel!"

11

THE LIGHT AT THE
END OF THE TUNNEL

Anne must have been hallucinating. A pinprick of light sat right in the center of all that nothingness. Her body felt so feather-light it was a wonder she didn't start floating. They were finally getting out.

BANG! A harsh noise rudely paraded through their moment of jubilation and relief. They all spun around.

"What was that?" rasped Diana.

The blackness before them offered no answer.

Callum glanced over his shoulder then did a double take. "No!" He dove in front of Anne. A flying boulder smacked him in the head, rendering him unconscious. Her heart jumped into her throat.

"Callum!" she shrieked. *Is he breathing?* She took a step toward him but halted upon noticing who was blocking their exit—Levian.

She clicked her tongue. "A pity, really. I did like him."

The commissioner unholstered his pistol, but another boulder loomed from the darkness and struck him. He collapsed.

"Harry!" Diana scrambled to his side.

Anne slapped her hand over her mouth. *No. Please, no.*

"Harry? Harry, can you hear me?" Diana whimpered, cradling his head and hovering her fingers over a bruise that was spreading just below his hairline. Seeming convinced that he was still alive, she glared at Levian and growled, "You monster."

"*I'm* a monster?" Levian snickered. "Have you looked closely at your rescuer?"

Anne's jaw clinched. "Callum is no longer the monster you'd have him be."

Levian staggered back a step and huffed. "Callum?"

Anne smirked. "Yes. *Callum.*"

"Hmm." Levian pursed her lips. "The man of which you speak perished long ago, scum."

"Are you certain of that?" Anne jeered. "Or did you not know your curse was incomplete?" Her gaze flickered to her sister and the commissioner. Was he alright? *He can't be dead. For Diana's sake, he can't be dead.*

Levian sighed impatiently. "Regardless, the scum failed. Surrender now. It is pointless to resist."

Anne scoffed. "You'd like that wouldn't you?"

"You are *not* leaving!" Levian exploded. "This is the day you die!"

Anne rolled her eyes. "You have no superpowers. How do you plan on stopping us?"

Diana winced at the boldness of her statement.

Levian sniggered. "Like this." A legion of Shatari emerged from the shadows.

"Oh." Anne gulped. "That explains the boulders."

Diana groaned. "You *had* to go and push her ego button."

Numerous boulders were hurled at them, but Anne was quicker. With a thought, the floor caught on fire, the flames licking the ceiling. The heat melted the deadly projectiles the minute they hit the firewall. The air filled with smoke as the flames fed on nothing but stone.

The soldiers looked at one another, dumbfounded, apparently having expected an easy victory. Rage dropping like curtains over their idiotic expressions, they set their faces towards the sisters and marched.

"Make it hotter," Diana yelled, alarmed.

Anne grunted, straining to increase the intensity of the flames. Her core heated up further, and the fire burned hotter and brighter as a result. The Shatari shuddered as they stepped into its territory.

Protecting her face, Diana started to withdraw, beads of sweat formulating on her forehead and arms. She snapped and an ice-cocoon popped into existence, which grew continually to compensate for Anne's ice-melting abilities. She also created ice-shelters for the commissioner and Callum.

That's when the shrieking started. "It's too hot! It's bright. It's bright!" The Shatari began to retreat.

"What do you think you're doing?" Levian thundered. "I will not suffer defeat!"

"It burns us," her soldiers croaked. "*Misery. Misery!*"

"Misery? I'll teach you misery if you fail me," she barked. "Press on. That's an order!"

Though howling and screeching, the Shatari pushed through. They evidently had a higher pain tolerance in Levian's presence.

"Diana!" Anne shouted. "We're having the same problem as before. My fire will slow them down, but it will not kill them. And they are much bolder with Levian being here!"

"Decrease the heat!" the cocoon ordered.

"Are you mad?"

"Just do it!"

Anne cooled her core. The flames went down. Diana evaporated her cocoon. Sweat was practically pooling at her feet now, and her hair was half-soaked. An object glistened in her hand—a thin sheet of razor-sharp ice. She flung it, with perfect aim, at a Shatari's throat, relieving him of his head. He toppled over and stayed there. No resurrections this time.

"Ha!" Anne exclaimed triumphantly. "How do you like that, you beastly imps?"

Diana proceeded to deal out the sheets of ice in rapid fire, a majority hitting their mark. One, two, three, four, five dead Shatari in a row. But more emerged from the flames. Did Levian have a never-ending supply? They were outnumbered, just like before. Diana was already heaving.

Anne's limbs began to tremble from maintaining the fire so long. "Diana, there's simply too many of them. You can't take on an army single-handedly! And I can't keep this firewall up forever."

Her sister's face scrunched up in concentration as she persisted in taking out Shatari. "Stand down! Let me try something."

"But your ice didn't deter them at all last time."

"Last time we were trying to kill them, not disorient them."

"Disorient them?"

"I have a plan. I'm going to create a blizzard."

Anne shot her a look. "A blizzard! You've never attempted something that big."

"Trust me."

She blew as if extinguishing a candle. The flames consumed themselves. The Shatari quaked and gulped down air.

Diana lifted her hands, fingers spread far apart, before they could recover, and, with a deafening cry, gave birth to a blizzard. The Shatari strained against the snow tornado, their eyes searching frantically for their no-longer-visible targets. Their dumb brains couldn't handle the madness. With a ripple of her fingers, she added honed icicles to her winter masterpiece, slicing the skin of their enemies.

They wailed and yelped but continued their advance halfheartedly, driven by the whip of Levian's snarling voice, "You *cowards*. Kill them! KILL THEM NOW!"

"Now that they're disoriented"—Anne put her hands on her hips—"what's this brilliant plan of yours?"

"Those...Shatari...will never...never stop," Diana panted. Sustaining the blizzard was taxing. "Levian won't...tolerate retreat. No matter what...we throw at them...they'll keep... coming. The only way this ends...is by...Levian's death. She's...our target."

"What makes you so sure we can? Even with her power severely weakened, it wouldn't shock me if she's death-repellent."

"We must...try. I...must try. With the blizzard—ow!—blinding...everyone, I...can get close."

"Are you *barking mad*? Just throw an ice spear at her or something. No need to get close."

Diana was doubled over now. "We cannot...risk a...a miss, Anne."

"Then let me do it."

"You'd have to use...fire, or I'd have...to deplete the storm for...for you to pass through. Either...way, we'd risk losing the element...of surprise. It's my storm. I can...get through. It won't...It won't hurt me."

"The-the blizzard?" sputtered Anne. "You're *barely standing*, and there's a maniac, psychopath, murderous, evil lady waiting to slit your throat! You think I'm worried about some baby snowstorm?"

"I'll be alright." Diana gave her a weary smile, a drop of blood slipping from her nose. "It'll be alright." She plunged into the wall of swirling snow, passing right by the oblivious Shatari soldiers.

"Diana, wait!"

No response. The snow whistled its clamorous song.

Wringing her hands, Anne stared at the unrelenting blizzard. The occasional smear of a Shatari would surface amidst the white, bewilderment still clinging to his face. Every now and then, a shimmer of a sword would pierce through as it stabbed its fellow in the mayhem. The soldiers were mistaking each other for their prey. What idiots.

Clever plan, Diana, but perilous.

And she waited...and waited...and waited, glaring at Diana's extraordinary diversion. The seconds ticked by. What was taking so long? Was Diana ok?

The angry snow started to dissipate, and a fuzzy image of the scene within socked Anne in the gut, knocking the wind out of her. Levian's fingers were wrapped fiercely around Diana's throat. Ashen, Diana gagged for air, her dangling legs kicking slightly as though to flee. Her discolored hands clawed uselessly at Levian's firm grip, and the vigorousness of her fight weakened by the moment.

Anne stood petrified. *Does Levian still have her poison?*

Terror imprisoned her soul and threw away the key, cackling with delight. A flash of memory, cold and cruel, showed her mother's marred body, the blood around her head glistening in the moonlight. Anne's legs had lowered her to the floor under the gravity of defeat, and strands of hair had clung to the strips of wetness on her cheeks. The keen edges of the broken glass had reflected the moon and manmade light alike. It would have been pretty, if not for the smudge of red on the edge that had been nearest to Anne. The knife—chill talons of remembrance sunk into her brain—was sharpest in her memory. It had protruded boldly from her mother's limp frame, like it had the right to be there. And the tingling sensation that had ignited under Anne's skin, the itch in her fingers, the push-and-pull tension in her muscles to undo it, to stop the blade. For it to *stop*. But the deed had been done. Like a gush of wind ripping off a single leaf, it was final.

Presently, Diana was dying—or something worse. Levian's fingers were squeezing. Diana's life was seeping, but her heart was still pumping. It was not yet final.

Anne would not lose her sister too. She simply wouldn't have it.

No...No, not again. Snap out of it, Anne. Do something!

"LET HER GO!"

Her arms shot out in front of her. Fire blasted from her palms, eating the snowstorm alive as every Shatari hit the floor and yowled for mercy. It gushed over the walls and ceiling, racing toward Levian. The blow nailed her square in the chest. She gasped and released Diana, who hit the ground, immediately rose onto one knee, and, reaching over her head, plunged her ice blade into Levian's chest.

In a howl of agony, Levian flung her head and arms back. The light that exploded in the room at last defeated the unyielding darkness.

Anne shielded her eyes as the Shatari's shrieks rung in her ears. It lasted half a second, then gloom swallowed the cave again. Forcing herself to take steady breaths, she parted her fingers cautiously to catch a glimpse of what the dickens just happened. The soldiers had been consumed by the light, it seemed, transformed into piles of ash. An ice statue of Levian sparkled in the torchlight, her anguish frozen in time. Legs tucked beneath her, Diana sat on the ground, one arm propping her up and the other hand holding her forehead by the temples.

Anne rushed over to her sister. "Diana, are you ok?"

"Yes, I'm alright." Diana got to her feet sluggishly and gaped at the Levian statue. "She's been frozen solid."

Putting her head back, Anne sighed in exhaustion and relief. "She's gone."

"Oh," Diana gasped. "Harry!"

As Diana scurried over to the commissioner, Anne knelt beside Callum. She tenderly shook him, and his eyes fluttered open.

"We're alive." He sounded shocked. "What—what happened?" He froze in the act of sitting up when he caught sight of Levian.

She laid her hand on his shoulder and whispered, "She's dead, Callum. You're free of her."

He squeezed her hand and released a deep exhale.

The commissioner circled the statue and said, "How'd you do it?"

"I stabbed her, but she would've transformed me into a Shatari if it hadn't been for Anne," Diana admitted.

"About that, you're not having any monstrous thoughts, are you, sis?"

Diana studied her skin then laughed. "No, I—I feel fine."

"She would not have been able to turn you," said Callum. "Being as weak as she was without the scepter, she could not create any more Shatari. Slight paralysis and pain, perhaps, but that would have been the end of it."

"What did you use to kill her?" the commissioner asked. "Things around here don't seem to take a hit from ordinary weapons."

"I created a knife," Diana replied.

"How did you know it would work?"

"I didn't. I just knew I had to try. I don't really know why it worked."

"Your rings," Callum said. "Have you been told where they came from?"

"Wasn't there something concerning elves? Oh!" Anne exclaimed. "The elves made them for that very purpose—to defeat Levian!"

"Correct," said Callum. "They were the only weapons on earth that could destroy her."

Straightening up, the commissioner half-turned his head towards the mines. "What is that noise?" The rumble of many running feet echoed through the hall.

"I think that's our cue to leave," Anne said and made a dash for the exit.

The soldiers soon caught up with them, but they did not attack. They just shot past them. Anne glanced behind her, and her jaw dropped. A fearsome dust storm was ripping each soldier to shreds as it advanced. One by one, the Shatari vanished into thin air. No matter how fast they ran, they could not escape the wave of destruction washing over them. The wave reached the Shatari near Anne, and they disappeared with a screech. The death of Levian had birthed the end of the Shatari.

They skidded to a halt at the cave's mouth. The last soldier vanished.

If all the others are dying, what will happen to Callum?

Anne gave him a nervous once-over. "Will you die too?"

He shook his head. "The curse broke upon my recollection. I am no longer Shatari, so I will not turn to ash. However, I will die eventually, for I have regained the mortality of man.... I am grieved by your care because," he paused, "alas, Anne. I must say farewell."

"*What?*" she exclaimed. "You're not coming with us? You can't possibly want to stay in this ghastly place."

"I do not," he admitted faintly, eyes downcast. "But I also do not belong in your world. How could I expect to come with you? It was I—it was by my hand—" He fought back tears that arose upon his unspoken words. "I killed your mother. I can't—how could I ever—? How could I live among you? How could you forgive me much less call me friend? How could I ever forgive myself? You know only of one death, but there is a shameful amount of blood on my hands. No, I must stay here. There is no life waiting for me."

"There *is* a life waiting for you, Callum. You can have a fresh start. Come with us! We can help you," Anne pleaded.

"You—you *wish* me to accompany you? But I—it was me—"

Diana interjected in a whisper, "Somehow, Callum, I can't find it in my heart to blame you for our mother. It was Levian and her curses. She had control over your mind. It was nothing you chose to do."

Anne nodded eagerly.

His head dropped. "That's not what I see."

"Maybe not. But it's in the past. You must forgive yourself."

"Why? How can I forgive myself?"

Anne gave an empathetic smile. "That's a difficult thing to do, I admit. Let's start with this then: *I* forgive you."

"As do I," her sister said.

Tears poured from Callum's eyes as he stared at them in absolute astonishment.

"Come on," Anne cooed, offering him her hand, "I can't promise it'll be easy. On the contrary, I can promise you it won't. But it's a chance."

"A chance for what?" he asked despairingly.

"To find the joy of life again, to find healing. Your family wouldn't have wanted you to give up."

He gazed at her hand an eternity before taking it and sliding it gently into his until their fingers interlocked, then all four of them stepped into the light.

During their hours in the cave, the woods had transformed. Buds decorated the bare tree limbs. Yellowhammer birds fluttered and chirped as they zigzagged between the branches. Sunbeams reached down and gifted the withered grass with a long-awaited breath of life.

"Would you look at that? The curse has lifted!" Anne beamed. "Callum—"

Wow.

Sunlight embraced Callum. Scars thinned and shrank until there was nothing but unblemished skin, whose color was returning to its natural state. The black clumps that were his hair smoothed into a silky, shoulder-length curtain that framed his face. He blinked, and his gray eyes changed to a piercing green. His armor was gone. Instead, he was dressed in medieval peasant's clothes. The man that stood before her now was—*handsome.*

His hands searched his whole person, patting his body until they arrived at his cheeks. Amazement shone on his face upon discovering that every mark had left. A relieved sob forced its way out. He grasped the fabric over his chest, and a smile played on his lips. When the scars on his face disappeared, had some of his soul's wounds healed as well?

"Wow, Callum," Anne breathed, "you look so different."

"Yes." He let his hands fall to his sides. "The curse had greatly altered my appearance."

"Well, the real you is certainly a dashing fellow." Out of the corner of her eye, she caught the commissioner whispering something in Diana's ear. She simpered and whispered something back. As she beamed up at him, he cradled her waist and pressed a kiss onto her lips.

"Easy now, lovebirds." Anne's abrupt statement caused the couple to jump apart. "Oh, sorry. I spoiled the moment, didn't I?"

The commissioner and Diana glanced at each other and started to chuckle.

Anne rubbed the back of her neck. "I'll take that as an 'of course, you did.'"

"It's all good, sis." Diana hooked her arm through Anne's as they strolled through the woods. Being a few steps ahead of the men, Diana said in a low voice, "I'm really proud of you, sis. You were very kind to Callum."

Anne shrugged. "It was the truth. I meant every word of it."

Diana patted her hand. "You have Mum's heart."

Anne jerked her head back a little. "What are you going on about? I'm more like Dad, with my temper and all."

"Yes, you have Dad's temper. But you offered Callum compassion and forgiveness, two things Mum was the very description of. And beyond that, your words to me in the cave. I see Mum's tender and wise heart flourishing in you. Never lose it, dear sister."

"Aw," Anne turned her blushing face downward, kicking a pebble as she walked. "You're pretty brilliant yourself, sis. The *best*."

Diana gave her sister a playful shove. "I mean it, Anne."

"I mean it too," Anne replied softly.

As the sisters walked arm in arm, she couldn't help but get misty-eyed. How she had missed her sister the past few months. To think, their strife was merely due to stubbornness and pride. Each of them stood alone only because neither of them attempted to bring harmony. Neither of them opened their mouths to reveal the darkness, and so lies appeared like logic.

She looked down at their linked arms. Life was too short to harbor resentment, to allow discord to carry on. She would never let her pigheadedness get in the way of her relationship with Diana again.

She had believed her family had died with her mother, but Diana, despite all her errors, stood waiting. They had both committed grievances against one another, and they had both missed the point. In spite of their squabbles, failings, and mistakes, they were still sisters. They were still family, small though it might be, and family was worth fighting for, worth fighting through the petty indifferences and serious conflicts. It was too valuable to let slip away.

Regardless of what transpired in the future, whether Diana would be there for her or not, Anne would never back off again. She would be there for her sister, no matter what. She would choose to love her through thick and thin, because that was what family did.

When they had reached the car, Diana said, "Ok, to the hospital with you, Harry."

"Yes," said Anne, "and afterward, to the clothing store. Callum, your clothes are *so* out of date."

Callum sighed but could not suppress his grin. "I thought as much."

As the laughter dwindled, a warm sensation swelled in Anne's chest. She had begun this journey feeling alone, and now she was surrounded with family.

12

FIVE WEEKS LATER

Diana opened her eyes. Sunlight gave her a warm kiss as its rays splashed over her blanket. Her lips broke into a grin. She was going on another date with Harry this evening. She slipped out of bed and tiptoed to the window. Like every morning, she watched another beautiful day begin. The red roses in her window box were in full bloom and looked heavenly in the sunshine. A bird fluttered above them, chirping a merry song to usher in the day. On the boulevard, drivers zoomed to work. Was Harry on his way or already in the office? She hummed a laugh. He probably arrived at work bright and early, the moment the first sunbeams hit the street. He wasn't one to do things halfway.

She skipped down the steps toward breakfast. Though spending the day with her sister was lovely, it drew on too long. Her anticipation for these evenings with Harry remained constant despite having been out with him several times before. When five o'clock finally arrived, Diana began to get ready.

As she was brushing her hair, Anne called up the stairs, "We have a guest."

"Harry?"

"No. You'll see."

Eyebrows furrowed, Diana set down the brush. *Who else could it be?*

She hurried downstairs. A handsome, black-haired man was standing in the living room with Anne.

"Callum!" Diana said in delight. "What a pleasant surprise."

With her and her sister's help, he had gotten settled and adjusted to modern society rather quickly. He had a home and a job and continued to learn about his new world every day.

"Thought I'd—what do you say—drop in? And see how you girls were doing."

"You're always welcome in this home," said Diana.

"Who else did you think it was when I said it wasn't Harry?" Anne asked.

Diana shrugged, suppressing a smile. "I never really know with you, sis."

Anne rolled her eyes playfully. "Har har."

The phone rang. Callum startled.

"I always forget that this—what do you call it again?—this *phone* makes that frightful sound," he muttered, hand over his heart.

Anne giggled and said, "I'll get it!" Rushing over to the phone, she picked it up and took the call.

"No problem. I'll let her know," she told the receiver. She hung up and announced, "That was Harry. He said he'll be a bit late. Police business, you know."

Callum and Anne sat in the living room while Diana pre-
pared tea in the kitchen. Returning to the living room and
setting the tray down, she tried to hand Callum a cup, but
he was preoccupied with the vase of roses on the tea table.

He gazed at the red petals bathed in the sunset's rays and
slowly removed one flower from the vase. "Do roses have
special meaning to your family? I noticed a row of them
growing beneath one of your windows."

"Yes," Anne responded after sipping her tea. "They were
Mum's favorites."

"Why do you ask?" Diana removed a biscuit from the tray.

He rubbed a petal between his thumb and index finger.
"My wife loved roses. She wore them in her hair all the time."

Diana immediately felt a pang of regret. She gulped
down the hot sweetness of her drink. "I'm so sorry, Callum.
I wouldn't have put them out if I knew—"

"Don't be sorry," he murmured. "I *want* them to remind
me of her. I don't wish to forget her."

Anne smiled mournfully, then took a deep inhale. "Tell
us another story, Callum, if you will. About your homeland."

He told them tales of times long past, and the sisters
taught him things about the modern world, just like every
time they met. Diana's thumb traced the rim of her cup as
she mused on the past five weeks. How strange it was that
the feeling of family could develop among friends over such
a short period of time.

At last, the doorbell rang.

Diana perked up. *Harry!*

She leapt to her feet and, before Anne could tease her
for her haste, went to get the door. Harry walked in, a wide

grin spreading across his face as his gaze fell on her. His blue tie brought out his eyes, and his new black suit coat fit him handsomely.

"Hello, Diana." He kissed her in greeting. "You look lovely."

She bit her lip coyly. "So do you."

Anne rounded the corner. "Hey, Harry!"

"Good evening, Anne. Evening, Callum. How are you doing?"

"I'm doing well," replied Callum. "I learn something new every day."

"Something to look forward to every morning, then. Any plans tonight?"

"Not really. I'm trying to catch up on all the history I missed, so I'll be reading."

"Anne?"

"Just a night by myself. I'm trying a new—" Anne's eyes widened. "Crikey! I forgot the shepherd's pie in the oven." She darted to the kitchen. There was a scream, a loud bang, and some smoke followed by coughing.

She reappeared, annoyed. "Aren't I daft? The whole meal's rubbish!"

"First time cooking shepherd's pie?" asked Harry.

Anne nodded, and Diana teased, "I think this might be a sign to stick with the old recipes, Anne."

"Yeah, yeah," Anne dismissed with a wave of her hand.

Harry circled his arm around Diana's waist and said quietly, "Feel like helping these two forlorn souls out?"

Diana sighed playfully. "I don't know..."

"Come on," Harry whispered. "I'll make it up to you with...an evening at the theater followed by a stroll through the park?"

"The theater, you say?" She beamed up at him. "Alright."

Harry addressed the others, "Would you two like to accompany us tonight?"

"Oh, I don't want to impose on your date," said Anne.

"It's alright," Diana said. "It's been a couple weeks since all four of us went out, and I rather enjoy it. Besides, Harry and I can still talk with you there."

"Brilliant!" Anne folded her hands under her chin. "Sounds lovely. What about you, Callum?"

"I–"

"You will, Callum, won't you? Please? You can't leave me alone with these lovebirds!"

Diana huffed in jest, putting a hand on her hip. "Well, I never."

"Alright, Anne." Callum chuckled. "I will save you this once."

"You're an angel, though this would make twice. Hold on. I need to fetch my purse." Anne disappeared onto the second floor.

"Siblings," Diana joked, shaking her head, "what are you going to do?"

As Anne returned, Harry asked, "Shall we be off then?"

"We shall," Diana said.

As they walked out the door, she held Harry's hand tight. Wounds had healed. Bonds had mended. Her family loved her. There was no doubt. But how had such darkness ended in such light? How had a tragedy ended in bliss? She gazed at the stars above her—lights only visible under cover of darkness. What could create such a paradox? Was there some mighty hand drawing up good from unholy waters? Was this journey designed as though to whisper, "There's more to this story called 'life.' There's something behind the curtain"?

Nevertheless, of one thing she was sure, as she held onto Harry's hand, she would never let go and neither would they. All was well...

13

THE MISSION IS COMPLETED

"And so, the Griffin sisters had a happy ending after all. Though they missed their mother dearly, the sisters loved their new family—be it the strangest family one had ever seen. Little did Diana know, that a few months later, one of her dates with Harry would end with the most magnificent question of all. By the year 1932, Diana and Harry were married, and two years after that, they had their first child, whom they named Tara. Yes, the war that was soon to come did bring them many sorrows, but they made it through together. Callum remarried a few years after the war and had a family of his own. Anne married shortly after him. Throughout the generations, these families remained friends. And they all lived happily ever after. The end." Grandpa Greg took a deep inhale, closed his eyes, and folded his hands in his lap, as though satisfyingly weary from another journey.

Rae beamed and stared off into space, thinking of the marvelous story that had just been told. "That was great, Grandpa," she exclaimed.

"Yeah!" Natasha agreed.

Jonny said, "It was cool!"

"What was your favorite part, Rae?" asked Natasha.

"I really liked the romance scene in the cell," replied Rae, and Jonny gagged.

Natasha said, "I thought all the clues were cool."

"I liked the wolves," said Jonny. "And the battles."

Natasha rolled her eyes. "Of course, you did."

"Well, children"—Grandpa Greg rose from his chair—"I think I'll turn in for the night."

Jonny's brow furrowed. "You never go to bed before us."

"You can't blame an old man for being tired." Grandpa Greg chuckled. "Good night."

As Grandpa Greg went upstairs, Mrs. Greenwood also left to go do something, apparently forgetting to order the kids to bed. So, the children seized the opportunity to stay up a little later. They climbed onto the sofa and watched the fire dance.

"Grandpa should write a book," Jonny said.

Rae looked at her brother. "What?"

"Yes!" agreed Natasha. "Grandpa has these stories written down—at least, that's what I think all those papers are. He should get them put into a book with a hard cover, title, fancy gold lettering, and everything!"

"That is a good idea." Rae's eyes lit up.

Jonny asked, "What would the title be?"

"How about 'Adventures in Otherworlds'?" Natasha suggested, gazing dramatically up at the ceiling.

Jonny tapped his chin with his index finger before saying, "I like it."

"Me too," said Rae.

Jonny sighed contently. "Tonight's story was great."

"Yeah, it was," Rae murmured. "I loved how it showed the importance of family and taught the lesson that the lies we believe can mess everything up."

"Is that what you're going to put in your journal, Rae?" Jonny teased.

"Oh, shut up," she said.

"Hey!" Natasha folded her arms. "That's my line."

"I wonder what Dad's surprise is?" pondered Jonny aloud.

"I don't know"—Rae yawned—"but I can't wait to see."

The three Greenwood children continued to gaze into the fire, all cuddled together. Sleepiness made their eyelids heavy, and eventually, they gave in. Mrs. Greenwood returned to put them to bed but found them already deep into their dreams. With a smile, she tiptoed away and left them in peace.

The moon shone high in the sky that quiet night. The Christmas tree lights twinkled radiantly along with the stars, which appeared as if angels had hung them in just the right places. There was no sound in Grandpa Greg's sitting room except the crackling of the fireplace and the soft breathing of three small children, who were off in other worlds on their own adventures.

THE END...FOR NOW

ABOUT THE AUTHOR

Leandra Massengill was born in Guntersville, Alabama in 2005. Though she has lived in various places around the world (Croatia, Germany, the United Arab Emirates, and Illinois), she currently lives in her hometown with her grandparents with plans to return to the United Arab Emirates with her parents and younger sister.

A graduate of Beacon of Hope Christian School in St. Augustine, Florida, she is a full-time online college student at Liberty University. Leandra loves stories regardless of the form they take and has a passion for writing and discovering new worlds between pages. Despite having dyslexia and dysgraphia, she was determined to write *Adventures in Otherworlds*, being heavily influenced by authors J. K. Rowling, C. S. Lewis, and J. R. R. Tolkien.

FOLLOW HER ONLINE
Instagram: leandramassengill_author
Facebook: Leandra's Dream